HUNTER SNIPER

A World War II Thriller

PACIFIC SNIPER SERIES BOOK IV

DAVID HEALEY

INTRACOASTAL

HUNTER SNIPER

A World War II Thriller

By David Healey

Intracoastal Media digital edition published 2023. Print ISBN 979-8-9872808-1-2

BISAC Subject Headings:

FIC014000 FICTION/Historical

FIC032000 FICTION/War & Military

"The world is not pretty. It's only the hard work of some people that makes it so."

—JAMES A. MICHENER, TALES OF THE
SOUTH PACIFIC

CHAPTER ONE

THE TROPICAL NIGHT sky was clear, lit by a waxing moon. A bat swooped across the face of the glowing orb, then another, hunters in the dark.

There was just enough light to give shape and form to individual trees and clumps of spiky kunai grass, but in a way, only half seeing something was worse. The longer you stared at a dark clump of shrub, the more it started to look like a sneaking Japanese soldier.

Listening to the night noises, Deacon Cole gripped his rifle and stared into the darkness. He didn't grip the rifle out of fear, but out of eagerness. The rifle felt like a living thing in his hands, and some part of him ached to shoot something. He wanted to feel the familiar jolt against his shoulder, the acrid whiff of gunpowder that was the best smell in the world this side of bacon frying. He wanted to feel the sheer power of that rifle and hear the *whunk* of a bullet hitting home.

Given that the jungle was crawling with the enemy, he reckoned that he'd have his chance soon enough.

He took his hand off the rifle just long enough to touch the bowie knife at his belt, reassuring himself that it was there and sharp as ever.

If the Japanese showed up, he'd be ready for them.

As if the shapes in the darkness weren't enough of a test of the imagination, it didn't help anyone's nerves that the jungle was never silent. Deke reckoned that if the night birds and insects went quiet, you might even hear the plants growing.

A few creatures and night birds stirred in the moonlight, their rustling through the underbrush and the sharp cries of hunters and prey setting the soldiers' nerves on edge.

Screech! Shreek! Aiieee!

These were primal sounds, echoing the jungle's cycle of savagery and death, a reminder of what awaited them all in this war.

The question was, What were the soldiers tonight? Hunters or prey?

Deke and the other soldiers were supposed to be the hunters, battle-hardened tough guys, but it was easy enough to sympathize with the prey when they heard the strangled, desperate cries of a dying creature. In this war, Deke reckoned that everybody felt like prey at one time or another.

"I can't tell if it's the Japanese sneaking up on us or just some damn bird making a racket," whispered Philly, off to Deke's right. The former city boy's voice was laced with exhaustion and nerves, sounding cracked, hoarse, and dry.

"I hope it *is* the damn Japanese," Deke replied, feeling wide awake and alert, his gray-blue eyes glinting in the moonlight as he scanned the darkness. There was no fear in his gaze, but something feral and predatory that searched the jungle with the anticipation of a hunter hoping for his next kill. "I just wish they'd hurry up and get it over with if they're gonna attack."

"For Pete's sake, Deke," Philly grumbled, a note of disgust in his voice. "Don't you ever get tired of this damn war?"

"Don't you worry about me," he said. "Just keep an eye out for the Japs."

"Yeah, wouldn't it be a shame if there weren't any out there? We might get some sleep for a change."

Deke didn't answer, only half listening to Philly. He stared intently through the scope, hoping for any glimpse of movement.

The strange noises made the soldiers uneasy, but it was just possible that their fears were unfounded. Philly had hinted at that possibility. After all, they were now near a section of Leyte Island in the Philippines that was supposed to be more or less secure.

For the last several days, they had forged their way across the interior of Leyte, fighting Japanese patrols whenever they encountered them. Their company had followed a narrow path through the hills and dense jungle. Their purpose had been to reconnoiter the jungle regions as much as it had been to harass the enemy.

Now they were approaching the coastal area of the island's western shore, near the city of Ormoc, where they hoped to be reunited with the rest of the division. Their mission now was to guard a small airfield and fuel depot that they had stumbled across.

The Japanese had a much larger presence at Ormoc than on the coast itself. They held the port city there and possessed a well-developed airfield, from which they continued to launch raids on the American fleet. However, the Japanese also had small airfields dotting the island, such as the one that Deke's company now guarded.

The Japanese had a smart strategy, because the scattered airfields were hard to find and target from the air. As it turned out, a Japanese Zero didn't need much of an airstrip to take off and land. Although the Zero was no longer a match for newer, more advanced American fighters, the aircraft was well suited to this jungle environment.

The nimble Zero had been the top dog in the early days of the war, back when the Japanese had attacked Pearl Harbor. Those were the planes that had sunk the ships at anchor and killed thousands of sailors, Deke's own cousin Jasper among them.

Incredibly, the Zero was built from canvas and wood, more a product of craftsmanship than mass production, in that a single team often worked to complete one entire aircraft at a time. This approach and the materials used now seemed an antiquated concept, but in the early days of the war the lightness of the Zero gave it the advantage of speed and maneuverability.

Since then, American aircraft had outpaced Japan's in terms of firepower and speed, but the Japanese planes remained a threat, especially now that the Japanese had resorted to turning their planes into airborne bombs and flying them directly into ships, something that they called *kamikaze*—a Japanese term that roughly translated to "divine wind."

The presence of these small airfields helped explain how Japanese planes still managed to take to the sky and harass the American fleet just offshore. No matter how many enemy aircraft the Hellcats managed to shoot down, there always seemed to be more.

Just a few days ago the airfield and fuel had belonged to the Japanese. Not anymore.

The question was, Would the Japanese try to take it back tonight?

Deke and the other soldiers waited to find out.

Each errant noise from the dark jungle surrounding them might very well be indicating a new threat from the Japanese, the sounds of the animals and insects masking the noise of the approaching enemy.

The moonlight was just bright enough to give Deke's dirty, stained uniform a dappled appearance, mixing light and shadow, like a jaguar's coat. The condition of his uniform testified to the fact that he had experienced more than a few fights. Even in the dim light, some of the stains looked suspiciously like dried blood —or worse.

"Just keep your eyes open," Deke eventually whispered in response to Philly. "For all we know, there might be a whole company of Japanese out there, waiting for us to let our guard down."

"Yeah, yeah, and it might just be a couple of pigs rooting around."

Farther down the line, a rifle cracked. The stab of the muzzle flash pierced the night. If there were any Japanese in the forest, they now knew exactly where the US line was located.

"What the hell are you shooting at?" a sergeant demanded.

"I thought I saw something, Sarge," a soldier stammered in response. Deke didn't recognize the soldier's voice.

"You didn't see nothin'. I've been starin' at this jungle the same as you," the sergeant said. "There's nothing to shoot at. Knock it off, Kowalski. If there are any Japanese out there, you just drew them a map of our position."

Deke thought that you couldn't blame the soldier for shooting at nothing. The moonlit night and jungle cacophony had set everyone on edge.

The American line settled back into uneasy silence. Some nights were like this, Deke reflected. Everybody was jumpy, figuring that something was going to happen. It was like a pot on the stove that was about to boil over. He kept his rifle fitted against his shoulder and his finger on the trigger, just in case.

Back on Guam, they had once opened fire on what had sounded like a Japanese patrol sneaking up on their foxholes. In the morning, they'd discovered that they had slaughtered a small herd of goats. They had felt foolish about it, but better safe than sorry.

They hadn't seen many goats on Leyte, but there seemed to be an abundance of wild pigs in the forests here, providing a regular source of pork chops for the locals.

Watching the dark forest, Deke didn't reply to Philly. The sniper was so alert, eagerly scanning for a target, that there was no doubt that he had more in common with the hunters in the dark night than with the prey. Sometimes Deke felt like his rifle was hungry and he needed to feed it with dead Japanese. When he thought about it, he realized that it wasn't the rifle that was yearning to kill.

He had come a long way from the mountain farm boy that he'd been. He supposed that they had all come a long way.

Deke remembered that, as a very young boy, he had been reluctant to walk out to the barn at night, afraid of what might be out there. Staring at the dark jungle, that boyhood fear seemed laughable now. There hadn't been anything in the dark to worry about back then—at least not until the bear had come down from the mountain. He touched the left side of his face and felt the deep scars left by that encounter.

The Japanese might actually be out there, like dozens of bears in the dark, with bayonets and rifles instead of claws and teeth. If they weren't there now, then it would be the next night, or the night after that. When it came to a Japanese night attack, experience indicated that it was only a matter of time.

Deke shook his head, clearing his mind, never taking his eyes off the trees. What he needed was sleep. They all did.

Nobody had slept soundly for several nights, mainly because the Japanese were well known for their nighttime attacks. Unlike their American opponents, they had trained to fight at night and take advantage of the cover provided by darkness. These tactics gave them an advantage against the increasingly superior numbers and firepower of US forces. Also, the US had mostly gained control of the skies over the Philippines, which meant that larger Japanese troop movements could be targeted by US planes during the daylight hours.

Truth be told, the greatest advantage for the Japanese and their nighttime attacks was likely the psychological advantage. Even if the Japanese were nowhere in the vicinity, the slightest sound in the darkness resulted in sleepless hours for the American forces hunkered down in their foxholes.

Deke and Philly were attached to C Company, led by Captain Merrick, a unit fighting its way across the Leyte Peninsula. The idea was to search and destroy any Japanese units that might be using the rugged jungle interior as cover.

The two of them had been among the forces that landed on Red Beach near the town of Palo, just before General Douglas MacArthur had waded ashore. With the fall of strongholds such as Hill 522, much of that coastal area was now under US control.

There was still a lot of fighting to do. In its infinite military wisdom, the army had decided that the snipers of Patrol Easy should be split up, with Deke, Philly, and Yoshio journeying across the mountainous jungle interior of the peninsula. The goal was to link up with US forces that had traveled by sea to capture Ormoc on the west coast of Leyte. The rest of Patrol Easy—Lieutenant Steele, Rodeo, Alphabet, Egan with his war dog, Thor—had been sent by ship to Ormoc.

Ormoc was a well-defended Japanese holdout on Leyte. It didn't mean that the Japanese had given up or completely lost the fight. They still fought savagely in units of diminishing size, refusing to surrender. It was beginning to seem as if Leyte would firmly be in US hands only when the last Japanese soldier was dead.

So far the trek across the peninsula had not been easy. They had confronted a Japanese unit that blocked their path and had managed to break through in a desperate fight across a jungle ridge. In that fight Deke had managed to outwit a deadly Japanese sniper named Ikeda. It had been a near thing, but Deke had seen to it that Ikeda had gone to meet his ancestors.

He still wasn't sure that the fight had been entirely fair, but Deke was learning that when it came to war in the Pacific, there wasn't any such thing as a fair fight. In the end, he was just glad that the Japanese sniper was dead, and Deke wasn't.

Deke had lived to fight another day—just barely.

"What's that?" Yoshio asked. Yoshio Shimizu served as their Nisei interpreter, a Japanese American who had opted to show his patriotism by enlisting, despite the fact that his family and many members of his community were now living in an internment camp.

Deke wasn't sure that he would have been as willing to fight for a government that had essentially imprisoned his family, but he understood better than most the need to prove oneself.

Like many who first encountered Yoshio and his distinctly Asian features, Deke and Philly had met their new squad member with some suspicion. That had been back on Guam. When they looked at Yoshio now, all they saw was a fellow soldier they could count on in a fight.

The only one of their little band who was missing was Danilo, a tough Filipino guerrilla who had been assigned—or possibly volunteered—as their guide through the jungle. He had slipped away to visit family in the area. It was a reminder that while the US forces and the Japanese battled over the Philippines, they were merely interlopers here. For men like Danilo, this was home.

Among the three present on the perimeter at the edge of the jungle clearing, Yoshio's ears remained the sharpest. The rest were all starting to go a little deaf from the gunfire, Deke in particular. It was an occupational hazard for a soldier.

Yoshio glanced toward the dark jungle sky, listening.

Deke couldn't hear anything at first. "What is it?"

Yoshio pointed upward. "Planes."

From high above, the sound of aircraft reached Deke's ears. This was a little unusual because, by and large, planes from the US did not fly at night during World War II. This wasn't some lone plane either. There were a lot of aircraft up there.

"I hear it too," Philly said. "Too high up for us to worry about, anyhow."

But Deke wasn't so sure. The sound of the planes seemed to grow louder, almost hovering overhead. Finally, several large transport planes came into sight, silhouetted against the starlight. To their amazement, parachutes began to bloom in the sky, drifting down like pale jellyfish toward the tropical forest.

"I sure as hell hope those are our guys," Philly said, sounding doubtful.

"Nobody told us about any parachute drop," Deke replied.

That wasn't unusual. In typical army fashion, the left hand often didn't know what the right hand was doing. But the US already had thousands of men landed. Why would they need to drop paratroopers?

The answer came like a gut punch.

Before the paratroopers had even touched down, they had opened fire at targets on the ground. A grenade exploded nearby, dropped out of the sky. These were surely Japanese paratroopers, as incredible as that seemed.

"Take cover!" somebody shouted.

But Deke was already up and out of the foxhole, running toward where most of the parachutes seemed to be coming down.

"Dammit, where the hell are you going?" Philly swore again, then ran after him. Yoshio had no choice but to follow.

Out in the open, Deke took a knee and swung the rifle up.

The scope of his Springfield sniper rifle gathered the light, and he quickly scanned the sky until he spotted the dark figure of a Japanese soldier in his jump harness, dangling beneath the parachute that had blossomed like a night-blooming flower.

Deke put his crosshairs on the silhouette and squeezed the trigger. The Japanese paratrooper hung limply. Deke's bullet had found its mark. Quickly, he searched the sky for another target, acquired it, and ensured that another paratrooper was going to be dead on arrival.

However, the paratroopers were not defenseless. The winking muzzle flashes from above indicated that they were shooting back. A bullet snapped the air not far from Deke's head, and he flinched, feeling his spine quiver. Hearing a bullet fired at you wasn't something he'd ever get used to.

"Like shooting fish in a barrel!" Philly shouted happily. He wasn't half the shot Deke was, but that didn't stop him from firing again and again at the descending paratroopers. The night breeze must have shifted, because the parachutes were suddenly carried directly over Company C's position.

"Shoot the bastards!" Captain Merrick shouted, as if his men needed any encouragement. "Shoot them down!"

Behind Deke, the rest of C Company had opened fire. Their semiautomatic M1 rifles had a much faster rate of fire than the Springfield sniper rifles. Even Private Frazier joined in with his Browning Automatic Rifle, stitching the sky with deadly bursts.

On the ground, the Americans opened fire with everything they had. A distant artillery piece had even been brought into play. The shells scattered the low-flying enemy transport planes but passed harmlessly through the descending parachutes. It must have been terrifying to be coming down in a parachute and hear the scream of an artillery round go past. The Japanese who made it to the ground would be plenty rattled.

Another grenade exploded and someone screamed. In the

dark it was impossible to see the grenades coming down. There wasn't any warning or any way to dodge what you couldn't see. Still another grenade went off, so close that Deke was temporarily blinded. He blinked and blinked to clear his vision, glad that he hadn't been hit by any shrapnel. The Japanese grenades were nothing to mess around with, being every bit as deadly as the American version.

The parachutes did not linger overhead. They soon disappeared beyond the treetops as the Japanese touched down. None landed in the field containing C Company, but they must have landed in another clearing. Deke could hear more shooting in the distance, but he couldn't tell whether it was the Japanese or the US forces.

"Come on," Deke shouted, and ran in the direction of where the greatest number of parachutes were raining down.

CHAPTER TWO

IN THE SKIES OVERHEAD, the artillery and antiaircraft guns had also done their work. The burst of flak resembled small black clouds in the moonlit sky. Having surprised the American forces on the ground, the Japanese planes had flown over nearly unscathed. Nearly.

As they watched, one of the Japanese planes was hit, began to trail smoke, and then burst into flame. Ponderously, the plane began to turn, parachutes spilling from it like seeds from a milk-weed pod. The burning plane turned toward the distant sea and slowly disappeared from sight, leaving a trail of glowing sky in its wake. The spectacle was mesmerizing, but the action at hand forced the men to turn their gaze away.

If the soldiers had known what they faced, they might not have run headlong toward where they had seen Japanese troops come down. The paratroopers were crack troops that had seen a great deal of action in China. It hadn't received much attention, because America was busy fighting its own war, but the Chinese had put up a tough fight against the Japanese invaders. Unfortunately, they had been outgunned and poorly supplied, but they certainly had a fighting spirit in defense of their homeland. The Japanese paratroopers had found that out the hard way, and now they faced American troops.

Just beyond the closest trees, the Americans heard rifle shots and submachine-gun fire.

"Doesn't sound like one of ours," Philly panted, struggling to keep up with Deke, whose lanky farm boy's legs ate up the ground.

"Everybody be careful," Deke called, not sounding nearly as winded as Philly. "Those Japs came down thicker than jam on a buttered biscuit."

"Whatever that means," Philly managed, then put his head down and, with a burst of speed, managed to catch up to Deke.

They burst into the clearing, Yoshio on their heels. Deke saw a paratrooper still struggling out of his harness and shot him.

Immediately stitches of muzzle flashes came from their right. Deke dropped to one knee to make himself less of a target and fired at one of the flashes. The enemy soldier went down.

More GIs spilled out of the trees right behind them. Deke heard a grunt of pain and saw one of the GIs fall. After all that they had been through the last few days on their journey through the jungle, the last thing any of them had expected was for Japanese reinforcements to literally drop out of the sky. Deke cursed when he saw another soldier fall.

Deke picked out another target and squeezed the trigger. Next to him, he heard Philly's rifle fire almost at the same time. That was two down.

The Japanese probably hadn't planned on making a fight in this spot, which was nothing more than a random clearing in the surrounding trees, but they were doing a good enough job of it.

The Japanese who were left decided not to stick around. Still firing, they retreated into the trees and lost themselves among the brush and undergrowth.

Deke wasn't about to let them go so easily. His blood was up. After the tension of the last few days, it was as if something inside him had snapped. With a snarl, he ran after the enemy.

"Deke, where the hell do you think you're going?" Philly called. There was a curse, and he heard Philly coming after him, muttering, "That stupid redneck is gonna get us all killed. Come on, Yoshio."

That was the last Deke heard before he crashed into the jungle underbrush. Green and lush as it looked, there was nothing soft or forgiving about the forest. Sharp-edged kunai grass at the edge of the clearing cut his hands as he pushed it out of the way. The spiky leaves of the smaller trees jabbed at his face and eyes.

Deke didn't care. He just wanted to go after the enemy.

Up ahead, in the darkness, he could make out the brush swaying this way and that as someone forced his way through. Deke put his rifle to his shoulder and pressed his eye to the scope. He caught a glimpse of helmet and fired. There was a grunt of pain. Almost immediately one of the paratroopers fired at Deke, the bullet passing so near that he heard it clip the stem of a palm frond as neatly as a pair of garden shears. *Damn, that was close.* Deke dropped, hoping the next shot would miss him by more of a gap, then fired at the enemy's muzzle flash. It was hard to say if he hit anything. All he could see now were the ghostly flashes that had played havoc on his night vision.

He stopped running, hearing noises behind him as Philly and Yoshio caught up.

"What the hell was that all about?" Philly wanted to know.

"Hush now, these woods are crawling with Japanese," Deke replied, then cautiously moved forward, his earlier battle madness having dissipated. He had gone about fifty feet when he came across the body of the Japanese paratrooper he had shot. The man had been solid and well fed; even his uniform looked new. Many of the Japanese they had faced on Leyte so far had shown the signs of meager rations and a struggling supply chain, although it had little impact on their fighting spirit. This man, on the other hand, did not seem to want for anything.

Deke frowned. He found it disturbing that the Japanese seemed to have an endless supply of men with which to feed their war machine. The brass wanted them all to think that the Japanese were just about licked, but that didn't seem so obvious on the ground.

He reached down and spent a moment examining the dead enemy soldier's rifle, noting that it was yet another Arisaka, but well oiled. You had to admit that the Japanese made a darn good rifle, even if the M1 had made the bolt-action weapons increasingly obsolete. So what if it had a slower rate of fire? No matter—it would kill you all the same.

Judging by the quiet behind them, it was also evident that Captain Merrick had not opted to lead the rest of his company into the forest in pursuit of the Japanese. Deke, Philly, and Yoshio were on their own.

Deke thought about how many parachutes he had seen drifting down. There had been a lot. An awful lot. He had been more than a little hotheaded in dashing into the jungle, but there was no telling how many Japanese might also be moving through the forest. It was likely that the Japanese paratroopers had a rendezvous point, and it wouldn't be all that smart for the three of them to stumble across it without any support.

"Let's get the hell out of here," Deke whispered, more than aware that there might be other ears out here, listening. "We need to find the rest of the company."

Yoshio seemed to have the same thought. Still, he took a moment to go through the dead paratrooper's pockets. He struck pay dirt when he found a map. Using the red lens of his flashlight so as not to spoil his night vision, Yoshio looked it over.

"What does it say?" Deke asked. The Japanese writing looked like chicken scratch to him, but he knew that Yoshio understood it well enough.

"I think it indicates targets they intend to hit," Yoshio said. "Captain Merrick may have a better idea. Anyhow, I don't think this is the place to spread out the map and read it."

"Agreed," Philly said. "Listen, Merrick held the rest of the company back at that clearing. Hopefully our guys won't think we're the Japanese coming back to get them and shoot us on the way out."

Deke couldn't argue with that. Slowly he turned and followed Philly and Yoshio back the way they had come, never taking his eyes off the dark jungle surrounding them, expecting at any moment to see an enemy soldier appear.

As they advanced through the jungle, it soon became clear that they were not alone. But it was not the Japanese they encountered. There were other threats in the night, ones oblivious to the war and indifferent to the struggles of the Japanese or the GIs.

Rounding a bend in the game trail, with Deke leading the way, they found two large green eyes staring at them. Deke froze, staring back without flinching. In the moonlight, the rest of the creature began to coalesce. They could see a powerful feline body, poised to launch itself at them.

They had come face-to-face with a large predator that was also stalking the night. It was a leopard cat, one of the few large predators in the Philippine jungles. Like as not, the leopard cat or its kin had been responsible for some of the death cries they had heard from the darkness tonight.

"What's that?" Philly asked, sounding startled by the strange sight of glowing eyes staring at them out of the darkness.

Behind Philly, Yoshio muttered something in Japanese. It might have been either a curse or a prayer.

"Don't move," Deke whispered.

"Shoot it!" Philly urged.

They were moving single file on the narrow trail, and Philly couldn't get a shot off without hitting Deke in the back.

"No shooting, goddammit. We'll have every Japanese para-trooper in the neighborhood down on our heads if you pull that trigger," Deke replied quietly. "Just keep still. Let's see what he does."

It was true that a gunshot would have alerted the Japanese, who were surely lurking somewhere in the forest. What Deke didn't say to Philly was that it was doubtful that he could have lifted and aimed his rifle before the jungle cat covered the distance between them.

He trusted that his reflexes were quicker, or at least as quick, as any Japanese soldier they might have encountered on the trail. But Deke doubted that he was as quick as a jungle cat.

Maybe it was his imagination, but the old scars on the left side of his face, even the deep ones that raked across his body, flared up, tingling and burning on their own, throbbing with each beat of Deke's heart. Those scars were evidence of the mauling that had almost killed him as a boy. They had also left one side of his face and most of his torso disfigured and ugly.

These were the scars that the bear that had come down from the mountain had left on him all those years ago. Deke hadn't been quick enough then to stop the charging bear, and he doubted that he would be quick enough now if the leopard cat sprang at him.

The seconds ticked by.

Ever so slowly the leopard cat seemed to make up its mind that the soldiers either weren't a threat, or weren't worth the fight. It wasn't like they could ask it. The animal gave one last good stare with its green eyes, flicked its tail, and melted off the trail and into the jungle.

Deke realized that he had been holding his breath. He let himself breathe again.

"I'll be damned," he said. "I've got to say, I'd rather fight the Japs any day than fight that thing."

When Philly didn't reply right away, he turned around and found that Philly and Yoshio had retreated by several paces. Only Deke had held his ground.

"Uh, yeah," Philly said, sounding sheepish.

Deke snorted. "Some help you two were."

"It looked to me like you had things under control."

"Come on," Deke said. "This war ain't gonna fight itself."

As they approached the small airfield, they could hear a gun battle taking place. *You had to give these Japanese paratroopers credit,* Deke thought. They had dropped out of the sky into a hostile landing zone and still managed to regroup quickly and launch an attack. The Japanese attack also appeared to be highly organized, because they had even managed to post a handful of troops to guard their flanks.

They found that out because they ran right into those guards.

Stabs of flame from muzzle flashes punctuated the dark forest ahead. If there was any question about whether those shots were intended for them, that question was answered when they heard the sound of bullets zinging through the night air around them.

"Come on!" Deke shouted, then surged ahead.

"Dammit, Deke!" Philly protested. "Let's wait for the others to come up."

It sounded as if the fight at the airfield was not only hot but going badly for their own boys. The sharp crack of the Japanese weapons sounded slightly different from the American rifles, and their bursts outnumbered the smattering of return fire.

Where the hell was the rest of Captain Merrick's company? Deke wasn't going to cool his heels while Merrick's men caught up. *Ain't no time for that.* If nothing else, the three of them might be able to take the Japanese attackers by surprise and do some good there. So far, Deke, Philly, and Yoshio were the only cavalry those boys at the airfield were going to get.

Deke wasn't waiting for anybody else, not if they hoped to have any chance of turning the tide of the fight ahead. He ran toward the sound of the firing, shouting, "Follow me!"

CHAPTER THREE

As Deke ran toward the sound of the fight, the game trail through the jungle narrowed and disappeared, the forest closing in on them like a cattle chute, but Deke kept running pell-mell, shoving aside branches, crashing through the greenery, a one-man bush hog.

It wasn't how he normally liked to move through the forest, but a kind of battle madness had come over him. He became aware of a constant snarl rumbling at the back of his throat. He wasn't even himself anymore, he realized, but just an elemental force racing through the trees toward the fight.

They were making as much noise as a herd of buffalo, but considering all the shooting going on up ahead, he doubted anyone would notice. At some point a big spiderweb draped across his face like a net. He clawed it away and kept going. He could hear Philly and Yoshio right behind him.

Their sheer momentum turned out to be a saving grace. If they had been moving slowly, the outcome might have been different.

A figure popped up ahead of Deke. He could see the silhouette, crouched, caught off guard. From the man's short stature, Deke knew at once that it was a Japanese soldier. One of the paratroopers, probably carried off course, trying to catch up with the rest of his unit.

Philly had seen him too.

"Jap!" he whispered hoarsely.

"Yeah, I see him."

The paratrooper looked like he was about to launch himself at them, but Yoshio said something in Japanese, *"Anata no yunitto wa dokodesu ka?"*

Yoshio was asking him, *Where is your unit?* Yoshio's words seemed to confuse the enemy paratrooper into thinking that he had run into more of his comrades, but the ruse did not last for long. The soldier scowled, then said, *"Anatahadare?"*

"He wants to know who the hell I am," Yoshio whispered, then replied in Japanese: *"Watashi wa tomodachidesu."*

Yoshio had told the soldier, *I am a friend.* Apparently it was the wrong thing to say, or perhaps Yoshio's accent had given him away. Sure, he spoke Japanese, but he didn't sound like he'd just come from Tokyo.

Something bright flashed in the paratrooper's hand. Either a knife or a bayonet. These paratroopers were essentially commandos and had plenty of training with bladed weapons.

No matter how much training he had, not using his rifle turned out to be a mistake.

The hand went up, ready to slash down, the blade once again catching a ray of moonlight, the razor-sharp edge glinting. As the blade started to come down, Deke twisted his lean body out of the way like a mongoose dodging a striking snake. The blade hissed past, cutting only air.

Deke didn't have time to aim his rifle but fired from the hip at point-blank range, so close that the muzzle blast stabbed out and scorched the paratrooper's uniform.

The sheer amount of muzzle energy generated by the Springfield packed quite a punch. He hit the enemy paratrooper square in the chest, the force of the impact lifting the smaller man off his feet. The paratrooper tumbled back into the jungle, bladed weapon spinning out of his hand.

Deke didn't stop to make sure the man was dead, although he had no doubt of it. His momentum carried him right past the crumpled body, and he kept going. Behind him, Philly and Yoshio didn't stop either.

They didn't encounter any additional threats, Japanese or otherwise, as they rushed to rejoin Captain Merrick's company on the airfield perimeter. Up ahead, he saw the trees thinning out and the clearing that indicated they had reached the airfield.

"Coming through!" Deke shouted for the benefit of the soldiers who might be apt to turn their guns on the sounds approaching from the jungle.

He needn't have worried. Captain Merrick himself stood nearby, standing tall even as Japanese bullets cut the air.

"Hold your fire!" Merrick shouted at the men ready to shoot at the trio that had burst from the jungle growth. To Deke he said, "Where the hell have you been?"

"Chasing Japs." Deke refrained from calling the officer "sir" on the battlefield—it was a surefire way to attract even more attention from any Japanese within earshot.

"There's plenty right here. Get busy."

Merrick's company had quite a fight on their hands. The night blossomed with explosions, stabs of flame, and brilliant streams of machine-gun tracers. It was like the Fourth of July and Hades all wrapped up together.

Amid the overwhelming noise of weaponry, they heard shouted orders—some in English, some in Japanese—the enemy was that close. The air smelled of cordite mingled with the fecund odor of the jungle at night.

Following orders, the sniper team took up position in a foxhole occupied by a dead man. Deke shoved the body aside without thinking, then slid his rifle to his shoulder and his eye to the scope. The flashes and bursts sprang closer, but the telescopic sight severely limited his field of view. This was exactly why he had Yoshio as a spotter.

"On your left!" Yoshio shouted.

Deke swung the rifle that way. Through the scope, he spotted the movement just where Yoshio had said it would be. A shadow separated itself from the larger shadow of a tree trunk. The Japanese soldier had been creeping up on their position. Before the enemy could fire, Deke squeezed the trigger and dropped him.

Off to Deke's right, Philly was also firing at a target using his own rifle with its telescopic sight. Yoshio was trying to spot for them both, but the action was too fast and fluid. He gave up and turned his full attention to giving direction to Deke—who was the better shot, anyhow. Philly would just have to satisfy himself blasting away at the enemy muzzle flashes.

There were a lot of those. The Japanese paratroopers had converged on the airfield to make their attack, and they seemed to be everywhere at once.

What we could really use is a machine gun, Deke thought.

He would just have to do what he could to help defeat the attack and defend this jungle airfield, one bullet at a time. Though highly accurate, especially in the hands of a skilled marksman like Deke, his Springfield rifle had a slower rate of fire due to it being a bolt-action weapon.

The US Army lacked any official sniper warfare training, unlike the Japanese or the Germans. It was a little ironic, considering the Americans' reputations as hunters and crack shots. Weren't they all supposed to be like Daniel Boone and maybe Wyatt Earp? The truth was far from that. However, a little training went a long way, which was why a few renegades like Lieutenant Steele had made the effort to train snipers and put real sniper rifles into the hands of men like Deke and Philly, with devastating effect.

For the most part, the US military doctrine saw itself as a blunt instrument, a hammer blow. Sometimes what you needed was an ice pick, which was exactly the purpose that a sniper served.

The real advantage of a sniper came at the fringes of a battle, or not even during a battle at all. A good sniper learned to pick off the enemy during moments when he least expected it: having a smoke, drinking from his canteen, a careless moment when he stood up to admire the view or joke with a friend. That was when a sniper delivered death, a fatal metallic pill to swallow.

A sniper remained unseen and unheard until that moment when a bullet came out of nowhere. A good sniper would fire one shot and then vanish like smoke before the enemy could pinpoint him. He left death and fear in his mysterious wake.

More than anything, Deke had come to realize, sniping was a head game to strike fear into the enemy in quieter moments. That wasn't going to happen during a full-fledged firefight.

"Ten o'clock!" Yoshio shouted.

Deke swung the rifle that way and saw a Japanese soldier running right at them. In the flickering light of the battle zone, Deke saw that the enemy wasn't carrying a rifle but was armed with a stick bomb. These were long poles with a high-explosive charge attached to one end. The Japanese called them *Shitotsub-akurai*. The explosive charge would detonate on impact, essentially being a primitive pressure-sensitive bomb.

It was hard to say what the purpose of the stick was, considering that the amount of explosive would certainly vaporize the soldier delivering the bomb. But if that length of stick gave the soldier some sense of hope that he would somehow survive the attack, so be it.

Through the scope, he could see the Japanese soldier's open mouth, screaming a battle cry as he charged.

Deke shot him.

Crazy bastard, Deke thought. *What was the point of that?*

Then a cold stab of realization went through him. Just beyond their foxhole several barrels were stacked. Then more and more barrels. Holy hell. They were sitting right next to the fuel dump for the airfield.

The berserk Japanese soldier hadn't been trying to break through their lines. He'd been intending to blow up the fuel dump. If he had succeeded, the explosion would have taken out most of the company. As for the airfield, it would be rendered unusable—most likely, at least part of the landing strip would be reduced to a large burned hole in the ground.

All three seemed to figure it out at once. They looked at the stacked piles of highly flammable aviation fuel, at the advancing Japanese paratroopers, and then at one another.

"Dammit!" Philly said. "I don't want to get blown up."

Yoshio muttered, *"Chikushō."* *Oh shit!* No translation was required to understand that it was not something that he would have said in front of his mother.

"Yeah," Deke said. "That last fella was close. Just don't let them get any closer."

But the Japanese seemed to have made up their minds that they were going to blow up that fuel stockpile, even if it was the last thing they did. Destroying the airstrip and the fuel dump appeared to be the paratroopers' primary mission.

Another Japanese soldier broke away from the paratroopers. Like the previous man, he was similarly armed with a stick bomb. He ran at a crouch toward the American position. Incredibly, he seemed to leap over a burst of machine-gun fire lit by tracers and kept right on going.

"It's another runner, ten o'clock," Yoshio said.

"I see him," Philly said.

He fired, but the man did not go down.

"He's still coming," Yoshio said.

"Dammit, I'm out!" Philly shouted, fumbling in the dark for another stripper clip. "You've got to get him, Deke!"

Deke was already tracking the enemy soldier through his scope. Hitting a moving target was no small feat, even for the best marksman. The challenge was compounded by the flickering, uncertain light of the battlefield. Also, Deke and the others were being shot at. Bullets sang above their helmets, and it took a huge amount of willpower not to duck down out of sheer instinct. There was a very real possibility that Deke would get shot in the head before he could squeeze that trigger.

Deke got his rhythm going, swinging his sights through the man to a point just ahead of him, moving the sight along, matching his speed. With any luck, the target would essentially run right into the path of the bullet.

Easy, easy—

He flinched at the nearby detonation of what sounded like a mortar. Yoshio yelped in pain.

Dammit. Deke got back on target. The Japanese runner was quick. He had already covered too much ground. There was time for just one shot before the runner covered the distance to the fuel depot and detonated that stick bomb.

Deke put everything else out of his head. Time seemed to slow down. He repeated the process of swinging through the man again, matching his pace, holding the crosshairs there. The runner reached the edge of the fuel dump, where a pile of barrels had fallen over and rolled across the airstrip.

The Japanese gave a keening cry, either of terror or victory, nobody could be sure.

Deke squeezed the trigger.

What happened next happened fast. The rifle kicked against his shoulder, the runner tumbled, the stick bomb hit the ground —and exploded.

A blast wave of searing air washed over Deke's face. Clumps of burning fuel spread across the field and even landed in the jungle, burning like will-o'-the-wisps among the trees.

But nothing else exploded.

As Captain Merrick's company concentrated their fire, the fight seemed to go out of the enemy paratroopers. Either that or many of them had been killed. Private Frazier opened fire with his Browning Automatic Rifle and swept the jungle's edge with a long burst. The effect was like a gale force wind scattering the embers of a forest fire. The enemy fire immediately became more sporadic, then died down altogether.

And just like that, the real fight had ended, the desperate one where the outcome had hung by a thread. All that remained now was the mopping up.

It was hard to say how long the battle had gone on. Time had a way of distorting during combat—nothing made sense. There was no real way of measuring it. The movement of hands on a man's wristwatch was meaningless. What seemed like hours were actually minutes, while the hours themselves ticked by like seconds.

The only proof of the passage of the long night came from the fact that the sky was already growing lighter. Pale streaks on the horizon promised another tropical dawn. However, down here in the closeness of the jungle, it was still plenty dark enough.

"So much for that," Philly announced. "Now maybe we can all finally get some sleep."

Normally Deke tended to be the wide-awake one, getting by on less shut-eye and watching the jungle while the others slept. But a sense of exhaustion suddenly hit him, hard as a knockout punch from Joe Louis.

He slumped down into the muddy bottom of the foxhole, closed his eyes, and fell asleep instantly, clutching his rifle to him like the only lover he had known.

CHAPTER FOUR

EXHAUSTION SET in after the nighttime fight against the incursion of Japanese paratroopers, so sleep came quickly, even for men who had only a helmet for a pillow. While Deke slept, a handful of men kept an uneasy watch. An occasional crackle of rifle fire was a reminder that they hadn't gotten all the paratroopers. But the enemy's back had been broken, and they had evidently given up on attacking the airfield again.

The soldiers slept as long as they could, but the rising sun and tropical heat soon began to rouse them. Deke had a momentary sense of panic when he didn't immediately feel his rifle in his hands.

He sat up, frantically looking around. "Where, where—"

His fingertips touched the familiar stock, which had slipped a couple of inches out of his grip while he slept. "There you are."

His rifle hadn't gone anywhere. He shook his head, worried that he was overreacting. *I'm just tired, is all.*

He had managed to snatch a couple hours of sleep. It wasn't enough, but it would have to do. He supposed that he was lucky to get even that much shut-eye.

Judging by the faint sounds of snoring nearby, several of the other men were still sleeping, Philly and Yoshio included. Watching the forms of the two sleeping men, Deke felt a surge of affection toward them, what you might call brotherly love. In fact, if he'd had brothers instead of his ornery sister, Sadie, he was sure this was how he would have felt toward them.

Deke was surprised to discover that sense of bonding toward Philly and Yoshio. After all, he had thought that those last few difficult years on the failing farm and then in the bleak boarding-house in town—not to mention the loss of his ma and pa, good people beaten down by a hard life—had leached out the last of any emotion in him. Whatever was left that the bear hadn't clawed out of him already.

Deke discovered that he'd been wrong about that. It had taken a war and all that killing and fighting to realize that there was still something human left in him. He still had a little broth-erly love left to give someone other than Sadie. *Don't that beat all.*

Deke shrugged, stuffed a cork in the cracked bottle of his emotions for now, and turned to matters at hand.

None of the sergeants came by with orders, which meant that Captain Merrick didn't appear to be in any hurry to move out, meaning that they would likely sit here guarding the airfield and fuel dump for a while longer, so Deke set to work cleaning his rifle. The gunfire he'd heard earlier had been distant, and there seemed to be a good chance that he could take fifteen minutes to disassemble the rifle for cleaning without needing it to shoot anybody.

Living in these conditions, it was easy to let something like cleaning your rifle slide, but as far as Deke was concerned, his rifle came first. He might need a shave, his face was dirty, his uniform slick with mud and who knew what else, but he'd have a clean rifle.

He tackled that chore even before he'd had anything to eat

for breakfast—a well-oiled weapon might mean the difference between life and death.

If Deke had felt some fondness for his foxhole mates this morning, it didn't compare to what he felt for his sniper rifle.

First of all, the well-made Springfield seemed indestructible. Its origins went back at least a decade before World War I, a conflict that had put the rifle to the test and honed its functionality to perfection as a combat weapon.

Deke's rifle had been manufactured the year before at the federal armory on the banks of the Connecticut River in Massachusetts. It was a Model 1903A4 Springfield rifle. The Weaver telescopic sight had been made in El Paso, Texas, with a magnification of 2.5, which meant that the details of the surrounding jungle terrain sprang much closer. Japanese and German optics both had a reputation for being more precise and finely made, but the sturdy Weaver scope got the job done.

The Germans and Japanese seemed convinced of their manufacturing superiority when it came to weapons, even if their output could not keep pace with US production, but in this case, American steel, wood, and optics had been combined into a superior rifle.

Finally, the rifle was a reliable workhorse, or maybe even a sturdy mule. The Springfield was highly forgiving compared to the semiautomatic Garand M1, with its more complex moving parts. It hadn't let Deke down so far. However, there was no sense trusting the rifle's reliable function to luck.

He set to work, field stripping the rifle and pulling the bolt free. The metal surface was indeed grimy with gunpowder residue and minuscule bits of metallic fouling. There was possibly mud mixed in there, and the ever-present tropical moisture wasn't helping. Deke set to work, knowing that it was nothing that a rag and gun oil couldn't handle.

The metal soon gleamed again and smelled of gun oil rather

than sulfur. As far as Deke was concerned, nothing smelled better than gun oil. Hell, if they ever put gun oil into an after-shave, he would have bought it.

Finishing up the rifle, once again ready for action, he set it aside. Deke felt tired, wrung out, even more than usual. He wished he had a cup of strong coffee, maybe with some sugar in it, but that wasn't going to happen. He settled for a long drink of tepid canteen water, the metallic taste sour in his dry mouth.

Most of the men had managed a few hours of sleep after an exhausting night, but it hadn't been enough. Their sleep banks were long overdrawn.

Next to him, Philly and Yoshio finally began to stir.

"Look at that, I slept on a rock and didn't even notice," Philly remarked groggily. He touched the small of his back and winced. "Must have been tired. I'll feel it today, that's for damn sure."

"You sure you didn't sleep on that rock with your face?"

"Very funny, country boy. Aren't you just a ray of sunshine?" Philly yawned. "Damn, when we finally get back home, the second thing I'm going to do is sleep for a week."

"What's the first thing you are going to do?" Yoshio asked, unable to resist.

"I'll tell you what, Yoshio. Since you asked. The *first* thing I'm going to do is look up Nancy Holland and see if she will give a war hero like me a warm welcome home. With any luck, I'll spend the week sleeping in *her* bed. When she lets me sleep, that is."

Deke snorted. "Good luck with that. When I get home, the first thing I'm gonna do is get something decent to eat. Maybe a big breakfast with sausage and gravy. Hell, I'd settle for a hamburger."

"Ice cream," Yoshio muttered dreamily. "Fresh strawberries with cream. Orange juice."

"You dopes can go home and eat hamburgers and banana splits if you want to," Philly said. "I'm gonna go home and eat some pussy. Maybe put a pickle on it."

Deke couldn't help but laugh at Philly's crude humor. The conversation of most young soldiers usually focused on the things they had to do without in the jungle—food, booze, and women—with the usual amount of bragging, boasting, and wistfulness mixed in. Philly was just saltier than most, and a bigger liar.

Now that the sun had risen above the hills to the point that the sunlight finally managed to flood across the small airfield, Deke looked above the rim of the foxhole at the morning view. His good mood evaporated at the sight before him.

Daylight revealed the full carnage from the previous night's battle. Several dead Japanese lay scattered across the airfield. Some were balled up into fetal positions they had assumed during their agonized dying throes, while others sprawled exactly where they had fallen, killed instantly, perhaps by one of Deke's bullets. He didn't feel any remorse, however. The Japanese would gladly have done the same to him.

These had been crack Japanese troops fighting a desperate battle, and they had sold their lives dearly. Maybe a few had slunk back into the jungle, but it looked to Deke as if most of the paratroopers had been killed here last night.

Deke looked around and saw where he had shot that Japanese bomber before he could reach the fuel dump. Seeing the number of avgas barrels now visible in daylight, Deke realized it would've made quite a bang. Most of the company would have been incinerated. Although Deke's bullet had brought him down, the dead Japanese soldier's body was in several pieces thanks to the bomb he'd been carrying. He spotted what looked like a leg, and a few feet away, a hand still gripped the remnants of the stick bomb.

Ordinarily such a scene would have been nauseating, but Deke now took it in stride. What were they all becoming?

If he needed any reassurance about the carnage, all he had to do was look at the spot where a few dead GIs had been gathered at one end of the company's position. The four bodies had been laid out in a neat row, their faces covered with coats or blankets, giving them some measure of dignity in death. A detail trooped past with entrenching tools to dig graves. Between the heat and the inadequacy of the digging tools, it was doubtful that the graves would be very deep. It was too far to carry the bodies, so a shallow jungle grave would have to do.

No such effort was made for the dead Japanese—they would rot where they had fallen. There was little doubt that the vultures and other scavengers would pick at their bones, because little went to waste in the jungle. Again, Deke felt a kind of numbness at the thought. After all, these bastards had been trying to kill them just last night.

With some bad luck, or if the night had been darker and they hadn't spotted the parachutes coming down, it might have been all of them lying out there. Deke still didn't feel like he hated the enemy, but more and more, he was starting to wonder.

"Damn these Japs," he muttered to no one in particular. The words simply vented like steam from a cast-iron radiator.

"What?" Philly asked.

"Nothin'." Deke shook his head. No point in trying to explain himself.

A sergeant came around, looking for Yoshio. That in itself was a little unusual. Having been attached to the company as scout-snipers, the three of them—along with Danilo when he was around—were officially part of the company, yet somehow were not.

Captain Merrick had seemed to realize that they knew their business and left them to it. Most of the time, their job was to lead the column down the jungle trail, on the lookout for any threats of ambush. When there was trouble, they were the first to deal with it.

"You're that guy who speaks Japanese?" the sergeant asked.

"Hai," said Yoshio, who was not without his own sense of humor.

The sergeant stared at him a long beat, not without a little malice. Yoshio looked Japanese, and he sounded Japanese—some GIs just couldn't get used to the idea that he wasn't the enemy, even if he was as American as they were.

"Yeah, well," the sergeant finally said, "Captain Merrick's got a prisoner. He wants you to question him."

Yoshio grabbed his rifle and helmet, which he'd taken off hoping for respite from the morning heat, and scrambled out of the foxhole.

Deke and Philly looked at each other, then grabbed their own gear and followed Yoshio out of the hole.

Captain Merrick had made his HQ in a foxhole near the center of the line of holes that delineated the company's position at the perimeter of the airfield. The only concession to it being the HQ seemed to be that the hole was somewhat bigger, was also occupied by a radioman and the company's last remaining medic, and, stretched across the top, had battered camouflage netting that struggled to block the harshest rays of the sun.

Crouching in the hole was Captain Merrick, leaning over a wounded Japanese soldier. The man was propped up against the sides of the foxhole. His arms hung limply at his sides, and it was evident that he wouldn't have had the strength to sit up on his own. The soldier who had been a terrifying enemy a few short hours ago was nothing but a pathetic dying figure now.

Merrick was crouched over the wounded man and leaning forward as if to hear what the captured Japanese had to say. The man was speaking softly, but in his own language, leaving Merrick looking frustrated. At least the man was talking. If they wanted to find out what the enemy soldier had to say, they didn't have much time.

The Japanese soldier groaned when Merrick touched him, but refused even a drink of water with a weak shake of his head. Deke always expected the enemy to be older somehow, battle-hardened warriors, but this Japanese looked like he might be nineteen or twenty, younger than Deke.

Deke could see a large open gash in the man's thigh, almost to the bone. Thick, dark blood had collected in puddles around the wound, despite an effort to apply bandages. The smells lingering in the bottom of the foxhole were not good ones—sweaty bodies, mud wet from the dying man's blood, a whiff of intestines.

Captain Merrick sat back on his haunches when he saw Yoshio slide into the foxhole.

"Sir," said Yoshio. "You wanted to see me?"

Merrick nodded at the wounded prisoner. "This one is singing like a canary, but I'll be damned if I can understand a word of that gibberish. You're supposed to be an interpreter, right? Maybe you can make out what he's saying. Headquarters has been on us to gather some intelligence. Something, anything, that they can use to give us an idea of how many Japs are still out here and what sort of supplies they have. See what you can find out."

Yoshio changed places with the captain, leaning over the prisoner. The man's eyes were shut—for all they knew, he might already be dead.

Although it was true that Yoshio was an interpreter, there had been precious few opportunities for him to use his language skills. Not many Japanese surrendered. The ones who were captured tended to be badly wounded, like this man, too weak to take their own lives or beyond caring.

Yoshio spoke a few words to the dying man, whose eyes flicked open in surprise at the sound of his native tongue.

He responded with a few halting words spoken quietly. To Deke's ears, Japanese was a surprisingly harsh and guttural language. It seemed to roll around in the chest and the back of the throat before the words erupted like short, angry barks.

"What's he saying?" Captain Merrick demanded.

"He says that he grew up on a farm outside the village of Shirakawa," Yoshio answered. "As a boy, it was his job to tend the chickens and cattle. He had hoped to return there after the war and marry the daughter of a merchant in the village."

"I doubt that HQ wants to know any of that, Private," Merrick said. "Ask him how many more paratroopers there are. Where is their base? Where do they intend to drop next?"

Yoshio translated the captain's questions into Japanese, but the wounded enemy paratrooper just shook his head and uttered a few guttural words in reply.

"Well?" Merrick demanded, having appeared to hang on every word. He seemed desperate to provide HQ with something that they could use.

"Sir, he says to look around the airfield. Do you not see the bodies fallen like flower petals? There are no more paratroopers coming."

"All right, I suppose that's something. Ask him how many planes left their base."

Yoshio leaned close to do as Merrick ordered. The paratrooper's words had been faint, and his chest barely rose up and down. Yoshio said something in Japanese, but there was no response. "That is it, sir. He is gone."

"Dammit! HQ will be glad to know that there shouldn't be any additional drops—if we can believe this Nip."

"For what it is worth, I believe that he was telling the truth, sir."

Merrick snorted. "You believe him, huh? What was he, a cousin of yours or something?"

"I interviewed my share of prisoners on Guam and now on Leyte, sir. Dying men tend to tell the truth."

"If you say so, Private. From one Jap to another, right?"

"Sir—"

"That will be all. You are dismissed, Private. The rest of you, we'll be moving out in an hour."

The three of them exited the makeshift company HQ and headed back to their own foxhole.

"Got to say, Merrick was kind of an asshole back there," Philly muttered once they were out of earshot of the captain.

Deke nodded in the direction of the burial detail. "I reckon you might be, too, if you were the one who had to write all those letters home."

"Aw, Merrick can go screw himself," Philly said. "We all know we can trust you, Yoshio."

Yoshio gazed out over the field of Japanese dead beginning to bloat in the heat and didn't say anything at all.

An hour later, as promised, the order came to move out, and they left the airfield and the stinking bodies behind.

CHAPTER FIVE

LEAVING THE AIRFIELD, Deke took point and led the company out. Guarding the airfield perimeter had been a brief respite. It might even have been easy duty if it hadn't been for the Japanese paratrooper attack. Nobody had planned on that one, of course.

They moved down the jungle trail. Before long, they were supposed to arrive in the vicinity of Ormoc and link up with the troops fighting the Japanese stronghold there. But first there were many long miles of jungle to traverse.

The path was easy going at first but quickly changed the deeper they went into the forest. Leaves and shrubs crowded in from both sides of the trail, creating a tunnel of green and gloom. On the forest floor, decaying leaves and half-hidden tree roots wove a tangle that made their footing unsure, trying to trip up weary feet.

The air was humid and warm, and even in the shadows far beneath the jungle overstory the heat of the sun felt like an oven directed at their heads and shoulders.

Deke licked his lips. The jungle tasted wilted, like spinach gone bad.

The GIs sweated through their fatigues, and sweat poured down their faces, attracting swarms of insects. Some of the bugs were no more than an annoyance, clogging eyes and ears. Others were out for blood. Deke itched all over from mosquito bites, some of which had left big red welts.

The mountains were Deke's natural habitat rather than the jungle, but nonetheless, something didn't feel right. Deke found himself glancing back over his shoulder toward the end of the column. Private Frazier was back there with his BAR as a kind of one-man rear guard. But the big man was plodding along in the heat and humidity, not paying attention to what was behind them.

Deke motioned for the company to halt. He put his eye to the telescopic sight and caught just a glimpse of movement in the shadows. The next moment, whatever he had seen was gone. Another man might have thought that his eyes were playing tricks on him, but Deke knew better.

Captain Merrick came hustling up. "What is it?" he wanted to know.

"There's someone following us," Deke announced.

The captain was sweating heavily in the heat, rivulets of sweat running down his unshaven face. He looked haggard, probably because he'd had even less sleep than his men, given the nightly threat of Japanese attack or infiltrators. These young captains of combat companies bore an incredible leadership burden. Along with the sergeants, they were the backbone of the army.

"Japanese?" the captain asked, frowning.

"Hard to say, other than that it was two-legged. Whoever it was slipped off into the jungle."

"This wouldn't be a good place for a fight, not with us spread out along this trail," Merrick said.

"I don't think it was a Japanese patrol. Just one man. I'm not sure what the hell he was up to."

"All right. I'll pass the word to keep an eye out," Merrick said, then hustled away.

The captain paused from time to time to give a quiet word of warning to the men. They had been glad of the short break, but the column soon got moving again along the jungle trail.

Watching him go, Deke decided that he liked Captain Merrick well enough. *Liked* wasn't exactly the right word. *Respected* was more accurate. Merrick had shown himself to be more than competent in taking the company through the jungle-ridden interior of Leyte. He had come to rely on and trust Deke, some of that invisible barrier between officer and enlisted man eroding. Merrick asked for Deke's advice on occasion and even listened to it, which in Deke's book made the captain a smart man.

The captain had managed to keep most of the company alive so far during this jungle trek, which was saying something. There were some exceptions. They had lost a few good men, including Dickie Shelby, who had died bringing them precious water when they had been pinned down by the Japanese. Merrick said he planned on putting Shelby in for a medal once he had time to sit down and write the commendation.

However, Deke had been taken aback by the man's clear prejudice against Yoshio. To be honest, Deke may have felt some similar distrust when he had first set eyes on Yoshio's Asian features. In every way, Yoshio resembled the enemy they were so desperately fighting.

He now saw Yoshio as a brother and knew that the man had his back. During their jungle trek, the captain must surely have seen that Yoshio was a good soldier, but his prejudice must have been deeply ingrained. Deke was willing to cut the captain some slack, considering that his company had lost a lot of good men.

Not for the first time that day, Deke realized that he felt even more worn out than usual. Even his bones ached. A throbbing had begun somewhere behind his eyes.

Just tired is all, he reassured himself. But he began to have the nagging thought that maybe this was the start of something worse. Was he coming down with something? Several of the men already had fevers, possibly even malaria, and he wasn't eager to join them.

Distracted by his thoughts, it was only at the last instant that he detected motion in the trees nearby and swung his rifle in that direction, fully expecting an attack by the Japanese. It would explain why he had seen someone lurking at the rear of the column.

But it was not a Japanese soldier. The figure that materialized from the leafy shadows was none other than Danilo, their Filipino guide. Apparently he had finally decided to rejoin them after visiting family in some nearby jungle enclave. In the short time that the column was halted, he had managed to transit the forest parallel to the trail silently and unseen until emerging almost at Deke's side.

Deke held his fire and swung the muzzle away from Danilo's chest.

"Dammit, another second and I would have blown a hole in you."

Danilo just laughed, his lined face crinkling. He did not seem concerned. The two men communicated mainly through gestures or a few brief words, because neither man understood the other's language.

The Filipino guide touched his own rifle, a captured Japanese weapon, as if to indicate that he had the drop on Deke long before he'd been spotted.

"Bang!" he said, laughing again.

"What the hell is wrong with you?" Deke wondered.

He realized that the figure he had seen tailing the column had been none other than Danilo. He had slipped off the trail; then, while the company was halted, he had moved quietly through the trees and emerged at the front of the column. Deke doubted that he would've been able to pull off that particular stunt had the tables been turned.

Danilo wore a floppy hat, a stained and ragged shirt that was two sizes too big for him, pants hacked off unevenly at the calves, and rope-soled sandals. In these parts, it was what passed for a guerrilla uniform. Danilo had rigged a piece of rope to serve as a sling for the Japanese rifle. He might not look much like a soldier, but he was one of the toughest men that Deke had met.

While Danilo respected Deke's skills, and Deke in turn respected the Filipino's, there remained a sort of competition between them as to who was the better woodsman. Danilo certainly had the home advantage.

"Bang! Bang!" Danilo said again, happily.

"All right, that's enough of that." Deke pointed at Danilo and then at the empty position in front of him. The gesture needed no explanation, but Deke added, "Why don't you go on and lead us, if you're so smart."

The Filipino seemed happy to oblige, apparently still pleased with himself for having gotten the drop on Deke—well, almost.

Captain Merrick must have been wondering what was going on, but Deke gave him a wave. The captain signaled back that they should move forward.

"Well look who turned up," Philly said. "I guess Danilo has been visiting the local senoritas."

It was impossible for them to get any details from their guide, but his smile seemed to indicate that he had, in fact, spent his time away from the company pleasantly. The Filipino started up the trail.

Deke was glad to let Danilo take point for now. They would trade off later, which had been their method for most of this jungle trek. By and large it was the most dangerous position. Considering that Deke was right behind him, having Danilo go first wasn't much of a buffer. Should something happen, chances were good that they would both buy it.

The two men trusted one another. So far Deke had been reluctant to let Philly lead the way. Philly had his attributes, but he was no woodsman.

If an ambush awaited the company, whoever was on point would walk into it first. The same held true for any nasty surprises, such as booby traps. This was why it was so important to have the company led by someone with skill at sensing ambushes and traps. One wrong step and—well, that might be your last step.

* * *

THEY WALKED for miles until it started to get dark. Except for a couple of false alarms—one of which turned out to be a wild pig—the day was uneventful.

Their hope had been to reach the sea and the coastal area around Ormoc, but so far that had not happened. It looked as though they would be spending yet another night camped out on the jungle trail.

By then Deke's head ached, and he felt feverish. Hot as it was, he felt even hotter.

"You don't look so great," Philly said to him, looking him up and down.

"I'm fine," Deke snapped. "Just tired is all."

"You look a little yellow," Philly insisted. "I hope to hell you don't have malaria."

Danilo had also seemed to notice. *"May malaria ka,"* he announced. *"Kailangan mo ng pahinga."*

"What's he sayin', Philly?"

"I understood the malaria part," he said. "I don't think the rest of it matters. Danilo here thinks you're coming down with malaria."

"What does he know?" Yet Deke's feverish brow was beginning to tell him otherwise. Getting sick out here wasn't surprising. Malaria and other fevers ran rampant. For some the malaria was debilitating, and for others it was an illness that nagged at them for weeks at a time.

Sometimes it seemed as though the germs had felled as many soldiers as machine guns.

The trouble was that there wasn't any bed rest out here in the jungle. There was no choice but to keep moving.

Danilo pointed at the ground, indicating that Deke should sit. Suddenly weary to the point of feeling dizzy, he was glad to oblige. Danilo draped a blanket over Deke's shoulders.

"Better eat something," Philly said. "Keep your strength up."

"I ain't hungry." Deke wasn't one to be picky, but he suddenly couldn't stomach the thought of another tin of rations.

Danilo had other plans for supper than C rations. He carried a small bag, hardly more than a sack, over one shoulder rather than a haversack like the soldiers. Other than his rifle and his bolo knife, everything that he needed to survive in the forest was in that bag. He didn't even carry a blanket roll.

Once they were camped out on the trail for the night, Danilo quickly built a small fire, using dry twigs and branches that made very little smoke. Even the fire was small. A man could have scooped it up and held it in both his hands. Like the true woodsman that he was, everything that Danilo did was about economy and efficiency.

"Tell him to throw some green leaves on there and keep the mosquitoes away," someone suggested.

"What, and let every Japanese soldier in the vicinity know we're here? Didn't you ever hear of sending smoke signals?" Philly shook his head. "I don't think it's a good idea."

As the flames licked up and began to consume the dry twigs and sticks, it was a reminder that there was a primitive comfort in a fire. Maybe it went back to the oldest days of the cavemen, Deke thought. Wherever there was a campfire, a man felt at home.

Once the fire was going, Danilo slipped into the forest and used his bolo knife to cut a length of bamboo. The sharp blade went through the bamboo in one swift chop. Deftly, he cut away one side of the bamboo to reveal the hollow interior, which he filled with a handful of rice grains taken from his sack and a dribble of water from his canteen. He replaced the bamboo "door" that he had cut away and put the bamboo over the coals. It was an ingenious way to cook rice without a pot.

While the rice steamed inside the bamboo tube, Danilo produced half a cooked chicken from his bag.

Philly gave a low whistle. "What else have you got in that sack, Danilo? A chocolate cake?"

Danilo just smiled. It was anybody's guess as to how much English he actually knew, but he seemed to understand them most of the time—he just chose not to speak in return. It was also possible that Danilo understood something that Philly did not, which was that silence was the first step on the road to wisdom.

The Filipino skewered the chicken on a stick and held it over the fire to heat up. Soon the skin began to crackle and brown, filling the lower part of the jungle canopy with the delicious smell of roasting chicken. Canned rations did not even begin to compare. A visceral hunger clawed inside the men's bellies at the smell of meat cooking over an open fire. Soldiers looked enviously in Danilo's direction and at the hot meal he was preparing.

"Hey, Danilo, I'll give you five American dollars for that chicken," one soldier said.

"Ten," said another.

Danilo ignored them and focused on cooking his meal to perfection. Of course, there just wasn't enough of Danilo's meal to go around. With what seemed to be a collective sigh, the soldiers went back to scraping out the congealed beef stew from the walls of the steel ration cans.

When the rice began to escape from the bamboo tube to show that it had finished steaming, Danilo took it off the fire. Using a large leaf for a plate, he heaped it with rice and chicken and presented it to Deke. Danilo put the rest on another leaf for himself.

Before eating, Danilo crossed himself, and his lips moved silently in a prayer. Deke recalled seeing the man in the morning, on his knees in prayer. Deke never had been all that religious. To see such a tough man humble himself before God made Deke wonder if he ought to do more himself to get right with the Lord.

All in all, the meal was an impressive display of jungle craft of an entirely different sort than tracking the enemy or managing to move unseen through the forest.

Deke nodded his thanks. By now he was almost feeling too weak to eat. The fever was really taking hold. The air temperature couldn't have been much less than eighty degrees, and yet he was shivering. His bones ached and his head hurt. He was deep in the grip of whatever bug he had caught.

He didn't have much appetite. Deke never had been a big eater, and lean as he was after weeks of island fighting on Guam and Leyte, he didn't have any reserves to spare.

But Danilo's generosity was like a healing tonic in itself.

Deke ate everything on the leaf, feeling like he had a belly full of real food for the first time in weeks. He thanked Danilo once again with a single nod, then wrapped himself in a blanket and slept.

Deke's dreams that night were feverish, all mixed up with the farm where he'd grown up and the jungle where he was fighting to survive. He had one dream where he was hoeing weeds in a long row of banana trees. In another dream Deke imagined that he was in the woods without his rifle and a bear was tracking him, keeping just out of sight. At another point the bear turned into the jungle cat that he had seen earlier. Deke was using every trick he knew to outwit the predators, but he couldn't seem to shake them. Strangely, the bear marked its territory by clawing Japanese characters into the trees.

Fever dreams, all right.

When he woke in the morning, he didn't feel a whole lot better, but at least he felt more rested. Danilo pressed a tin mug full of steaming homemade tea into Deke's hands. It tasted bitter and smelled like boiled socks, but the brew seemed to clear his head and lessen his fever.

The company's lone remaining medic came by and checked Deke over. Japanese snipers had picked off the rest of the medics during the fight on the ridge.

"You'll live," he announced.

"What have I got, Doc?"

The medic shrugged. "Take your pick. Malaria, dengue, encephalitis, or maybe just your garden variety jungle fever."

"You've got one hell of a bedside manner, Doc."

"Hey, I've got news for you. This ain't a bed, and I ain't a doctor."

Deke managed to grin. "And here all I thought I had to worry about was dodgin' bullets."

"All I can give you is an aspirin," the medic said. He nodded at the mug in Deke's hands. "What did that Filipino fella give you?"

"Some kind of tea, I reckon."

The medic wrinkled his nose. "Well, it smells like it will kill off that fever, so drink it down. These people know how to treat these things. They've been doing it for centuries, right? Then take two aspirin as a concession to modern medicine. Whatever you do, don't make me carry you."

"Do not worry, I will carry him if I have to," said Yoshio, who was listening nearby.

"Nobody needs to carry me, dammit," Deke said. He gulped down the dregs of the bitter tea, swallowed two aspirin, and lurched to his feet. The surrounding greenery spun alarmingly, then settled into a dizzy spell that left Deke struggling to keep his balance. He felt queasy as hell.

If the Japanese decided to launch an attack, Deke realized that he would be an easy mark. He didn't seem to have the strength to lift his rifle.

"Here, give me that," Philly said, slipping Deke's rifle over his own shoulder. Yoshio picked up Deke's haversack. Danilo nodded approvingly, then moved forward to lead the column up the jungle trail toward Ormoc and the sea.

Captain Merrick came by, checking on his men. Some were walking wounded, their wounds stiff with the morning dampness. One thing for sure, the jungle and the Japanese had beat this company to hell.

Merrick stopped in front of Deke, frowning at him. "Dammit, Deke. You picked one hell of a time to get sick. You can't seriously expect the rest of us to fight the Japanese all by ourselves?"

Deke grinned. "You can just prop me up to stop the bullets, sir. Glad to make myself useful."

"Hopefully it won't come to that," Merrick said. "With any

luck, we'll link up with the rest of the division today outside Ormoc. They might even be able to offer you and the rest of these poor bastards more than a couple of aspirin."

"Sounds good to me, sir."

Merrick turned his attention to Yoshio.

"What I said the other day, when we were interrogating the prisoner, I was wrong. I got a little hot, is all. Glad to have you on our side, son."

"That is why I am fighting, sir. To show everyone that I am an American. That my family is as American as them."

Merrick offered his hand and Yoshio shook it, then moved on.

Watching Captain Merrick go, Deke said, "It's about time that Merrick got his head out of his ass. You don't have anything to prove to me, Yoshio. You're a damn good spotter. I would have been dead ten times already without you watching my back."

Philly had been listening to the exchange and snorted. "That's high praise coming from the likes of Deacon Cole. What about me?"

Deke grinned. "Jury's still out on you, city slicker."

The captain stopped to give other men a kind word. Lord knew they needed it. It was part of an officer's role to instill confidence, and Merrick was doing a good job of it. An officer had so many concerns and so much to worry about that praise was usually at the bottom of his list.

However, the captain's confidence may have been premature. They didn't know it yet, but they were going to have one more fight on their hands today.

CHAPTER SIX

THE HEAT of the day was growing as the morning was force-marched toward afternoon. Around them, the jungle felt sullen as a wife whose husband had forgotten their anniversary. Sure, things were quiet now, but sooner or later, there would be hell to pay.

Sweat dripped into the men's eyes under their helmets, which felt more and more like heavy steel buckets with each passing mile. Most of them had given up on waving away the insects that buzzed into their faces. It wasn't worth the energy. Instantly, more bugs would appear.

"Everyone stay sharp," Captain Merrick cautioned the soldiers in a low voice, moving along the column threading its way through the forest. "If there are going to be organized Japanese forces anywhere, we'll find them as we get closer to Ormoc. They'll be dug in around there and looking for a fight."

"Is that a bad thing, sir?" asked Lieutenant Gurley. Even after several days of hit-and-run fighting in the jungle, the young lieutenant hadn't lost his gung-ho attitude. "Aren't we here to kick those Japanese in the teeth?"

"To be honest, Lieutenant, I'd rather dodge the Japanese and link up with the rest of the division," Merrick said. "There's safety in numbers. Once we get near the beach, we'll be dealing with much larger enemy units. In case you haven't noticed, we're a little worse for wear. These are damn good men, but they've sure taken a beating."

Lieutenant Gurley nodded, although he looked disappointed. The captain had spoken quietly, intending his words for Gurley's ears only. However, some of the men had overheard the exchange and tended to agree with Merrick. They had done their part. Now it was time for somebody else to step in and pick up the slack—or to fight alongside them at the very least.

"I never thought I'd be looking forward to seeing a beach again," Private Frazier said. "Then again, I wouldn't mind having one more crack at the Japanese."

One look at Frazier confirmed that his words weren't intended as boasting or bravado. He was soaked through with sweat, and he must have been just as dog-tired as anyone. The big man was carrying his BAR slung over his shoulder so that the weapon hung at his waist, ready in an instant to deal with any enemy threats. He was like a one-man destruction squad, a veritable two-legged tank.

Not all the men had Frazier's fighting spirit. As the company plodded along, Captain Merrick had seemed to sense the lethargy overtaking his men and was doing his best to prod them to maintain their situational awareness. He knew that one of the best ways to come out ahead in a fight was not to stumble into one.

The problem was that his men were just going through the motions, more like sleepwalkers than soldiers. It was understandable if his men were beat, considering that they had been operating on little sleep and lousy food. Not to mention that they had already fought two significant actions against the enemy during this jungle trek. They had lost several good men during this mission.

There was no doubt that the captain was just as exhausted as his men, but a good officer did not have the luxury of slacking off. It was his job to see the mission succeed and keep as many of his men as possible alive during its completion.

They were under constant threat of attack from the Japanese —and whatever else the jungle managed to throw at them. He knew well enough that any lapse in vigilance would leave them vulnerable.

The Japanese were not the only danger.

There was the jungle itself, which was challenging enough without the enemy lurking in it. There were roots on the trail to twist a man's ankle, snakes, multicolored spiders so big that they caught birds in their webs and ate them, stinging centipedes, plus sharp-edged kunai grass and spiky cantala shrubs that cut bare skin like a knife.

The sweltering heat draped over them all like a soggy net. Sudden downpours left them shivering.

Given all the above, a swift death from a Japanese bullet almost seemed like a mercy.

There was also illness lurking here. The captain looked in Deke's direction and frowned, as if aware that his most dependable set of ears and eyes was now among the walking wounded, down and out with some sort of jungle fever.

"Hang in there, boys," Merrick said. "Keep your eyes open while you're at it."

* * *

DEKE FELT like his head was wrapped in gauze—or possibly spiderwebs. Maybe he had walked smack-dab into one of those big webs hanging across the trail and he hadn't even noticed. He focused on putting one foot in front of the other, which was the best that he could do.

As they moved up the trail with Danilo on point and Philly just behind him, they were on the lookout for the Japanese.

"Hey, Danilo, just remember to shoot first and ask questions later," Philly said.

Ahead of him, the Filipino guerrilla threw up a hand to indicate that he had heard Philly. Whether or not he understood anything other than his name remained an open question. Danilo hadn't spoken any English, but he seemed able to understand it—when he wanted to. It all added to the air of mystery that seemed to hang around their Filipino guide.

"That's what I like about you, Danilo," Philly continued. "You don't say much. Hell, you talk even less than Deke."

Normally Deke would have been the one leading the unit down the trail. Sick and feverish, he was struggling along behind the others. Every movement seemed to take extra concentration, as if Deke was trying to operate in a dreamy fog.

Yoshio was nearby whenever he needed a shoulder to lean on —which was more and more often as the day wore on.

"I can't believe I've dodged all these Japanese bullets so far, only to get laid low by some jungle bug," Deke said.

"Oh, how the mighty have fallen," said Yoshio with a patient smile. "You just take it one step at a time, my friend. You will be feeling better before you know it."

"So you're a doctor now too?"

"I am the closest thing you are going to get to a doctor anytime soon, so take my word for it."

Deke wasn't so sure about that, but he didn't have the energy to argue. Increasingly, he appreciated Yoshio's quiet inner strength.

The young soldier had been through so much—from seeing his family put into an internment camp to dealing with blatant prejudice against anything and anyone Japanese—an understandable response in the middle of a war against the Japanese Empire.

Having seen his own family farm lost to the bank during the Great Depression, Deke reckoned he knew a thing or two about what it was like to be uprooted and put off your land. The experience had shaken the Cole family and stolen their heritage. For a mountain person, land and family was everything.

The Japanese American offering Deke his shoulder had gone through much the same experience, thus giving Deke something in common with a person that he never would have expected.

Yoshio never griped, so neither would Deke, no matter how sick he got. He smiled to himself, thinking that maybe that loudmouth Philly ought to learn a lesson or two from Yoshio.

He took Yoshio's advice and concentrated on putting one foot in front of the other up ahead. Each step was an effort. From time to time he did allow himself to lean heavily on Yoshio, but the Nisei never complained. As far as Deke was concerned, those who thought that Japanese Americans were second-class citizens had another think coming.

He appreciated Yoshio's sturdy shoulder and steadying hands, but what he really wanted to do was put his head down and sleep for about a week. That just wasn't possible under the circumstances.

Gradually the trail widened somewhat to the point where the forest fell away. It was an encouraging sign that they were leaving the thickest of the jungle behind and approaching civilization near the far coast that had been their destination all along.

But they weren't out of the woods yet—literally and figuratively.

They approached a large coconut grove to one side of the trail. Perhaps the trees had been planted with the intention of cultivating them, but now it was hard to say if that had been the intent or if this was simply some random grouping.

The years of Japanese occupation had left a manpower shortage so that many crops had become overgrown and abandoned. The Japanese occupiers had been keenly focused on food production to support their army and perhaps even for export home. In their minds, "food" was synonymous with "rice." Their production efforts—in other words, the labor of the Filipinos— had focused on the rice fields.

Agricultural efforts other than rice took second place under the Japanese. Consequently, the Philippines were littered with abandoned fields and farms, their cultivation interrupted by the war. In the tropical climate, it did not take long for the landscape to revert to a jungle state.

Seeing the coconut grove ahead, Danilo called a halt and surveyed the grove with what looked like suspicion. The lines on his face deepened in a frown.

After all, the landscape before him seemed like a textbook position for an ambush, but there wasn't any sound or clue that the grove contained anything but fallen coconuts and neglected trees. The Filipino stood for a long time, studying the grove.

The vegetation deeper among the coconut trunks appeared dark and impenetrable, a tangled gloom into which the sunlight didn't reach. The stillness of the trees gave the impression that the grove was holding its breath. The only movement came from the leaves stirring in the slight breeze and the occasional flicker of a bird moving through the underbrush.

"I'm with Danilo. I don't like the looks of this place," Philly muttered. "There could be a million Japanese hiding in there, or just a bunch of weeds and birds."

"Hush now," Deke managed to say. Sick as he was, he could also sense that something wasn't right, but they would have to leave it in Danilo's hands for now.

Lieutenant Gurley came up. Whether it was intentional or not, the young officer tended to project an air of importance by being noisier than he needed to be—he tended to puff when he walked, his footsteps heavy, there being no effort at stealth. "Captain Merrick wants to know what's going on."

"Danilo is trying to sniff out any Japanese in those trees, that's what," Philly replied.

"Tell him to get a move on. The captain doesn't want us waiting around."

"You'd better tell him yourself, sir."

The use of "sir" was a small transgression, but the GIs knew that Gurley was one of those officers who would rather get shot at than let military decorum go by the wayside.

With a grunt of annoyance, the lieutenant moved up beside Danilo, pointed down the trail, and said, "Let's go."

The lieutenant turned and made his way back along the column, noisy as ever.

Slowly and cautiously, Danilo moved forward again. Philly was right behind him with his own rifle at the ready. The column began to pass the overgrown grove. It seemed as if everything was going to be all right—until it wasn't.

Just when the center of the company was passing the trees, flames of gunfire erupted from among the trunks. The flashes indicated rifle fire, but there was also a Nambu machine gun in there somewhere.

The bursts of machine-gun fire raked the center of the column and cut down a handful of men before the others could hit the ground.

"Everybody down!" Captain Merrick shouted, his voice managing to cut through the sound of gunfire. It was a good quality in an officer to be able to be heard on the battlefield— maybe even the most important one. "I want return fire on those bastards right now."

The men did as ordered, operating almost by instinct at this point. For a few moments they were too stunned to move, overwhelmed with shock and fear. Then, as if a switch had been flipped, their training kicked in, and they began to return fire. Though exhausted, they were all battle-hardened veterans who didn't need to be told how to fight back against the Japanese.

While the enemy had taken them by surprise, it didn't take long for the GIs to begin their own withering return fire. They shot back at the muzzle flashes in the gloom. Leaves and twigs rained down, but the Japanese kept firing.

Bullets tore through the foliage, and leaves and twigs rained down from the trees. The Japanese kept firing, and the GIs kept shooting back, the staccato burst of bullets joined by the sound of shouting and the occasional scream.

It was an intense and chaotic fight, the air thick with smoke, the tropical day suddenly filled with fire and thunder.

"Here I come, boys!" cried Private Frazier, firing his BAR from the hip as he advanced toward the grove. There were now so many falling leaves that it looked as if a whirlwind had taken hold among the trees.

But his magazine was soon spent, and in the face of heavy fire, he was forced to throw himself to the jungle floor. He rolled among the leaves, fumbling to get another magazine into the ammunition-hungry BAR.

The problem was that the column was now pinned down effectively by the ambush. There was no way to go except forward on the trail. Certainly there was no going back.

Deke found himself on the ground but had no recollection of getting there. He had been in something of a daze when the ambush broke out, and it was Yoshio who'd saved his bacon by grabbing hold of Deke's shoulder and pulling him down just before the machine gun swept the line.

Several men behind them were felled or scattered by the

burst of fire. Deke struggled to get up and reached for his rifle, but it wasn't there. He suffered a moment of panic, realizing that Yoshio was still carrying the weapon over his own shoulder.

"Get down, you fool!" Yoshio cried out in a rare show of exasperation. "Just keep your head down and try not to get shot. Let someone else fight this war for a change."

Deke realized that he didn't have the energy to argue, much less fight back against the enemy onslaught. He simply pressed his face into the muddy trail, hoping this wouldn't last forever. The smell of the earth and even the cool dirt against his face felt soothing. *Ashes to ashes,* he thought. *Dust to dust.*

It was a hell of a thing to be in a war and be too sick to fight.

Seeing that they were pinned down, Lieutenant Gurley decided that he'd had enough. Wielding a submachine gun, the lieutenant sprinted forward with it toward the coconut grove, screaming a mad battle cry and peppering leaves and trunks with a hail of automatic fire. It was brave, if foolish.

His attack suppressed the ambush just enough that it enabled the soldiers to pick themselves up out of the dirt and get into better positions.

Their rate of fire increased against the Japanese in the grove. It was impossible to say just how many enemy soldiers were hidden in there. They certainly did not outnumber the Americans, but there must have been at least a couple of dozen Japanese pouring fire at them. Also, the enemy had the advantage of cover, while the GIs were caught out in the open.

Lieutenant Gurley hadn't slowed down, but was still charging at the enemy position. The lieutenant's plan seemed to be to run all the way into the coconut grove and get in among the trees to scatter the Japanese.

"Look at that bastard go!" Philly shouted in amazement.

For the briefest of moments, it looked as if the lieutenant might succeed and turn the tide to put the Japanese on the run.

But in battle tides are treacherous. The fortunes of war swirled and ebbed at the whims of fate and chance. For the young lieutenant, the tide suddenly turned against him.

He had just reached the perimeter of the trees when a bullet caught him and spun him around. Gurley stumbled but kept going. Then he was hit again, finally collapsing with his submachine gun underneath him, the weapon's hot barrel still smoking.

His death hadn't been for naught. The sight of the fallen lieutenant enraged the soldiers, filling them with new resolve. Two more men followed Gurley's example, leaping up and sprinting for the coconut trees. One man named Simmons went down almost immediately, caught by Japanese fire.

The other soldier got close enough to hurl a grenade that reached deep into the grove and detonated with an ear-shattering blast. Shredded greenery and shards of wood whirled out from the center of the blast. Then that soldier also went down.

"Goddammit!" yelled Captain Merrick. "I don't want any more heroes. First Platoon, I want you to move around and flank that coconut grove. You boys in Second Platoon, see if you can get around there and hit them from the rear. These Japanese have got to go."

"Yes, sir!"

The two platoons moved off, leaving the rest of the company to slug it out with the Japanese in the coconut grove.

His orders given, Merrick hunkered down with the rest of the men and returned fire. However, the Japanese were far from beaten. They kept up a steady fire of such intensity that bits of leaves directly above the GIs fell like green snow.

All that Deke could do was keep his head down and hope that it all ended soon.

He did not have to wait for long. Clearly there were not that many Japanese in the coconut grove. They had to spread out to meet the new threat on their flank. No sooner had they done that than they found themselves attacked from the rear.

"Move up! Move up!" Captain Merrick shouted.

Private Frazier led the way, blasting the Japanese with his BAR. It was an impressive display of firepower, bullets chipping chunks from the trees and knocking down Japanese defenders.

Hit from all sides, the return fire from the Japanese began to slacken. The GIs were close enough by now to use their hand grenades effectively.

Thump! Thump!

There was no hiding from the blasts, which were followed by screams of pain from within the grove.

Finally, the last few shots were fired as the enemy guns fell silent.

Philly was among those men who waded into the grove to make sure the job was done. There was a shot or two, and he emerged a few minutes later.

Deke raised himself up from the dirt long enough to watch Philly come out. In fact, there seemed to be not one, but two, versions of Philly. Deke blinked his eyes to clear his feverish imagination.

"I counted a dozen dead Japanese," he reported. "They put up one hell of a fight."

The battle of the coconut grove was over. They had lost Lieutenant Gurley, and four men had been killed, plus another handful of walking wounded. It was a heavy price to pay for passage past a coconut grove that none of them would ever see again. Yet there had been little choice but to fight. Even if the GIs had managed to bypass the grove, it would only have meant that the Japanese would have been free to attack them from the rear.

The American dead were quickly buried near where they had fallen. The enemy dead were left strewn on the ground.

"Let's move out," Captain Merrick said. "I want to link up with the rest of the division before nightfall, if we can. Let's see if we can find the beach. I've had just about enough of these woods."

Once again, Danilo and Philly took point. Yoshio helped Deke to his feet, and the diminished column made its way up the jungle path toward the smell of salt air.

CHAPTER SEVEN

LIEUTENANT STEELE sometimes wondered how many beach landings he could make before his luck ran out. In the lieutenant's opinion, luck wasn't like a fountain, but more like a bottle of top-shelf scotch. In other words, there was a finite amount of it. You poured a few drinks, maybe spilled some here and there, or shared the bottle around, and before you knew it, the bottle was empty.

He knew from personal experience that there was nothing sadder than a bottle of empty scotch—except a bottle of empty luck.

He'd already been through the landing at Guadalcanal, then Guam, and twice on Leyte. Incredibly, he was about to take part in a *third* landing on Leyte as part of the task force intent on capturing Ormoc from the Japanese.

The question was, How full was that bottle of luck that he'd been swigging across the Pacific? He was sure it was down to the dregs, and there still seemed to be a whole lot more war to fight.

Steele even went so far as avoiding card games, for fear that he would use up some of whatever luck he had left. He knew maybe that was silly, but he was going to save his luck for fighting the Japanese.

Not that Steele or any of the other soldiers in Patrol Easy had any choice in the matter of going back into combat. A soldier went where he was sent, no questions asked. He'd had just about enough of beach landings, but nobody had asked him how he felt about it.

As an officer—a low-ranking one at that—he knew it was his job to follow orders and make sure those under him did the same. In other words, he kept his doubts and complaints to himself.

They'd already had a few false alarms, and they were sitting ducks out here on the big blue Pacific. They would have to rely on the antiaircraft guns aboard the USS *Leo*. Though the guns bristling across the deck appeared formidable, Japanese aircraft had still managed to elude these defenses on occasion.

He welcomed it when Rodeo interrupted his thoughts, which were turning gloomy. "How much longer are we gonna be on this floating tin can, sir? I can't wait to get back on dry land."

It was true that the cargo attack ship had few creature comforts, especially with so many men crowded onto the deck. This was a short run around the southern tip of Leyte, and as many men and as much equipment as possible had been jammed aboard.

The vessel had been designed strictly for function, which was to carry supplies across the Pacific and fend off any Japanese attacks as needed with its guns. The ship rolled somewhat gracelessly in the waves, fighting the currents in Leyte Gulf. More than a few of its passengers had become seasick as a result.

Rodeo had referred to the ship as a tin can, which was an apt description. "Tin can" was usually a nickname for US Navy destroyers, but Steele and Rodeo were soldiers, not squids, so they could call the ship whatever they wanted.

"Can't wait to get back on dry land, huh? Spoken like a true ground pounder," Steele said. "But I'd say this tin can beats walking, wouldn't you? Don't tell me you wish you were hiking across the peninsula with Deke, Philly, and Yoshio?"

"No thanks to that, sir. I hope those guys are all right."

Steele nodded in agreement.

Not long after they had helped seize Hill 522 and the town of Palo, the scouts and snipers of Patrol Easy had been split up. Deke and Philly were now making their way across the interior of Leyte, a jungle region crisscrossed with rugged terrain—not to mention lots and lots of desperate Japanese who would be dug in and looking for a fight.

Dividing the patrol had not been Steele's idea, but as with this sea voyage, nobody had asked his opinion.

Still, if anyone was going to survive a cross-country patrol through the jungle interior, he thought that it would be Deacon Cole. Together with that tough Filipino guerrilla, Danilo, they would be a match for any Japanese they encountered. As for Philly—well, at least he had Deke to look after him, the lieutenant mused.

Rodeo also seemed to be pondering the scenario of a jungle trek. "You know what, Lieutenant? As long as the Japanese don't shoot it full of holes, I guess I like this tin can just fine. It's better than swimming to Ormoc."

"There you go," Steele said. "Anyhow, next time you want to complain, do me a favor and bitch to somebody else. Like maybe a seagull."

"A seagull, sir?"

"Or a mermaid. Hell, you can complain to a mop bucket if you want to, just so long as I don't have to listen. Better yet, go find a poker game or something. Maybe go clean your rifle. You're bothering me."

Rodeo grinned. "You got it, Honcho."

Rodeo took the hint—the lieutenant hadn't exactly *ordered* him to get lost—and made himself scarce, losing himself in the crowd on deck.

"Honcho" was what he had instructed the men to call him instead of "lieutenant." It didn't matter so much here on the ship, where protocol required the use of "sir" and saluting when appropriate. Besides, there weren't any trigger-happy Japanese spying on them at sea. But back on land, addressing an officer using his rank or saluting him was like signing his death warrant at the hand of Japanese snipers. The Japanese had been trained to seek out and target officers.

Considering that he liked his head just fine without a bullet hole in it, Steele had come up with the "Honcho" business.

The nickname was something of a joke on the Japanese, considering that "Honcho" came from a Japanese word for "chief." They hadn't seemed to figure that out yet, and it was just fine with Steele if they remained in the dark.

Tall, with gray hair showing at the temples, Steele was on the wrong side of forty for a lieutenant. There were probably younger generals. His men couldn't decide if that meant he had pulled strings to avoid the headaches of rising through the ranks, or if he had royally pissed somebody off to the point that he was never going to be promoted. The men under his command generally bet on the second scenario, although they would have been wrong in Steele's case.

He had no plans to be a career officer—he'd be more than happy to go back to civilian life. In fact, having lost an eye on Guam while tangling with a Japanese sniper, he had a valid excuse to be shipped back stateside. But he felt that there was unfinished business regarding the war.

On the rare occasions when Steele had tried to explain it out loud, he had fallen back on simply stating that he was doing his duty. He supposed that summed it up as well as anything.

But it went deeper than that. He thought that the United States of America was a big, messy, imperfect country, but a place where a man could still say and do what he wanted. Just try getting away with free speech in Germany or Japan. If that wasn't worth fighting for, he wasn't sure what was.

Being an officer had a few perks—and plenty of headaches. He had found the right balance by getting himself put in charge of these scout-snipers, a job that nobody else wanted and that the army didn't seem sure needed doing. That job, and not getting shipped back home after being half blinded on Guam, had required pulling strings and calling in favors.

What did he have to go home to? Not much.

Steele stood at the rail of the troopship and looked out at the Pacific. It was a bright, clear day, and the sea was blue and calm. Hell, it would have been a pleasant cruise if it hadn't been for the Japanese Navy patrolling the waters, and the threat of planes with those big red meatballs on their wings flying overhead.

Steele felt the big ship shift its stance in the waves so that its rolling changed. He was no sailor, but it was clear that the ship had changed course.

They had never really lost sight of land, but now they were drawing closer again. He could see the distant hills of the island. The wind had also shifted, blowing out of a different quadrant. The breeze smelled vaguely of the jungle, tinged with salt air.

The change in course hadn't been his imagination. Orders began to be shouted as officers organized the men on deck.

It wouldn't be long now.

They would all be going ashore, hitting the beach yet again.

Along with the other officers, Steele had already been briefed on their mission. In addition to the men of Patrol Easy, he had also been put in charge of an entire platoon. It was not an assignment he had asked for or wanted, but the battalion commander had looked around in desperation, spotted Steele's lieutenant's bar, and that was that. Thanks to the sharp-eyed Japanese snipers, there was a growing shortage of officers.

If he wasn't careful, he might even wind up getting promoted.

He turned and looked at the soldiers milling around on deck. They mostly ranged in age from their late teens to their twenties and early thirties, young men who were about to go into battle. Steele realized that calling them *men* was a stretch in some cases, considering that some of these GIs barely looked old enough to shave.

Some of them were nervous, others excited. They were in good physical shape and ready for the fight. They were dressed in new khaki uniforms, each man with a loaded rifle and bandolier of ammunition over his shoulder. Most were veterans of other beach landings, but a handful were green replacements.

Steele approached his platoon. Another combat veteran, Sergeant Bosco, had been more than capable of getting the men organized. Steele figured his job was to stay out of Bosco's way.

"Sir," Bosco said respectfully, and stepped back, leaving Steele alone in front of the platoon. It was an opportune moment for last-minute instructions before they got into the boats and the actual landing operation began.

"I wish I had a few words of wisdom to offer you," he said, looking around at the men. The inexperienced soldiers eyed him expectantly. The expressions on the faces of the combat veterans appeared sullen, which Steele could understand. They seemed to be thinking, *Another damn beach landing. Let's just get it over with.* "Well, I can give you some words, anyhow. Not much in the wisdom department. When we get to shore, keep your heads down and keep moving forward. If you stay on the beach, you'll get killed. Do what Sergeant Bosco tells you. Sergeant, anything to add?"

"No, sir," the sergeant said gruffly. He sounded surprised to have been asked.

The moment stretched on, and the men were still silent, unmoving. *Was he supposed to say more?* Steele paused and looked out over the sea for inspiration, the sun-dappled waves glaring back at him. Some of the faces were still watching him expectantly, as if maybe he hadn't said enough, so he turned back to the men. "I'll tell you this, men. Our job is to beat the Japanese, pure and simple. No matter what happens on that beach, if you stay focused and do your job, we're going to come out all right in the end. It's going to be tough. I'm not going to lie about that. Like I said, stick together and do your job. When you see a Japanese soldier, shoot him before he shoots you. Do that, and you might just have a chance of making it back home again. That's all I've got to say."

The men remained silent as they listened to him. Some of the men who had done this before nodded, seemingly satisfied. They might not know their new lieutenant, but the eye patch was the best medal he could be wearing, and they appreciated that he hadn't given them a load of crap. *Short and sweet.*

The cargo nets were lowered, the landing craft pulled alongside, and it was time to go ashore.

* * *

THE THING about a beach landing was that nobody knew what the hell to expect.

The officers could plan all they wanted, but things tended to go to pieces as soon as a few big waves scattered the boats and the Japanese opened fire with guns that had supposedly been knocked out.

As usual, the navy had lent a hand by shelling the beach and inland areas. It was anyone's guess whether the impressive show of fireworks had softened up the Japanese—or simply let them know that they should be expecting company.

The shelling let up before the boats began racing in toward the beach. Mercifully, there was not much return fire, aside from a few artillery rounds that plunged into the sea, almost like a token effort. Maybe the shelling had wiped out the Japanese defenses, after all. None of the incoming craft were hit.

The ships themselves wouldn't be sticking around. The presence of the Japanese Navy and enemy planes made it too risky for the invasion fleet to allow itself to be bottled up close to the shore. Once the troops were away, the big ships would head for open water.

A coral shelf prevented the boats from carrying them all the way into the beach. Instead, the soldiers had to splash ashore from a hundred yards out, wading through the breakers. Fortunately, the sea was calm and the breakers were manageable—not usually big enough to knock a man down.

Steele was the first one out when the metal gangway splashed down. He'd heard some machine-gun fire coming from the tree line. It didn't take much imagination to picture being ripped in half by a burst from shore. But the tracers were reaching out toward other vessels, poor bastards. So far it looked as though he and his men would be able to get off the boat in one piece.

Despite all their training, some of the men froze when the ramp came down. Steele shoved at the nearest man to get him moving.

"Let's go! Let's go!" Steele shouted, leaping to one side as men spilled down the ramp and hopped awkwardly into the foaming sea. Most were so loaded down with the gear on their backs that they resembled stooped-over, two-legged turtles.

He saw Rodeo and Alphabet go by, carrying their sniper rifles wrapped in plastic to protect them from the salt spray and sand. Private Egan jumped out with his war dog, Thor, held tightly on a leash. The water was over the dog's head so that Thor had to swim for it, Egan shouting encouragement while he also struggled through the deeper troughs of water. In fact, for a moment it looked like Egan was in greater danger of drowning than the dog. But Thor surged ahead, the tension on the leash managing to keep Egan on his feet in the surging sea.

All around them, similar scenes were repeated from dozens of other landing craft, the massive landing operation forgotten as each man fended for himself in the waves. This was always the hard part, when the whole damn operation threatened to come undone.

The Japanese weren't entirely absent. A smattering of bullets dappled the surface of the sea like rain. At the next landing craft over, a couple of men were hit and went down, the red stain of their life's blood spreading through the white foam.

For the briefest moment, Steele felt awed by the utter magnificence of the scene—the rows of landing craft beached on the coral or sand, foaming waves, soldiers in khaki struggling through the water as a few streamers of tracer fire burned even brighter than the tropical sun. He stood there in the water, letting the spectacle of it all imprint on his brain. If he lived another fifty years, he would never forget this sight.

But there was no time to dwell on the scene, not if he wanted to live another five minutes.

"Follow me!" Sergeant Bosco shouted, leading the way across the coral shelf.

To call it a "shelf" was something of a misnomer, because that gave the impression of the coral being smooth and level. The coral posed many hazards. Unseen underwater, deep potholes in the coral waited to trip a man and send him face down into the surf. When loaded down with gear, getting back up again wasn't easy. Some of the deeper kettles in the coral could drown a man.

It didn't help that the coral was sharp and abrasive, acting like crushed glass when it came in contact with hands and knees and shins. The raw, scraped skin burned like fire in the salt water.

With all the men off the landing craft, the lieutenant headed for shore.

There was some sporadic enemy rifle fire, mixed with bursts from a few of the dreaded Nambu machine guns, but no concerted effort to keep the Americans from coming ashore. Even the heavier enemy artillery fire had mostly fallen silent. The Japanese had stopped short of putting out the welcome mat, but the situation could have been far worse.

Steele slogged through the water, trying to get ahead of his men. He stopped to help a soldier who had fallen. The man was discovering the hard way that it was entirely possible to drown in three feet of water when you couldn't get your feet back under you.

Steele dragged the man upright so that the soldier came up, sputtering for air. The lieutenant didn't wait for him but kept going toward the beach. There was no stopping now. He had to keep the momentum going.

Some of the GIs had already reached shore and were throwing themselves down on the sand, partly to avoid enemy fire and partly because they were exhausted by the effort of reaching dry land.

He didn't let them rest for long.

He stood there on the beach, well aware that he was a six-foot-tall target but knowing that if he threw himself down on the sand, the men would stall.

"Move out!" he shouted. "We're not staying on this beach."

Sergeant Bosco got the men moving, shouting, "Let's go! Let's go!"

Bosco had to drag some of them to their feet and shove them

in the lieutenant's wake. It wasn't that the men were afraid, just confused and already worn out.

Egan and Thor were among the men advancing toward the tree line, the dog panting but not barking despite all the excitement. *Good dog,* Steele thought. The war dogs had been trained not to bark except when the Japanese were around.

He saw that Rodeo and Alphabet had shucked the plastic off their rifles and were using the telescopic sights to scan the tree line for targets, just as they had been trained to do.

Alphabet fired, and one of the machine guns that had been pecking at the men on the beach fell silent.

"Good shot!" Steele shouted, not sure whether Alphabet had heard him or not, then ran on. Once again, he was well aware of being a target as he raced ahead of the soldiers.

He looked back once and saw the men following him, spread out in a line. It went against every fiber of a man's being to run toward gunfire, and yet they were doing it, every last one of them.

He felt a surge of pride even though he barely knew the soldiers of the platoon that he had been assigned to command. At the moment that didn't matter. *Damn, these were good men. Every last one of them.*

Turning his attention to the terrain ahead, he ran toward the line of vegetation where the jungle met the beach, shotgun at the ready. With the exception of his two snipers, most of the men were equipped with the M1 rifle, a fine weapon. But for close-quarters fighting in the dense vegetation ahead, it was hard to beat a twelve gauge.

Once again, he half expected a flurry of shots to tear through his guts, but there was mostly silence. A few enemy rifles cracked, snipers hiding in the trees or in spider holes carved into the sand, a kind of hors d'oeuvre for the fighting that would surely follow.

Reaching the tree line, he passed the base of a tree where, incredibly, a Japanese sniper had tied himself into the upper branches. The man had no hope of escape but was still resolutely firing at the hundreds of soldiers coming ashore, working his bolt-action Arisaka rifle between shots.

The sniper had clearly intended to die at his post, so the lieutenant decided to give him what he wanted.

Steele raised the shotgun and gave him a blast of buckshot. The enemy sniper slumped down, dead, but remained in the tree thanks to the ropes he had used to tie himself there. Back on Guadalcanal, Steele remembered how some of the dead Japanese snipers had been left in their trees until they had turned into skeletons picked clean by the magpies and scoured bare by the sun and wind. That didn't take long in the tropics.

A grenade exploded nearby, a muffled blast that was the result of being tossed into a spider hole. The explosion indicated that another lone enemy sniper had been dealt with, the narrow hole becoming his grave.

Other than a handful of snipers clinging to the beach area, there was little resistance. They had seen this before. The Japanese were here, all right, but knew that they couldn't hold the shoreline, not when the naval bombardment would have hollowed out any defenses and blasted them to pieces.

No, the enemy would be farther inland, well dug in, waiting for them.

Now that they were entering the jungle itself, Steele continued to take the lead, and he took it upon himself to find a path forward for his platoon. He didn't want to hand the job off to Sergeant Bosco, who had plenty of bravado and kept the men in line, but who lacked the finesse that being on point called for.

There might be trip wires, mines, or spider holes waiting for them, and one wrong step could spell disaster. Not for the first time, he wished that he had Deke with him. That hillbilly seemed to have a sixth sense for traps and trouble.

But Deke was somewhere in the interior, fighting his own battles. Steele would just have to manage on his own—one eye or not.

Satisfied that they didn't seem to be walking right into a trap or ambush, he looked back at the men of the platoon and waved them on. He could sense their uneasiness, as they seemed to be waiting for the other shoe to drop. The soldiers moved ahead cautiously.

He couldn't blame them. They had good reason to be nervous, Steele thought. When it came to taking a beach and the island territory beyond, there was nothing easy about it.

Aside from the sniper up in the tree, they had seen precious few of the enemy.

The question remained, Just where the hell were the Japanese?

Steele had a sneaking suspicion that they would soon find out.

CHAPTER EIGHT

IN HIS HEADQUARTERS aboard USS *Nashville*, General Douglas MacArthur studied the maps that had been secured to the steel bulkhead. One of the maps displayed the entire Pacific theater of operations, its surface showing a great deal of blue water dotted with chains of islands that, until a few short years ago, had been unknown to the average American, such as the Marianas, the Marshall Islands, and the Gilbert Islands.

Some of the names had become not only familiar but synonymous with terrible battles: Guadalcanal, Guam, Saipan. Thousands of young American lives had been lost in those places, fighting the Japanese Empire.

Other islands were so small that it required a fair amount of squinting to make out their names on the map, considering that the smallest were little more than a grove of trees on an elevated pile of sand that managed to keep above the tide line—if just barely.

The general knew all too well that just because an island was small on the map did not mean that it was insignificant. Peleliu was one such example. Measuring just five square miles, about one-fourth the size of Manhattan, the fight for Peleliu had cost the lives of more than thirteen hundred marines.

Some had called the American campaign "island hopping," and that was an accurate description.

After all, Japan itself was an island nation that had built its empire largely of other Pacific islands, along with several swaths of the Asian continent that held the precious natural resources that Japan needed to feed its industries and its war machine—raw materials such as rubber, metals, and all-important oil to fuel its ships and planes.

The map showed how many more islands there were to go as US forces pressed ever closer to the Japanese home islands, especially Iwo Jima, the smaller Ryukyu islands, and Okinawa. Adding those islands to the list of American conquests promised to cost so many more lives on both sides that the very thought of the battles to come was daunting.

MacArthur was a commanding general, but he wasn't a monster. He both understood and dreaded the price that would be paid. He often thought of General Ulysses S. Grant, whom some had seen as a butcher for his willingness to grind down his own army in search of victory. That reputation had always cast a shadow on Grant.

Could he do what Grant had done? In the end, MacArthur knew that he might not have much choice.

There had been rumors at the highest levels that the United States was developing a superweapon of such destructive power that it would strike fear into the Japanese Emperor's heart. Even a general as high ranking as MacArthur didn't know the details, but he didn't have a lot of faith that anything less than the equivalent of Zeus's thunderbolt would bring the Japanese to their knees.

Pacing his office, he paused long enough to put his hands on his hips and glare at the territories on the maps still held by the Japanese, as if willing the enemy to surrender.

* * *

MacArthur's chief of staff came in. Born in Maryland, Dick Sutherland had been raised in West Virginia and had come to the army by way of Yale. Thirteen years younger than MacArthur, he had helped chase Pancho Villa in Mexico and fought the Germans on the Western Front during the Great War. Smart and capable, he was a tough taskmaster who oversaw the headquarters staff with an iron fist and an unrelenting attention to detail. It might be said that he was the general's hatchet man and lobbyist, which hadn't won him any friends in Washington.

The two men had experienced their ups and downs. They had even come close to falling out over MacArthur's disapproval of Sutherland's mistress—the wife of an Australian army officer —until Sutherland had come to his senses. Sutherland remained fiercely loyal to MacArthur—if a Japanese assassin had burst in, he wouldn't have thought twice about taking a bullet for his boss.

He saw MacArthur looking at the maps yet again.

"Kind of makes you wonder why they don't surrender, doesn't it?" Sutherland asked.

"No," MacArthur said. "You know damn well that we wouldn't surrender either. We have to keep hitting them until they can't hit back anymore."

"From your lips to God's ears."

Sutherland left some papers on MacArthur's desk and went back out, leaving the general to his ruminations.

The map that held the most interest for the general showed

operations on the island of Leyte, where thousands of his troops had recently landed.

"Sir?" Another staff officer who was far junior to Sutherland poked his head cautiously through the door. They all knew that the general didn't like to be interrupted, but from time to time, one of them appeared to update the maps.

"Go on," MacArthur said.

As swiftly as possible, the man made a few marks on the map and retreated with a palpable air of relief from the general's inner sanctum. Tall and imposing, MacArthur's regal appearance tended to have that effect on his staff. He was not one to engage his staff in hale and hearty conversation.

The fact that he called his junior staff by their rank and not their actual names had convinced them that the general did not consider them worthy of notice.

It was interesting that officers in different branches of the service seemed to favor a certain "type" or look. Senior naval officers preferred a thin appearance, skinny as the fox-faced Lord Nelson in an old oil painting. Sometimes it almost seemed as if those navy boys were having a competition to see who could be the leanest.

Army generals tended toward bulkiness, and MacArthur was no exception. Heavy through the shoulders and chest, with a thick neck, six feet tall, he somewhat resembled an old bull and could project an air of intimidation.

Early in the war, he had picked up the nickname "Dugout Doug" for keeping to his bunker while his troops fought on Bataan. Those who questioned his courage seemed to have forgotten that as a young officer, he had single-handedly killed several enemy soldiers in combat, both in Mexico and in the Philippines, sometimes against overwhelming odds.

Alone again, the general nodded with satisfaction at the updated map. Truth be told, he had most of the maps committed to memory, but they gave him something to look at while he strolled around the confines of his office. The general did his best thinking on his feet.

The lines showed his own forces were advancing and that the areas under Japanese control were shrinking. In other words, things were moving in the right direction. This was progress.

The only place where the positions were murky remained in the jungle interior of the island, where small US patrols battled like-size Japanese forces. Again, the general knew that "small" did not mean insignificant to the men fighting and dying in those battles.

He was sure that the Japanese commander, General Tomoyuki Yamashita, had similar maps on the damp walls of his cave or bunker or wherever the hell it was that he had gone to ground. The picture presented by Yamashita's maps would be far bleaker, MacArthur knew.

MacArthur had successfully landed on Leyte, returning to the Philippines. His return had been a promise made and kept. Now that he had set foot on shore, he had to seize the rest of the nation from the Japanese.

He had not shifted his headquarters from USS *Nashville* to the shore, though that might have been more symbolic. From the general's point of view, remaining at sea was strictly a practical consideration. The truth was that the ship enabled far better communication thanks to its powerful radios and electronics.

Simply staying in touch with commanders across the vast Pacific counted for a great deal in terms of military success. Also, the ship provided comfortable quarters and decent food.

There were also interservice rivalries to consider. MacArthur thought there was sound advice in the old saying about keeping your friends close and your enemies closer.

Being a guest of the navy was a bit like staying at a hotel

where one didn't need to be concerned about practical matters such as changing the sheets or cleaning the bathroom. MacArthur found that he could focus all his energies on the needs of his forces.

The shore was a short boat ride away whenever he needed to get there in person. For now, the reports coming in and the occasional updates to the maps provided all the information he needed.

The maps were carefully marked with troop positions, both those of his own men and, to the extent that observation and intelligence reports allowed, the disposition of the enemy troops.

Enemy. It was a powerful word, he thought. He knew that it came from the Latin word *inimicus*. Julius Caesar would have used the word to describe the Gauls or the barbarians of Germania.

The word implied a certain amount of hostility, even hatred. MacArthur searched his mind, then shook his head. He didn't feel hostility. Instead, he thought of the Japanese as his adversary or opponent. People like Admiral "Bull" Halsey crowed about "killing Japs" to the delight of the press and presumably of the folks back home as well, a growing number of whom had lost husbands, sons, or young men from their communities in the Pacific conflict. It was understandable if they wanted some blood.

Back home, the US government had even seen fit to round up Japanese Americans and put them in camps to keep an eye on them. That action had been motivated in part by hatred and bigotry toward the Japanese.

MacArthur didn't feel the same way. However, MacArthur's equanimity toward the Japanese went only so far. In particular, he was concerned about the treatment of American POWs held by the Japanese.

Long before the invasion of Leyte, reports had come in of Japanese cruelty to their prisoners of war. The prisoners were generally American, British, or Australian. The cruelty involved starvation, beatings, and brutality of all stripes, even murder. He believed that captured soldiers should be treated with honor.

The very thought of the Japanese cruelty toward his men was one of the only things that really angered MacArthur. When it came to the enemy, it was the one issue that made his blood boil.

It was why he had made a statement about the treatment of POWs and punishment for those who harmed them one of the cornerstones of the speech that he had made on the beach a few days before. Once the Philippines were more secure, he planned to locate and liberate the POW camps as quickly as possible.

To some extent, his landing on the beach had been staged for publicity purposes, but those words of warning to the Japanese regarding the treatment of POWs hadn't been hot air. MacArthur meant them deeply. He had issued a warning to the Japanese, and he planned to stand by it. He wanted them to understand that, make no mistake, there would be punishment and retribution for harm to American POWs.

"I have no shortage of rope to hang every last one of those sons of bitches if necessary," he had once told Sutherland.

On the other side of the coin, there were relatively few Japanese taken prisoner, given their adversary's determination to die for the Emperor. The Japanese were indoctrinated that surrender or capture would bring dishonor on themselves and their families, perhaps for generations to come. They were told that a man who surrendered could never return home again. Given these high cultural stakes, you couldn't blame the average Japanese for refusing to give up.

Nonetheless, at least a few Japanese had the sense to surrender or were captured. But bitterness flowed both ways. He knew that sometimes Japanese prisoners did not make it back to the POW compound behind the lines. He frowned on such things and discouraged it. He wanted his soldiers to be men of honor, right down to the lowliest private. They needed to practice self-control.

Then again, MacArthur had seen the bodies of men killed by the Japanese. Some of the bodies had even shown signs of torture. The sight had sickened him. He could understand why Japanese prisoners sometimes didn't survive for long in combat areas, but the general did not condone it. Americans were better than that.

Once Japanese prisoners reached the POW compound, they were treated well. They were given food, clean clothes, medical attention. It was another sign of American power that they could be generous and magnanimous toward prisoners of war.

After all, US forces were winning. The maps indicated that MacArthur was driving back the Japanese on all fronts. One thought that troubled him almost as much as the Japanese was the disposition of the US Navy. He was in constant operational contact with naval forces, and they certainly had a common enemy, but the two branches of the service were always trying to make an end run around the other.

The way that MacArthur saw it, the navy would gladly have tried to win this war on its own and taken all the credit for it. To be fair, the same attitude was probably true of the army.

The truth was that he didn't always know everything that the navy was up to. To that end, he had a plan.

If his junior staff believed that MacArthur never bothered to learn their names, they were sadly mistaken. There was not much that escaped the general's attention.

He leaned into the hallway and bellowed, "Oatmire!"

* * *

WORKING in a cramped room two doors down, Captain Jim Oatmire heard his name being shouted by the general and very nearly threw up his recent breakfast of powdered eggs and black coffee.

Holy crap!

Having been summoned from on high, Oatmire had no choice but to come running, his footsteps echoing through the metal hallways of the ship. Other officers glanced at him but were careful not to meet his eyes. They just figured that Oatmire was running toward his doom.

Oatmire had gone ashore with a small contingent of General MacArthur's staff during the general's initial landing on Leyte. He hadn't exactly been in combat, but he had been close enough to hear the shooting.

Come to think of it, so had the general. MacArthur hadn't appeared to be troubled the least bit by the sounds of combat.

Since then Oatmire had found himself back aboard USS *Nashville*, wielding nothing more lethal than a sharp pencil and dodging nothing more dangerous than the mess hall's version of meat loaf.

"Sir?" asked the breathless young officer, who like most of the other junior staff remained in awe of the general. That awe and apprehension was clearly written on his face.

"Pack a seabag, son. I'm sending you as a liaison over to USS *Kalinin Bay* with the Seventh Fleet. The captain is an old friend of mine, and I'll lay on some story about interservice learning and cooperation. He'll probably smell my bullshit from a mile away, but he'll laugh about it. I just need you on that ship. I hear they're heading out to pay a visit to the Japanese Navy."

"Yes, sir." Oatmire's blank look indicated that he still had no idea what the general had in mind. What the hell was interservice learning and cooperation, anyhow? "What do you want me to do while I'm there, sir?"

"Relax, Oatmire, you're not being transferred to the navy. Not yet, anyhow. I want you to observe and report back to me." A smile creased the general's face. "You're going to be my fox in the navy henhouse. In other words, son, you're going to be my spy."

CHAPTER NINE

THERE WAS a reason that Oatmire had joined the army rather than the navy. The reason was that he preferred dry land rather than the sea.

He was reminded of this preference while being bounced around in a small launch that was crossing a very large expanse of ocean. He suspected that the boatswain was doing his best to hit all the waves sideways, thus maximizing the rocking and bouncing of the boat to unnerve the ground pounder huddled miserably in the bow.

Oatmire felt his stomach begin to churn. He tried not to dwell on the extra helping of reconstituted powdered eggs that he'd had that morning, washed down by a mug of the navy's thickest black coffee.

His mood was not helped by the salty spray that pummeled him in the bow. In fact, he seemed to be doing a good job of blocking the spray and thus preventing any of the actual navy personnel from getting wet, God forbid.

"How much farther?" Oatmire shouted, the breeze threatening to whip away his words.

"The ship is just over the horizon, sir."

"All right. For a minute there I was worried that we were headed back to Pearl."

"No, sir, we wouldn't have enough fuel for that."

Oatmire checked for a smile on the boatswain's face, but the man had said it deadpan, as if he had taken Oatmire's wisecrack about crossing the Pacific seriously. On top of that, the sailor had been concerned only about the lack of fuel, and not the lack of *size* of the launch.

"Good to know."

Oatmire shook his head, managing to take a fresh face full of cold sea spray in the process. *Sailors.* Everybody said it was the marines who were trouble, but he wasn't so sure about that.

He wouldn't have been surprised if someone in the navy brass really had decided to send MacArthur's aide all the way back to Hawaii in an open boat, just as a way of poking a stick in the general's eye.

Disconcertingly, USS *Nashville* was slipping out of sight. Though massive in person, the distant ship seemed insignificant on the blue Pacific. A vast sky studded with puffy clouds swept down to meet the sea at the horizon. They were much too far out to sea for any glimpse of Leyte, of course.

The launch rode up a wave and sliced down in the trough, then up again, wild as any roller-coaster ride. His head spun, and he suddenly felt himself losing the skirmish with his queasy stomach.

He leaned over the side and heaved up his breakfast. He sat up and wiped his mouth with the back of his hand. At least he'd had the good sense to lose his breakfast over the downwind side of the launch.

The boatswain made no comment, perhaps out of a sense of interservice diplomacy. Oatmire suspected that he'd been trained to ignore seasick army officers, lest they be even further embarrassed.

Oatmire groaned. He thought back to the conversation he'd had with his closest friend on the staff when he had suggested that perhaps someone else would be better for the job. *Any*body else. But they both knew his orders weren't going to change. These orders had come from General MacArthur himself.

"What I don't get is, why me?" The look on Oatmire's face made it clear that he still didn't understand his situation.

"Look, Oatmire, if MacArthur sent Sutherland on that ship, those squids would all be on their best behavior. They'd never say anything in front of him. Besides, MacArthur would miss him too much. He *is* the chief of staff, after all. You, on the other hand, nobody is even going to notice. Hell, nobody is even going to miss you here."

"Thanks a lot."

"You know me. Just trying to cheer you up."

Oatmire's thoughts were interrupted by a change in the engine noise. The launch that had been bravely pushing through the Pacific chop suddenly slowed to a crawl, nearly wallowing in the waves. Oatmire had thought that going slower would be a good thing, but he realized that he was mistaken.

He looked up, but there was nothing on the horizon. "What's going on? Why are we slowing down?"

"We've got two aircraft incoming, sir. I don't think that they're ours."

Following the sailor's glance, he saw the two planes. "I'll be damned."

The aircraft remained at high altitude, so it was impossible to determine whether they were friend or foe. Maybe someone with sharper eyes could tell the difference, but squinting over the sights of a typewriter had taken its toll on Oatmire's vision. However, the fact that there were only two planes was suspicious. American aircraft generally flew in squadrons, but the Japanese were flying sorties with smaller numbers of planes, reflecting their dwindling forces.

One thing for sure, if they were Japanese, the launch would be defenseless if they came by for a strafing run. One good burst from the machine guns of a Zero would reduce them to splinters, or at least put enough holes in the hull to ensure that their journey wouldn't last much longer.

The boatswain had slowed to eliminate any wake, which was the most telltale sign of a vessel moving on the surface, even one as small as this.

Oatmire held his breath and kept quiet, as if the pilots could hear him all that way up. It would seem as if their small boat would hardly be worth the effort, but it was hard to say how vengeful a Japanese pilot might be feeling.

Once the planes had started to slip from sight, the boatswain reengaged the throttle, and the launch began making headway once again.

The small boat resumed its bouncing journey, but Oatmire kept one eye on the sky in case the planes returned.

He doubted that his adventures with the United States Navy could have gotten much worse, but he was wrong about that.

* * *

FINALLY, a brooding gray silhouette appeared on the horizon.

"There she is, sir," the boatswain said helpfully, evidently just in case army officers were blind in addition to being prone to seasickness.

"I see her."

Since the incident with the aircraft passing overhead, Oatmire had been more than alert. He studied the ship ahead with interest.

He was glad to see that the ship was large, which would be some countermeasure against the Pacific swells, but that was as far as the allure went.

He remembered once seeing a tall ship, a massive wooden vessel with canvas sails, rigging like gossamer, and a carved and painted figurehead portraying a Romanesque woman or maybe a minor goddess. Even a landlubber like Oatmire had been struck by the beauty of that ship, almost like a massive swan sweeping silently across the water. The navy vessel on the horizon did not resemble that majestic tall ship in any way.

"What the hell is that?" Oatmire asked.

"That's the USS *Kalinin Bay*," the boatswain replied, sounding puzzled. "Didn't anyone tell you where you were going?"

"I was told that I was visiting a ship. That looks like a giant floating shoebox."

For once, the boatswain cracked a smile. "You wouldn't be far wrong, sir. The *Kalinin Bay* is an escort carrier. What we call a Jeep carrier or baby flattop."

The boatswain then launched into a surprisingly detailed explanation of a Jeep carrier, which had very little to do with Jeeps, although there might be some of those stowed in the hold for transfer to Leyte. Instead, this was a small carrier intended for just twenty-seven aircraft and with a complement of more than nine hundred men, including pilots and aircrew. The so-called Jeep carriers could be built relatively quickly and deployed to Pacific outposts, where the resources of a full-size carrier would be wasted. More than fifty of these Casablanca-class escort carriers were now scattered around the Pacific, forming a small navy in themselves. The boatswain stopped short of explaining that *Kalinin Bay* was named for a remote body of water in Alaska.

In comparison, a full-size aircraft carrier such as the famed

USS *Enterprise* transported up to ninety-six planes and more than twenty-two hundred personnel, almost as much of a floating city as a ship.

The smaller carrier had been built for utility rather than looks. Oatmire had thought that USS *Kalinin Bay* resembled a giant floating shoebox, which was an apt description. Though shorter in length than the mighty USS *Nashville*, the Jeep carrier somehow looked bulkier due to its sheer sides. Oatmire stared with some apprehension at the rope ladder that hung down the side of the ship, blowing around in the ocean breeze like a loose thread.

"Here we go, sir," the boatswain said. "My advice is, don't look down. And don't stop climbing."

The launch nosed up against the steel skin like a baby whale nudging its mama. Oatmire looped his seabag over his shoulders, swayed unsteadily with the weight, then lurched forward. A wave had slapped them away from the ship, opening a gap between the launch and the dangling ladder. For a moment it seemed as if Oatmire might fall into the sea and never be seen again. But the skilled boatswain yanked at the throttle and the rudder, closing the gap so that when Oatmire did fall, he managed to grab the ladder and hang on for dear life.

Oatmire knew that he couldn't stay there forever, feet planted in the bucking launch and wet hands grasping the ladder. He forced himself to start to climb.

Below him, the launch pulled away.

"Good luck, sir!" the boatswain shouted, and then the small boat headed back across the sea.

Fueled by sheer terror and adrenaline, Oatmire managed to climb the ladder. The ladder was not secured at the bottom, which meant that from time to time it swung out over the water like a pendulum when the ship rode a large swell. "Dear God," Oatmire muttered, holding on for dear life until the pendulum swung back and smacked him against the steel skin of the ship. At the top, hands reached down and helped him over the side. Oatmire flopped onto the deck and lay there gasping like a freshly caught fish.

As he caught his breath, Oatmire began the first of his naval observations.

First of all, he noted that there was no fanfare. Apparently the ship's captain hadn't even taken the time to be there to greet him—that was how far down the pecking order Oatmire was in the scheme of things.

The ship was apparently already at anchor and had not stopped expressly for him. The business of the ship was going on around them, sailors busy coiling lines and mopping up oil spills from the flight deck. Other sailors were busy doing jobs and working on equipment that Oatmire couldn't even identify. He felt more like a landlubber than ever.

The arrival of a junior army officer did not warrant any sort of ceremony and was scarcely noticed, even if he was coming from General MacArthur. If it had actually been MacArthur arriving on the ship, it would have been a different story. The ship's officers would have all been on hand to greet him, and most of the ship's crew would have been gathered in formation, all wearing their best uniforms. Of course MacArthur wouldn't have bothered to go aboard a Jeep carrier, no more than a chef would have stopped to eat at a roadside diner.

"That last step is a doozy," said a voice that clearly sounded amused, and Oatmire looked up to see a naval officer reaching down to assist him with getting upright again.

"Let me help you with that, sir," a sailor announced, and Oatmire felt himself being relieved of the weighty seabag. He lurched sideways as he adjusted to not being weighed down.

Oatmire regained his balance and found himself looking into the smiling face of a lieutenant commander. The man was about average height and build, with what seemed to be a friendly disposition.

"I'm Tom O'Connell," the lieutenant commander announced, extending a hand that Oatmire shook. Oatmire understood that it was a rank equivalent to an army major, which meant that O'Connell technically outranked him. "Welcome aboard."

Oatmire couldn't help but grin back. "So you're going to be my babysitter, sir?"

O'Connell laughed. "If you want to call it that. Officially, I've been assigned to be your liaison, mainly because they don't know what else to do with me. The ship I was on got sunk by the Japanese back at Ironbottom Sound, and they put me aboard this carrier. They already have a full complement of officers, so I end up with a lot of 'and other duties as assigned' by the captain. No need to call me 'sir,' by the way—I'm just here as your tour guide."

It was an honest and straightforward introduction. Oatmire couldn't help but smile again. "I've got to say, that sounds a lot like my job back at HQ, which is probably why I got sent out here."

"Why exactly are you here?" O'Connell was friendly enough, but Oatmire noticed that the naval officer had quick, intelligent eyes. Maybe his lack of other duties wasn't the only reason he had been assigned to chaperone an army officer. Like most career officers, he was probably an Annapolis graduate. Not much would get past him.

At any rate, it was a fair question to ask why he was on board. "I'm a liaison. General MacArthur wanted to promote interservice—"

O'Connell cut him off, looking amused. "Liaison, huh? You mean you were sent here to spy on us. In that case, let me show you around. We're not as big as the *Indianapolis* or even the *Nashville* that you just came from, but there's still plenty to see."

Oatmire didn't bother to argue about being called a spy. He still wasn't entirely sure why he was there or what he was looking for, but he thought that he would know it when he saw it.

"I'd appreciate a tour," Oatmire agreed. "As long as it doesn't involve climbing any other ladders."

"Don't worry. Coming up the side of that ship was the most excitement you're likely to see. The Seventh Fleet is strictly supply and logistics. If you wanted to see some action, you should have gotten yourself sent out to Halsey's Third Fleet." O'Connell waved a hand to indicate the ocean beyond. "They're at least sixty miles out. They're the ones who are tangling with the Japanese right about now."

"Quiet is fine by me," Oatmire said. He took a step, realizing that his legs still felt rubbery after the climb up the ship's ladder. He took another step and staggered.

O'Connell moved to steady him. "You know what? There's officially no booze allowed on board, but the officers do keep a little scotch on hand for medicinal purposes. I'd say you could use a drink."

"I think I *could* use a drink—strictly for medicinal purposes," Oatmire said.

"That's the spirit," O'Connell said. "Right this way."

"I have to admit that I'm suddenly liking the navy a lot more than I did a minute ago."

CHAPTER TEN

AT THAT MOMENT, little did Oatmire or anyone else aboard USS *Kalinin Bay* know that the Japanese were about to launch a vast and desperate gambit to crush the American landing efforts at Leyte. Events being set in motion would result in the largest sea battle in history.

The Japanese effort spanned vast distances across the Pacific, putting at risk almost all that was left of their navy. But as with so many gambles in military history, with the risk went tremendous potential rewards.

Oatmire, O'Connell, and USS *Kalinin Bay* would find themselves in the middle of it.

* * *

BY THAT POINT IN 1944, the Japanese fleet had been decimated by losses at Midway, the Eastern Solomons, Santa Cruz, and the Philippine Sea—where it had lost nearly four hundred aircraft. Those pilots and aircrew, not to mention the planes, could not be replaced.

Meanwhile, American production prowess had geared up almost faster than the United States could have hoped for, producing new aircraft and ships at an astonishing rate. The growth of the United States Navy was almost exponential.

The Japanese built excellent aircraft and ships but could not replace the huge numbers that had gone down in flames. At that point Japan was losing the war, but it had not yet lost.

There were still Japanese planes, but the overall loss of Japanese aircraft leading up to the Philippines campaign was devastating.

Although their numbers of seaborne aircraft were greatly diminished, their navy remained relatively strong. They still possessed large numbers of submarines, heavy cruisers, and battleships—including two of the most formidable ships in the world.

It hardly required a military expert to see that the odds were not in Japan's favor. The chief factor was aircraft. Admiral Yamamoto had been visionary at the outset of the war in understanding the value of aircraft carriers and aircraft as the path toward winning the war of the future. When the battlefield was mainly composed of islands and the vast Pacific itself, these resources were vital.

Their other great weakness was that, simply put, they were running out of the oil they needed to fuel their ships. Oil flowed from their oil fields around Indonesia to Japan itself. The loss of the Philippines would cut that off, creating the nautical supply route equivalent of a vasectomy. Put in those terms, there wasn't a man who didn't flinch at the thought.

As the Japanese high command saw it, the best way to crush and thwart the invasion of the Philippines might be to smash the invasion fleet that provided the supply and logistics support.

Although it might seem obvious to an armchair admiral, the Japanese had not previously used this strategy of targeting the logistical apparatus of the invasion forces. With a little luck, the Emperor's ships might even be able to get in close enough to unleash their massive guns on the American troops on shore.

To that end, the Japanese developed a simple but devious plan to fool the Americans.

* * *

MOST OF JAPAN'S remaining aircraft carriers had been recalled to Japan itself for refitting. The bulk of Japan's remaining naval power, including the massive battleships *Yamato* and *Musashi*, were in the vicinity of Singapore.

Under October skies, the Japanese carrier fleet set sail from Japan on a path toward the Philippines. US Navy submarines quickly detected the movement and relayed the information. This information caused a great deal of excitement in American quarters.

US Navy forces around the Philippines consisted of the Seventh Fleet, composed mainly of older vessels. Their task was to provide logistical support for the US Army landing forces on Leyte. Consequently, these ships were operating closer to shore. The USS *Kalinin Bay* that Oatmire found himself aboard with Lieutenant Commander O'Connell was part of this Seventh Fleet force.

The Third Fleet with its large aircraft carriers was nearly sixty miles off the Leyte coast. This was the force commanded by Admiral Halsey from his flagship, the carrier USS *Enterprise*.

Perhaps the Japanese understood Halsey too well. They knew that he was a proud and pugilistic commander known for his personal motto, "Hit hard, hit fast, hit often." Perhaps it was thus no surprise that they seemed to know that Halsey would be unable to resist turning all his attention to the force of aircraft carriers leaving Japan.

But the Japanese had a trick up the sleeves of their kimonos.

Little did Halsey know that the carriers were almost empty, their decks bare, most of their planes gone.

The carrier fleet was being used as bait.

The trap had been set.

Admiral Halsey fell into it, rushing his Third Fleet even farther from Leyte to meet the carrier fleet head-on. He couldn't wait to unleash his Curtiss Helldivers, which moved at 294 miles per hour, against the Japanese, delivering a knockout punch.

Operations on Leyte would be left without vital air support as a result. Defense of the waters around Leyte would be left up to the aging "second-rate" ships of the Seventh Fleet.

Meanwhile, withdrawing from Singapore, the Japanese battleship fleet began to move north toward the Philippines, intending to strike a crushing blow against the workhorse Seventh Fleet and the US landing forces.

This force represented much of the remaining might of the Japanese Navy: thirteen destroyers, one light cruiser, seven heavy cruisers, and five battleships—including the mighty *Yamato* and *Musashi*.

The two battleships on their own may have been enough to sink the Seventh Fleet. They were massive, approaching nine hundred feet long and two hundred feet wide, with several eighteen-inch guns—the largest ever used in naval combat.

In comparison, USS *Kalinin Bay* was equipped with a single five-inch gun.

The Japanese force split in two to come at the Seventh Fleet in a pincer movement. Half the force steamed through Sulu Sea and Surigao Strait toward Leyte Gulf. The other half of the enemy fleet moved through the tangled islands of the Sibuyan Sea and then into San Bernardino Strait.

It was shaping up to be an epic naval battle—or a slaughter.

* * *

CAPTAIN OATMIRE HAD FINISHED up his medicinal scotch and received a tour of the *Kalinin Bay* courtesy of Lieutenant Commander O'Connell. He watched a couple of planes take off and land, which was something of a novelty to see up close. The trio of planes had launched to scout Japanese positions on Leyte. The ship was too far out to sea to offer any glimpse of land, but it was just a hop, skip, and a jump for aircraft to get there.

"They'll drop some bombs while they're at it and give the Japanese a headache," O'Connell commented.

It was approaching sunset, the sun giving a golden glow to the sea, when the planes returned. They were just in time—the fighters did not typically fly at night.

Watching the landings gave Oatmire new respect for naval aviators. It nearly boggled the imagination to think about landing a plane on the deck of a ship that would be little more than a speck in a very large ocean. He was reminded that every soldier, sailor, marine, submariner, and aviator in the US armed forces thought that he had it tough—and he often did—until he took a moment to think about the job that the other guy was doing.

"Here they come," O'Connell said. "Looks like they all made it back. Thank God for that."

Oatmire watched the plane grow from a dot on the horizon to an aircraft swooping down onto the deck and shook his head. Damn, that was something to see.

Not long after sunset, Oatmire was only too happy to adjourn to the bunk that he had been assigned in the junior officers' quarters. It wasn't much space, but he was already used to that from USS *Nashville*. He read for a bit from a paperback copy of *Last Laugh, Mr. Moto*, a detective story by John P. Marquand. Oddly enough, the popular series featured a Japanese detective. Marquand had written the book before Pearl Harbor, so its publication had been up in the air until government officials had determined that the detective was sufficiently bumbling to allow continued publication of the series.

The pages were only a little waterlogged from his trip across on the launch. He'd managed to get through only a page or two, and then he'd fallen into a deep sleep.

* * *

EARLY-MORNING DAYLIGHT WAS COMING through the single porthole, open to the sea breeze to keep the tropical heat at bay in the cramped quarters. Despite the morning cool, the porthole was failing miserably at its job.

But it had not been the morning light or the heat that had awakened Oatmire; rather, it had been the klaxon calling the crew to general quarters.

"Here we go again," he muttered, sitting up and promptly banging his head on the bottom of the bunk above him.

Aboard the *Nashville*, he had experienced more than one general quarters. Those alarms had always been due to air raids. Usually they hadn't amounted to much. General MacArthur's staff found those alarms to be little more than an annoying interruption of their work.

Oatmire figured that it would be more of the same here on *Kalinin Bay*.

The other officers he'd been bunking with scrambled to get dressed.

Oatmire rubbed his head and took his time getting his pants on. As a visiting army officer, he had no real duties on the ship. Eventually, he followed the others up on deck.

O'Connell was waiting to shove a helmet and life vest at him. The serious look on the normally jovial Boston Irishman's face told Oatmire that something was going on even before O'Connell explained.

"We have Japanese ships on the horizon," O'Connell said.

"Anybody have binoculars?" Oatmire asked, some boyish part of him not a little excited. He had yet to see a Japanese ship.

"You don't need binoculars," O'Connell said, pointing.

Oatmire looked in that direction and saw not a lone ship, but several. "It looks like an entire Japanese fleet!"

"This is one time I wouldn't argue with a ground pounder," O'Connell said. "That definitely looks like a Japanese fleet."

"Where the hell did they come from?"

"Sneaked right up on us from the other side of Leyte. I'll tell you one thing, that took some sailing."

"Damn" was all Oatmire could manage in response. Even from this distance, he could see the telltale Japanese pagoda silhouettes of the ships and even a glimpse of the Rising Sun flag.

Water foamed at the bows of the enemy ships. They were headed right for the US task force.

"Better get that helmet on. Maybe put your fingers in your ears."

"What—"

Oatmire was suddenly deafened by the firing of the Jeep carrier's five-inch gun. A jet of flame shot out toward the enemy fleet.

He could feel the ship turning under his feet, struggling to make itself a more difficult target. But a big, floating shoebox like *Kalinin Bay* was not nimble. It did its best.

He soon understood why. There was a roaring sound like a freight train or maybe a tornado, and then an enormous geyser erupted off the stern of the ship. That was soon followed by more roaring and splashes as an entire Japanese salvo arrived. Oatmire suspected that if the ship hadn't managed to maneuver, those shells might have turned the carrier into swiss cheese.

The small carrier was also getting her bow into the wind. Across the deck, pilots raced for their aircraft. Even as more shells came in, first one plane, then another and another, managed to claw their way into the morning air and head toward the enemy vessels.

The Jeep carrier was accompanied only by a couple of destroyers. They were hopelessly outclassed and outgunned by the big enemy ships headed their way.

In an almost suicidal attack, one of the destroyers raced toward the Japanese, every gun firing. Oatmire had borrowed some binoculars and watched, amazed, as the destroyer made a direct hit on the nearest Japanese vessel. He whooped, expecting to see the enemy ship go up dramatically in flames.

To his astonishment, the shell from the US ship exploded but bounced off, doing no more harm than a firecracker makes against a sidewalk. The Japanese ships were just too heavily armored for the destroyer's smaller gun to penetrate.

"Look at those brave bastards go," O'Connell muttered in amazement.

Oatmire was reminded of a mouse trying to fight a bunch of cats. "Who are they?"

"That's the *Johnston*."

The destroyer had gotten right in among the Japanese fleet, firing in all directions, hitting them with everything from its five-inch gun to antiaircraft weapons. The feisty ship even hurled depth charges whenever it came close enough to an enemy vessel.

Other destroyers followed the example of USS *Johnston*, but held back from getting right in among the Japanese fleet. The attack had slowed the enemy onslaught, enabling *Kalinin Bay* and the other escort carriers nearby to get their planes into the sky.

These were not nearly the numbers of aircraft—or the savage dive bombers—that USS *Enterprise* and the rest of the Third Fleet carriers could have launched. However, the Third Fleet was much too far away to help them now.

Even a small number of planes was more than the Japanese possessed. Theirs was strictly a naval force. The aircraft attacked furiously, as if their lives depended on it—which they did.

Flak filled the sky, creating a rainbow effect of colorful bursts. The explosions made sharp popping sounds that jabbed at his eardrums between the firing of *Kalinin Bay*'s 40 mm cannons and 20 mm machine guns. It could have passed for a Fourth of July display if the intent hadn't been so destructive. Japanese ships were each assigned a separate color as a more effective way to track their own antiaircraft fire in a joint action. It was a simple but ingenious method to manage each individual ship's fire during the heat of combat.

Somehow the US planes managed to avoid the flak, although one or two planes were hit. One moment they were racing across the blue sky, and the next moment they were cartwheeling in flames. Oatmire shuddered at the sight.

The smoke from the burning planes smudged the sky, and the sound of explosions echoed across the ocean. The crew on the USS *Kalinin Bay* stayed at their battle stations, their hearts pounding with fear and adrenaline. They had been caught by surprise, and they had to fight with every fiber of their being if they hoped to survive.

Oatmire continued to watch the naval battle unfold through the binoculars. For a few amazing minutes, it had almost seemed as if the *Johnston* and her intrepid crew might turn the tide of battle all by itself. But flames were now coming from the intrepid destroyers, showing that it had been hit not once, but probably multiple times.

The larger ships were not ignoring USS *Johnston*. Instead, she had been surrounded by several Japanese destroyers. They were ganging up on the American vessel, pouring fire into the wounded ship.

They were killing her.

Oatmire groaned and swore helplessly. He couldn't imagine what it must be like to be one of the crew on that ship, being hit from all directions. The destroyer began to list to one side, its deck covered in smoke and flame. Then the stern dipped under the waves and the ship went under.

There must have been survivors, because one of the Japanese destroyers hung around to strafe the waves with machine-gun fire, ensuring that no one from USS *Johnston* would live.

This went beyond warfare. This was murder and revenge, all rolled into one.

Sons of bitches, Oatmire thought.

He pulled the binoculars away from his eyes. The slaughter was more than he could bear to watch.

But the sacrifice of USS *Johnston* and her crew had made a difference. Given the gift of time, the escort carriers' planes were hitting the Japanese hard. It was a reminder that naval warfare now depended more than ever on aircraft. Without air cover, the Japanese were taking a merciless beating.

Slowly, the Japanese ships began to turn and retreat. They had lost the momentum of attack. Little did they know that if they had only pressed forward and really brought the *Yamato* and *Musashi* into play, they might have utterly annihilated the Seventh Fleet and done untold damage to the landing operation on Leyte.

After the war, the Japanese admiral would reveal that he had thought he must have run into the Third Fleet after all, rather than the beleaguered Seventh Fleet. Their furious defense had convinced the Japanese that they had encountered a much larger force.

* * *

IT WAS another week before Oatmire made the return trip to USS *Nashville*. He hadn't been meant to stay that long, but in the excitement over the Japanese presence, nobody had worried much about inconveniencing an army captain.

Once he had cleaned up and put on a fresh uniform, he found himself reporting to General MacArthur himself. It was a little unusual in that normally his written report would be "passed up the food chain." In this case, the general wanted to hear it straight from the horse's mouth.

MacArthur seemed to have forgotten his concerns about what the navy boys "were up to." Instead, he wanted details about the sea battle that Oatmire had witnessed. The general asked a few questions but mostly appeared rapt as Oatmire described the actions of the destroyer in almost single-handedly taking on the Japanese fleet.

The rest of the story, which General MacArthur already knew, was that *Yamato* and *Musashi* had not made it far from the Battle off Samar that Oatmire had witnessed. First, the *Musashi* had been targeted and sunk by repeated bombings from US aircraft.

Then had come a reckoning for *Yamato*. Although the ship had taken an incredible amount of punishment, she was no match for the relentless air attacks that she faced. Eventually, the ship that was the pride and joy of the Imperial Navy also slipped beneath the waves.

All told, the Japanese had lost several ships. Oatmire had been privy to some of the reports coming in. Estimates were that the Japanese had lost more than twelve thousand sailors and aircrew across the smaller fights that made up the sea battle of Leyte Gulf.

Allied forces—the Australian navy had also played a role—

had not gone unscathed, but had also lost ships and as many as two thousand sailors and aircrew. If things had gone differently in the Battle off Samar, the outcome might have been far, far worse for the efforts to take back the Philippines.

Because the general wanted more than reports, but an actual eyewitness account, he asked Oatmire a few additional questions, then signaled that the meeting was coming to a close.

"Any other thoughts you want to share, Captain?"

Oatmire considered, then said, "Yes, sir. I just want to say, thank God for the United States Navy!"

General MacArthur frowned. It was not exactly what he wanted to hear or expected, but in this case, even the general seemed ready to admit that Oatmire had a point.

"You might just be right about that, son. Now, dismissed!"

CHAPTER ELEVEN

DEKE and the rest of the company crept cautiously toward the coast, expecting at any moment to meet more Japanese resistance. They were battered and bruised, and more fighting was the last thing any of them wanted.

Even the fight at the coconut grove had cost them dearly. Lieutenant Gurley had been a good man, and so had Private Simmons. They had now joined the long list of soldiers who would not be coming home from the Pacific. The consensus was that Gurley had been a good man, but too eager. Fighting the Japanese wasn't like in the comic books. It was good to keep that in mind if you wanted to stay alive.

"Damn shame about Lieutenant Gurley," Philly remarked. He had drifted back to join Deke and Yoshio in the middle of the company moving along the jungle trail, content to let Danilo take point.

"He ought to have known better than to charge right at the Japanese," said Deke. "There's nothin' worse than a dumb officer."

"You know what, Corn Pone? The thing about you that we

can always count on is that you don't like anybody." Philly's tone suggested that he'd held the dead lieutenant in somewhat higher regard. "I do believe that you are the angriest son of a bitch I've ever met."

"I might be angry, but at least I'm not a dead son of a bitch. Not yet, anyway. Always remember that the Japanese can shoot just as straight as we can. An officer like Gurley can get every last one of his men killed. We're lucky that Captain Merrick has got more sense than that."

"If you say so."

Deke had no real love for most officers. In Deke's book, many officers were just part of the system that kept a good man down. They ranked right up there with bankers and factory owners. There were exceptions to the rule, he thought, like Captain Merrick and Lieutenant Steele, men who knew their business. Another exception might even be MacArthur himself, who seemed to know how to go about winning the war.

"I think that Lieutenant Gurley was frustrated by the enemy," Yoshio said. "He wanted them to come out and fight. It was his own version of a banzai charge."

"Well, he's dead now, and so is Simmons," Deke pointed out. He had meant to just point out the facts but was surprised to hear the note of anger in his own voice.

The fight at the coconut grave had been an unpleasant surprise. It had shaped up to be their last combat action before leaving the jungle behind. If only they could have avoided it, then several more of the company's men would have survived.

It was small consolation that they had killed all the Japanese who had ambushed them. In fact, it was quite a lopsided victory. But it would have been better if the fight hadn't taken place at all. You certainly couldn't blame Danilo for the ambush. In fact, it was his alert eyes and ears that had kept the Japanese ambush from being far worse.

Deke could understand what Yoshio meant about the lieutenant charging the Japanese position out of anger and frustration. Some of the others had done the same thing. But rage didn't make you bulletproof. As it turned out, those men had died all the same. It was only the stealthy flanking movement that had snuffed out the Japanese attack, not the foolhardy charge by Lieutenant Gurley and the others.

And why had they died? To capture a little grove of overgrown coconut trees? No—that was the wrong way to look at it, Deke decided. They had died fighting the Japanese, pure and simple. The place and the circumstances didn't matter. This was a war that was being won by increments.

Meanwhile, something that Philly had said was still gnawing at him.

"Hey, Yoshio," Deke said. "Do you think I'm angry all the time?"

"Well, not *all* of the time," Yoshio said. "Just *most* of the time."

Deke chewed that over in his mind. Back home, there had been a lot of people he was angry at, but mostly he had been angry at himself. Here in the Pacific, he could unleash that anger on somebody else—the Japanese.

And that was just fine by him.

* * *

ALL MORNING, they had been moving toward the sound of fighting. Machine guns, mortars, even some artillery. The sounds indicated that this wasn't just another skirmish at a coconut grove, but the sounds of a substantial fight taking place. Without doubt, they must be approaching the Japanese bastion around Ormoc.

His fevered mind convinced Deke that he could already

smell the scent of spent gunpowder and blood, burning crops and the sap of the broken trees. In places, patches of jungle still pressed close to the trail, so that a thousand tiny branches seemed to scratch at his face and bare hands. He felt each one of them, his feverish skin extra sensitive, each brush against the leaves and branches seeming to have a different texture and shape, like running his hands over rough-cut lumber or rubbing his face with sandpaper.

He shook his head to clear it and took a drink from his canteen.

The fact that he was itching to get back into the fight made Deke realize that he felt marginally better, the fever starting to release some of its grip on him. At least the jungle wasn't spinning quite as much as it had been. He had been popping aspirin like gumdrops and washing the pills down with more of Danilo's tea. One or the other seemed to be working, or maybe it was a combination.

Sometimes, after having dodged so many bullets, Deke got to feeling invincible. Anyhow, nobody wanted to think that he could die. Getting killed was for the other guy. It was a convenient fiction that kept a man going, because if you believed that you were going to die in the next minute or the next hour, you'd curl up in the bottom of a foxhole instead of doing your job as a soldier. The fever was a reminder that death lurked in all sorts of ways, lest Deke get too bold.

Up ahead, Deke could see Danilo leading the way along the trail, several feet ahead of the nearest soldier. The Filipino guerrilla reminded Deke of the jungle cat that he had seen, all the man's senses on high alert, like some creature of the forest.

Deke considered that he knew almost nothing about Danilo other than that he was one of the guerrillas who had served with Father Francisco to fight the Japanese occupiers in any way possible. He didn't know how old Danilo was, if he had children, or how his family might have suffered under Japanese occupation.

The man had made an effort to nurse Deke back to health in his own rugged way. Would Deke have done the same for him? He realized that he might not have, at least not before Danilo had done so much for him. He felt ashamed about it. When it came to the Filipinos, Deke realized there was so much that they took for granted about these generous people.

Danilo signaled a halt. They saw him crouch, rifle at the ready.

"Dammit, it's probably more Japanese," Captain Merrick could be heard muttering as he hurried forward. "Frazier, get that BAR ready."

Private Frazier hurried forward, shouldering his way past the other men in an attempt to catch up with Captain Merrick at the head of the column. Instead of gunshots, however, they were met with a booming American voice that demanded, "What's the password?"

Danilo looked at Captain Merrick, who shouted irritably back at the unseen sentry: "I don't know the damn password!"

There was a pause in which everyone held their breath. The moment was tense, considering that more than one incident of so-called friendly fire had been caused by nervous or overzealous sentries. "How do we know you're not Japs?"

"Do we look like Japs to you, soldier? We don't know the damn password because we've been hiking through the damn jungle. Goddammit."

Two GIs emerged from the cover where they had been hiding, their rifles almost casually pointing in Merrick's direction. As the captain moved forward, they lowered their weapons. More men appeared, and one of them turned out to be an officer. In keeping with policy, there was no exchange of salutes or formalities. Not that most officers needed any. It was easy to tell an officer by the way he carried himself. When it came down to it, Merrick held himself the same way—a little stiff, a little apart from the enlisted men.

No wonder the Japanese snipers keep picking off our officers, Deke thought. *They make awful good targets.*

"We were told that we should be expecting a patrol that had been cutting across the peninsula," the officer said. He looked over the battered column. "It looks as if you and your boys caught hell."

"You have no idea," Merrick said. "I guess you've been having a regular Sunday picnic over on this side of the coast."

The other officer snorted. "If your idea of a picnic is getting shot to hell on the beach and then fighting Japanese all over the place, then yeah, I guess it has been one helluva picnic."

Captain Merrick collected directions to headquarters, and then the other officer and his sentries stepped aside to let the company pass. From the looks on their faces, Deke could see that he and the rest of the company must have seemed like a wreck. It sounded as if they weren't going to get much in the way of relief.

"Everybody stay alert," Merrick warned. "We didn't come all this way just to get mowed down by the Japanese—or our own guys, for that matter."

Before long, the jungle began to fall away as they reached cultivated fields. They passed through a small village, abandoned except for a few dogs that yapped at the men. The fact that their rib cages stood out like wires indicated that the dogs were starving.

One of the men tried to give one of the dogs a few scraps to eat, but Captain Merrick scowled at him. "Knock it off. There's nothing that you can do for these dogs, except maybe shoot them and put them out of their misery. You want to feed somebody, then save it for the villagers. I'll bet they're just as hungry."

However, the villagers did not show themselves, apparently having fled the fighting. Deke wished them luck. Right now there didn't seem to be many places to go to avoid the fighting. The Filipinos' homeland had been turned into a battleground. He supposed that it was unavoidable. Like the old saying went, you had to break a few eggs to make an omelet. In this case, the omelet was returning peace and freedom to the Philippines.

"Look, sir, over here!" a soldier called.

The soldier pointed out the bodies of two women. Their clothes were ripped asunder, and it appeared that they had been bayoneted. Nearby lay the carcasses of two dogs and a goat. It appeared that they, too, had been stabbed to death. The awful smell of decay lingered.

The captain stood over the bodies of the two women, nose buried in the crook of his elbow, studying them. One had graying hair, while the other woman appeared younger. Maybe they had been mother and daughter? Then the captain retreated several steps away and seemed to take several gulps of fresher air.

They had all seen dead civilians before, usually people caught in the middle of war, killed by accident. There were always going to be casualties when artillery shells landed in towns and villages. Some of those stray shells had been American. That was how it was when you were fighting a war, but it was a damn shame, and everybody felt bad about it. Even among these battle-hardened GIs, none of them could fathom the intentional killing of a civilian. They were caught up in a noble cause, fighting to liberate these people.

They knew that the Japanese took a different view. They had seen how civilians were used by the enemy as human shields in Palo. But seeing the two dead women felt different. The women had been bayoneted like the livestock, either out of anger or for sport. Nothing accidental about it.

The captain had shown himself to be mostly calm and steady,

but just for an instant, his worn features twisted into something like anger.

"The Japanese did this," Merrick said, raising his voice so that all his men heard. "Killed these two women like they were dogs. Never forget who we are fighting."

One by one the men trooped past the gruesome scene, unable to avoid looking at the bodies. The sight couldn't help but evoke thoughts of wives, sisters, mothers, and daughters back home. These dead women had certainly meant the world to someone. They had been murdered for no good reason at all.

"Damn these Japanese," Philly muttered. "Damn them all."

CHAPTER TWELVE

LEAVING the village and the grisly scene behind, they advanced through a countryside that bore the marks of war. They passed shattered trees, the smoldering ruins of modest houses and outbuildings, and scorched craters left by artillery shells.

If it hadn't been for these scars of war, it would have been a lovely green countryside. Given time to heal, it would be lovely again. But for now the stink of charred wood and cordite seemed to linger in the air. It looked as though a giant had walked through the area, twisting and uprooting trees as he went.

The broken trees and craters were the result of the navy bombardment before the beach landing by US forces. Judging by the number of craters, it must have been an impressive show of firepower. The navy seldom failed to disappoint in that regard. They had big guns, and they welcomed a chance to use them.

What the navy had been shooting at and how much good the bombardment had done was hard to say. Most of the shells seemed to have struck empty fields and patches of forest. There certainly weren't any Japanese bodies. The Japanese must have pulled back and hidden themselves deeper in the interior jungles, safe from the bombardment.

"I sure hope those squids have some shells left," Philly said. "They might need them to shoot at the enemy. This looks more like target practice to me."

"Don't you know that's the part that we're here for?" Deke pointed out.

"And what part is that, exactly?"

"The actual shooting-the-enemy part."

Philly gave a short laugh. "You must be feeling better. That crap Danilo gave you to drink must have done the trick."

"You know what they say—what doesn't kill us makes us stronger."

Deke still felt shaky, but he was stronger than he had been. Yoshio was still carrying his haversack, but Deke had taken back his rifle. It was slung over his shoulder, and he doubted that he could have used it effectively, but he couldn't bear to be without it. The weight of it tugging at his shoulder felt reassuring.

By now the path had become a sandy road. Few of the roads in the rural areas of the Philippines were paved. The road was packed down hard in places, but in others the loose sand gripped at tires and made walking difficult. During one of the frequent heavy rains, the road would be a quagmire.

As the road continued, the surrounding forest fell away to reveal open stretches of marsh and cropland. The soldiers felt open and exposed as they passed through the fields abandoned by the local farmers. There was also the nagging thought that the open fields would provide any Japanese defenders with broad fields of fire. But so far they had not encountered any of the enemy. Perhaps the naval bombardment had not been wasted energy, after all, if it had driven off the Japanese. Deke remained wary, just in case they were walking right into an ambush.

They began to pass soldiers going in the other direction. At first it was a shock to see other GIs after being on their own for days. The sight of their own troops meant that the beach landing on this side of the Leyte Peninsula had been successful.

These men didn't have the appearance of fresh troops. For most of them, it was their second beach assault in the Philippines. The soldiers had taken part in the landing at Red Beach on the other side of the peninsula. They were then crammed into transports and sailed around the tip of the Leyte Peninsula —under constant threat of Japanese attack at sea—before taking part in yet another landing in the campaign to seize Ormoc. In fact, they looked almost as beat up and weary as Captain Merrick's company did from their jungle trek.

Deke looked for any familiar faces, knowing that Lieutenant Steele, Alphabet, Rodeo, and Egan had taken part in the landing effort. However, it was hard to tell one weary face from another. The soldiers were wet and grimy from head to toe, hardly recognizable as Americans. He had to wonder if he would even recognize any of his old companions. Deke reckoned that he didn't look much better after the jungle trek.

The other soldiers were so tired that they barely gave Merrick's men a curious glance. Danilo had dropped out of leading the column and fallen back to walk alongside Deke, Yoshio, and Philly. He didn't seem to want to call attention to himself, perhaps because he was the only Filipino guerrilla in sight.

At the beach itself, the soldiers emerged onto the white sand and the welcome sea breeze that seemed to carry away the fetid odor of the jungle and their filthy uniforms. Although they were in the full sun after the shade of the jungle, it didn't seem as hot because of the breeze. Deke's broad-brimmed hat also helped keep the sun off. He had gotten that hat from a grateful wounded soldier that he had helped on Guam and had long since abandoned his helmet in favor of the bush hat.

As expected, the beach was a beehive of activity. Stacks of equipment were everywhere, along with a handful of trucks that soldiers struggled to get out of the sand. The few company command posts and makeshift hospital areas were marked by tarps or camouflage netting that had been set up to offer protection from the elements. The tarps flapped wildly in the ocean breeze, threatening to blow away. The soldiers' hold on the beach appeared tentative at best.

Beyond stretched the bright-blue sea without a single ship in sight. Curiously, there were no support vessels offshore. The Japanese still controlled much of the air and waters on this western shore. The landing ships had pulled back to the open sea and the protection of the US fleet and carrier force.

Merrick called a halt, and the company flopped down on the sand, glad to take a load off their weary feet. A runner was sent to the nearest hospital tent, and medics soon appeared, bearing stretchers to carry away the worst of the wounded.

"You ought to go see a doc," Philly told Deke. "See what they can do about that fever. Hell, if you've got malaria, that might be your ticket to one of the hospital ships. They might even send you all the way back to Hawaii."

"Hell no," Deke snapped. "I'll be right as rain in no time."

"If you say so," Philly said doubtfully. Philly appeared excited by the prospect of *someone* getting sent home, even if it wasn't him. "I've got to say, if it was me, I'd be trying to get somebody to punch my ticket out of here."

"Well, I ain't you," Deke said harshly.

"All right, don't get sore."

"Look around, Philly. We've barely got a toehold on this place. Does it seem to you like we can send soldiers out of here?"

"Look, I just don't want to have to carry your ass back here in a couple of days if you get sicker." Philly sounded exasperated.

"Besides, you might not have any say in it once Merrick remembers that you're sick as a dog."

"Just keep your mouth shut," Deke said. "Merrick has got more on his mind than one sick soldier."

Arguing with Philly had tired Deke out. He stretched in a tire track in the sand, pulled his hat down over his face, and promptly fell asleep.

It soon became apparent that Deke's prediction about manpower was coming to pass. The medics patched up the walking wounded and sent them back to their units. The division was going to need every man who could hold a rifle for this operation. There simply weren't any reinforcements to be had.

Captain Merrick went off to headquarters to make his report. Meanwhile, the company awaited orders and slept wherever they had managed to stretch out in the sand, oblivious to the fresh sunburns they were getting. Considering that most of them were already deeply tanned, it might have been said that their sunburns were getting sunburns. Some turned red as boiled lobsters, but they were just too tired to care.

Four figures approached across the beach—or five, if you counted the large dog that trotted beside one of the men. They appeared to be battle-hardened veterans, but what really set them apart was the fact that three of them carried rifles with telescopic sights, instantly marking them as scouts and snipers.

The tallest man in the group stopped from time to time to talk to soldiers that they passed. His body language indicated that the officer appeared to be asking questions. Finally, a sergeant pointed at the company sprawled across the sand. The tall officer headed in that direction.

He walked past the prone soldiers, who didn't so much as acknowledge him, because most of them were in various stages of sleeping or resting. When he approached the small knot of men who had set themselves apart from the rest of the company, he seemed to have found what he was looking for. One of the three men was not sleeping but sat in the sand, watching the officer approach. It was Danilo, whose face broke into a smile as he recognized the officer.

The officer was about to kick the boot of one of the men who had fallen asleep gripping his rifle, but hesitated with his foot drawn back, and instead used the toe of his boot to tap the bottom of Philly's boot.

"Hey!" Philly complained, sitting bolt upright in the hot sun. "What's the big idea?"

"Wake up, Philly. I knew better than to kick Deke—he probably would have shot me."

Philly blinked a couple of times at the tall officer. "I'll be damned. Is that you, Honcho? Or am I looking at a ghost?"

"It's me, all right. I can't believe that I'm saying this, but I'm actually glad to see you, Philly. I was getting so that I almost missed your wisecracks and bellyaching."

"I'll do my best to make up for it."

"Let me emphasize the word *almost*. Anyhow, I didn't think that I'd ever see you sorry bastards again."

"You know us, Honcho. Always turning up like a bad penny or yesterday's meat loaf."

"Better make that *sir* here on the beach," the lieutenant said. "There are too many other officers around way above my pay grade, and they get touchy about that sort of thing. Save the pet names for the jungle, when there are Japanese snipers around."

Philly snapped to attention and gave him a salute. "Yes, sir!"

Steele just shook his head.

Behind Lieutenant Steele, Rodeo, Alphabet, and Egan approached. They shouted greetings at Philly. "Look at these lazy bastards! It figures that we'd find them snoozing. Good thing we weren't Japs!"

"Aw, shut up, you dopes," Philly replied good-naturedly.

"While you were on a pleasure cruise, our asses were hiking through the jungle. Let me tell you, it was uphill both ways, with the Japanese shooting at us the whole time."

Egan had to hold back Thor, who started barking in excitement.

Yoshio and Deke had been awakened by the commotion. The new arrivals were slapping Philly on the back. Yoshio sprang up and promptly found himself hugged by Rodeo. Alphabet slapped him so hard on the shoulder that he staggered. It was a sign of the easy brotherhood between soldiers, where even being Japanese didn't matter to men who had lived and fought together.

The soldiers were more reserved toward Danilo but still gave the Filipino welcoming grins. Danilo returned their grins and nodded at them.

Deke got to his feet more slowly, unfolding himself like a rusty jackknife struggling to open. The bright sun amplified his gaunt features, the scars on his face making him look even more haggard.

"What the hell happened to you?" Rodeo asked, sounding a little taken aback.

"Just tired, I reckon."

"He's got malaria," Philly said. "But he's too damn stubborn to go see the doc."

Deke shot Philly an angry look for letting the cat out of the bag. Philly was only stating what was obvious, which was that Deke had been ravaged by the jungle fever.

"You're all a sight for sore eyes," Lieutenant Steele announced. "Now that we're all in the same place again, let me see what I can do about keeping us together. I can tell you one thing for sure, which is that we're in for one hell of a fight to take Ormoc from the Japanese."

"That's good to hear," Deke said. "It's been at least a day or two since I shot at any Japanese. I'm getting out of practice."

Steele shook his head. "I hate to tell you this, Deke, but you're not going anywhere except to the hospital tent."

Philly barked out a laugh. "How about that, Deke? The minute that we're all back together, Honcho here tries to get rid of you."

"Just for that, you can take point next time, Philly. If the Japanese are going to shoot somebody, it may as well be you."

Ordinarily Deke might have stalled for time, but he didn't have the energy to put up much of a fight. He was soon dragging himself toward the medical area, wondering if this was going to be it for him on Leyte.

CHAPTER THIRTEEN

CAPTAIN MERRICK RETURNED WITH ORDERS. He gathered the men who had managed to snatch a little sleep on the beach. Some regretted the fact that they now had sand not only in their gear but in cracks and crevices that would make it difficult to get themselves sand-free anytime soon. A shower was out of the question, and there wasn't even time for a quick dunk in the ocean.

"We're moving out," Merrick explained, looking around at the company. "There's a harbor about a mile north of here that we need to guard, just in case the Japanese decide that they want it back. And knowing the Japanese, they *will* want it back."

Merrick told the men to be ready in ten minutes, then waved Lieutenant Steele over. The two men had met outside Palo, when the orders had come to divide the scout-snipers and some of Patrol Easy had been attached to Merrick's unit.

"I heard you had it rough landing on the beach," Merrick said.

"And I heard your trek through the jungle wasn't any walk in the park, sir," Steele replied. The lieutenant had taken off his helmet, and with his gray-flecked hair and weathered face, he looked at least ten years older than the captain.

Merrick grunted. "I don't think anybody had an easy time of it. Then again, I always prefer dry land to a boat ride. I'm a ground pounder through and through."

"Yes, sir."

"Listen, I'd sure hate to part company with Deke and Philly, not to mention Yoshio and Danilo," Merrick said. "The four of them are damn good soldiers. It looks like our walk through the jungle is over, but any chance that I could get them to stay?"

"We don't have any orders yet." Steele nodded at the pandemonium on the beach. Everyone seemed to know what they were doing, but it was hard to see any real organization or order yet. "I don't think anyone is too worried about a handful of snipers."

"You know what, I lost a lieutenant in that last fight we had, in a coconut grove, of all places," Merrick said. He shook his head as if trying to clear it of that painful memory. "I sure could use you and your men. Besides, the damn Japanese really thinned out our ranks."

Lieutenant Steele seemed to consider the question. "It sounds as if you're headed to fight more Japanese."

"Sounds about right," Merrick replied.

Steele smiled. "Then count us in."

"Welcome to the club, Lieutenant."

The two officers shook hands; then Merrick hurried off to make sure that the company obtained a few last-minute supplies: bullets, more rations, and another medic that he cajoled out of the hospital tent.

But when Merrick returned, he was accompanied not just by the medic, but also by the familiar figure of Deacon Cole. He staggered a little in the sea breeze, as if it might blow him over.

The others were surprised to see him.

"What the hell are you doing here?" Steele demanded. "Shouldn't you be on a cot somewhere?"

Merrick spoke up. "The docs are under orders to send anyone who can still walk back into the field. We're that short-handed. Maybe in a few days, if we get reinforcements, some of these boys can rotate out. Now let's move out."

This time there was no jungle trek. Instead, the company followed the coastline, sticking to the beach. While it was true that the going was easy, they felt exposed out in the open. Fortunately, so far, Japanese forces appeared to have retreated deeper into the interior. There wasn't so much as a potshot taken at them.

"How about that, the gang is all together again," Philly said. "Just like old times. You missed us, didn't you, Honcho?"

"Stuff it, Philly," the lieutenant said, then grinned. "Gee, I haven't said that in a while. *Now* it feels like old times."

The lieutenant shared the fact that Patrol Easy would be sticking with the company, at least until receiving orders otherwise.

"Right back into the fire, huh?" Philly complained. "No rest for the weary. I thought I might sit on the beach for a while and work on my tan."

It was a measure of the patrol's informality that Steele deigned to explain the circumstances to Philly. "You know how the army works," the lieutenant said. "If someone important sees us standing around long enough, they'll either put us to work guarding these piles of supplies or send us on some hare-brained mission to capture some Japanese general hiding in the hills. Or we can go with Captain Merrick. Which would you prefer?"

Deke spoke up. He was still feverish, and the hot sun on the beach felt broiling. He welcomed the idea of getting back under the trees and some shade. "I don't want to stand around here guarding boxes of Jeep parts and bandages. I say we go where we can fight some Japanese."

"There you have it," Steele said. "Get ready to move out."

* * *

NOW THAT THEY were reunited and unofficially attached to Captain Merrick's company, the scouts and snipers moved out to help protect the small harbor where the Malbasag River ran out into Ormoc Bay.

Deke had hoped for some shade, but he was disappointed to find that their route followed the beach. The soft sand made for hard going—it was almost as bad as slogging through snow in its own way. Worse than that was the feeling of being totally exposed, out in the open. Fortunately no Japanese snipers seemed to be around, because nobody was shooting at them. Still, the hot sun was enemy enough.

Just north of the harbor they were assigned to guard was Ormoc itself, where the Japanese still held the town and the nearby airfield. US forces had pushed right up against the Japanese lines, establishing their own perimeter at what came to be known as Camp Downes. Although the Japanese had fallen back from the actual coastal area, it was clear that they were dug in and intent on fighting for every inch of ground around Ormoc.

The Japanese had not given up, not just at Ormoc but on the northern areas of Leyte into which US troops had not pushed yet. The enemy forces had determined to make a stand there no matter the cost. Of course Leyte was just the start, one of the many Filipino islands. The grand prize itself would be Manila, where bitter fighting was expected.

Despite their heavy losses, including the naval defeat in the waters off Leyte, the Japanese were determined to wrest the

Philippines back from the invasion forces. At the very least, they intended to inflict such heavy losses that it would leave the American forces damaged and licking their wounds for some time to come.

To that end, Japan's ships loaded with supplies and transports filled with troops continued to steam toward the Philippines, converging on the fight like moths to a flame. Like those moths, they seemed headed for their own destruction. Most of the vessels never reached shore, but were bombed and sunk. The sheer number of Japanese troops lost at sea was tremendous, numbering into the thousands. Oblivious, the Japanese high command sent more men to die.

These heavy losses were inflicted by the superior air power and naval forces of the United States, especially in the wake of the decisive battle of Leyte Gulf. There was not much left in terms of a Japanese Navy to defend its supply chain across the vast Pacific.

However, the Japanese still had some teeth. There were enough airfields within Japanese control that they were able to harass both US ground and naval forces.

This situation soon became apparent to Patrol Easy and the rest of Merrick's company as they set up a defensive position at the small harbor in the distance.

With his sharp eyes, Deke was the first to notice the vessel. The sun was going down, and the sea had taken on the color of gunmetal, interrupted by the dark blur of the distant ship.

"What the hell is that?" Deke asked. He put his rifle to his shoulder so that he could get a better view of the ship through the telescopic sight.

It appeared to be a small troop transport, all alone on the ocean. Although it could technically be called a small ship, it appeared to be more akin to a floating shoebox—an ungraceful vessel cobbled together with wood and metal, then filled to the brim with troops.

"I hate to say this," Honcho said once the lone ship had been brought to his attention. He studied the distant vessel through binoculars. "But I don't think that's one of ours."

"Japanese? You've got to be kidding me," said Philly.

By now word had spread, and the rest of the company was intent on the ship. They all watched in wonder as the lone transport continued its journey toward shore.

"Don't tell me those guys are planning a one-ship invasion," Steele muttered. "They can't seriously think that they can take back an island with one ship."

"It sure looks like that's what they're planning to do," Deke said.

Incredible as it seemed, the ship kept right on coming. It was just possible that in the evening light, whoever was at the helm of the transport could not see that the shore was, in fact, occupied. Or if they could see troops on shore, maybe they had assumed that those troops were Japanese.

Just a day or two before, after all, there would have been Japanese troops here. They had since retreated to defend Ormoc.

There was a lot of confusion in war for all sorts of reasons. It wasn't called "the fog of war" for nothing. It was even possible that the transport had outdated orders or had been out of communication, its radio knocked out or malfunctioning. After the devastating naval battle, whatever the case, the crew of the Japanese transport seemed uninformed.

It was even possible that the officers on the ship were well aware that they were sailing into a suicide mission but had no intention of turning back. The Japanese mindset was a mystery.

Captain Merrick watched in as much disbelief as any of his men.

"Hold your fire," he ordered. "Let's make sure those buggers are Japanese before we go and sink one of our own ships. Where's Deke? Deke, you've got sharp eyes. Tell me when you can see a flag on that ship."

Their fingers itchy on their trigger fingers, the soldiers waited. They didn't have any artillery, but a mortar squad set up to greet the incoming vessel if needed.

At least two heavy machine guns were lined up, their sights zeroed in on the vessel.

"Come on, come on. Just a little closer," muttered Private Frazier, balancing his BAR across a chunk of driftwood. "Come to Papa."

Silently, almost eerily, the dark hulk of the vessel approached. The men on shore could hear the steady thrum of its engine carrying across the water, directly toward the harbor entrance. Aside from a few small fishing boats moored here and there, the harbor itself was otherwise empty. The muddy water of the Malbasag River ran out to mix with the clear ocean water. The vessel was still far enough out that the water was quite deep, well over a man's head. The swirling currents where the river's flow met the sea looked treacherous.

Lieutenant Steele had his binoculars out and was studying the ship intently. "I'll be damned." He whispered the words in disbelief. "It *is* a Japanese vessel, all right. Deke?"

"I can see their damn meatball flag, Honcho."

Soon, even without binoculars, the men on shore could clearly see the enemy flag silhouetted against what remained of the bright sky above the darkening sea.

"Steady, steady," Merrick shouted. "Here they come."

The vessel was picking up speed, apparently intent on racing into the harbor and up onto the shore so that its Japanese troops could disembark. As the ship came closer, they were able to see a few helmets appearing above the straight-sided gunwales. Clearly these were not troops expecting a battle. They were just curious to see what awaited them on shore.

Deke was feeling well enough that he could put his rifle to his shoulder and fix his crosshairs on one of those helmets.

"Don't shoot till you see the whites of their eyes," some witty bastard said, and a few men nearby laughed.

Captain Merrick was having none of it. "Everybody shut up. This is no joke. Get ready. When I give the order, I want you to put more holes in that boat than a screen door."

Silence fell over the company as they tensed up before the hell that they were about to unleash.

So far the Japanese had not opened fire on the shore. Surely the transport was equipped with at least a machine gun. They seemed about to be taken by utter and complete surprise.

"Fire!" Captain Merrick shouted.

No sooner had the order escaped his lips than the entire company began shooting at the barge. The air seemed to shimmer with bullets. Tracers from the machine guns raced across the water and tore into the transport at the waterline. The heavy bullets ripped open the lightly built structure as effectively as a can opener, so that water began to pour into the transport. The gap was made worse by the force of water as the vessel continued rushing forward. Soon the vessel began to list badly to one side.

If the lookouts on the vessel had thought that the troops on shore were friendly, they had received a rude awakening. Too late, a machine gun began to answer from the Japanese.

The weird blue tracers from the Japanese gun danced across the harbor toward shore. Near Deke, a soldier cried out as one of the enemy rounds found its mark, but his cry was instantly cut short as he was hit again by the Japanese gun.

Private Frazier had unleashed the full fury of his BAR and emptied it into the vessel in one long burst. He slapped in another magazine and went to town on the vessel. He was shouting something as he fired. It was hard to make out the words, and maybe there weren't any—it was almost a high gleeful sound, very nearly a girlish squeal of delight, which sounded strange coming from such a big man.

Japanese soldiers were now leaping from the vessel into the water, but they were loaded down with their heavy equipment— packs, rifles, ammo, grenades, bayonets, even swords—every- thing they had anticipated that they would need for the landing. They were soon pulled under and lost from sight.

Even the ones who managed to swim weren't safe, because the soldiers on shore targeted them with their M1 rifles. Although the water was growing darker in the fading daylight, the sand-colored Japanese helmets and uniforms stood out against the dark backdrop, making them easy targets.

Deke fired just once or twice, but then lost steam. The rifle seemed to grow heavier with each shot, the bolt harder to work.

Around him, soldiers had left the cover of their foxholes and were standing up to get a better angle of fire into the waters of the harbor. Deke was reminded of a firing squad. Captain Merrick had even drawn his .45 and was squeezing off shots.

Although the Japanese machine gun had claimed a few casu- alties, it had fallen silent, leaving the enemy transport defenseless.

This wasn't a battle; it was a massacre.

The horizon was alive with explosions and gunfire, each pop and crackle signaling that a man might be dying.

Deke felt no pity toward the Japanese. If the tables had been turned, they would have shown no mercy to the Americans. For the soldiers, this was payback for buddies lost in the fighting. Considering that they had been resupplied just a short time ago on the beach, there was no shortage of ammunition.

He sat down and let the others do the shooting. This was no

longer what he would have called precision work. This was shooting fish in a barrel.

The smell of gunpowder burned his nostrils, and smoke stung his eyes, but Deke couldn't tear his gaze away from the scene before him.

The Japanese vessel was now settling deeper into the water, its forward motion halted. The merciless fire from shore continued. Soon enough there was no sign of life aboard the transport or in the surrounding water, just a few bodies floating on the surface.

"Cease fire!"

Gradually the fusillade came to an end with a few final gunshots. The men on shore stood staring out at their handiwork.

"I'll be damned," Philly said, surprise evident in his voice. "We just sank us a ship."

"That's got to be a first," Lieutenant Steele replied. "It also means that the Japanese will be getting that many fewer reinforcements."

"Amen to that," Philly said.

CHAPTER FOURTEEN

SINKING the Japanese vessel had brought a sense of elation, but it was fleeting. The sighting of the enemy vessel seemed to raise even more questions. If the Japanese had sent one boat, would they send others? Had there been landings that they hadn't seen, meaning that enemy troops might be circling around behind them?

"Over here!" shouted a soldier who was exploring farther down the waterfront. He had reached a cove that had been concealed around a bend in the shoreline.

Their fears regarding the Japanese presence were confirmed when someone found tracks in the mud and sand where another enemy craft had apparently landed. The number of footprints and the impressions left by the equipment that had been dragged ashore indicated that a contingent of Japanese had escaped their detection.

The tracks were so fresh that water was still oozing into them from the surrounding mud. The Japanese must have landed undetected, possibly just before the arrival of the US troops at the waterfront or when their attention had been focused on sinking the Japanese landing craft.

"The Japanese landed here, all right," Lieutenant Steele said. "The question is, Where did they go?"

Considering that they hadn't immediately attacked, it was most likely that the Japanese had slipped away toward Ormoc to bolster the defenders with more men and supplies. But the ship that had brought them to shore couldn't simply have vanished in such a short amount of time.

Deke swung his gaze out to sea.

"Look!" he cried, pointing toward a dark speck riding the swells beyond the harbor. They could just make out the outline of the distant vessel. The vessel was definitely going away rather than approaching. It wouldn't be long before the vessel disappeared over the horizon.

After an uneasy night getting what sleep they could, new orders arrived. Although they had not come under further attack during the night after the incident with the barge, they could still hear random firing in the distance. It seemed to be a promise of things to come, letting them know that the Japanese weren't finished yet.

In any case, their assignment to guard the harbor proved to be short lived. General Bruce, the division commander, apparently did not see fit to let his battle-hardened troops rest easy. Captain Merrick's company received orders to move out, and a company of fresh troops was moved into position.

"Maybe we did too good of a job, considering that we even sank that Japanese barge," Philly grumbled. "We killed the hell out of those Japanese, that's for sure. Not a one of them made it to shore."

"Not a one of them," Yoshio repeated hollowly. He didn't have to elaborate on the fact that none of the Japanese had even been allowed to shore.

"It ain't like they were gonna surrender," Deke pointed out in an effort to make Yoshio feel better, but it didn't seem to do much good.

While the sinking of the enemy barge had buoyed most of their spirits because it had been such a lopsided victory, it may have come as no surprise that Yoshio did not seem to share in that jubilation. Enemy or not, the men they had slaughtered in the harbor—there was no other term for it—were Japanese, and Yoshio must have surely been affected by that. He knew better than to admit it out loud and kept his thoughts to himself.

Merrick's company found itself moving inland. Aside from the unlucky troop transport, they had yet to see any Japanese troops even with the proximity to Ormoc. They approached a small village called Ipil, about halfway between the harbor and the city of Ormoc itself.

Once again Patrol Easy had taken point, this time with Danilo in the lead. Right behind Danilo were Egan and Thor, in hopes that the dog would smell the enemy if Danilo didn't spot them first. The rest of the soldiers in the company seemed reassured by the sight of the dog, but Deke preferred to put his faith in Danilo.

Deke didn't mind seeing Danilo leading the company, considering that he still didn't feel completely himself. His fever had mostly abated, but he still felt too weak to be effective. He longed to close his eyes and sleep for a day or two, but he knew that he wasn't going to be that lucky. Like he'd been told back on the beach, every man was needed in this fight for Ormoc.

"Everyone says that the Japanese are dug in tight," Rodeo said. "Do you think it's true?"

"We'll find out soon enough," Philly pointed out.

The company had some help as it moved out in the form of the "Long Toms" from the 226th Field Artillery. The 155-millimeter field guns helped to pave the way ahead of the company's advance. The shells screeched overhead, then landed in the distance with a dull thud that still managed to shake the ground even at this distance. Plumes of black smoke and dust rose into the air.

"I just hope they have good aim," Philly said. "I sure don't want one of those dropping on my head."

"It would give you quite a headache, all right," Deke agreed. The shelling also made him anxious, but not for the same reason as Philly. He preferred to be able to hear what lay ahead of them, and listening for any sign of the enemy, from the silence of the jungle birds to a shouted order in Japanese, was helpful. As things stood, only the roar of the shells coming in and exploding filled his ears. In his experience, the Japanese were usually so dug in that shelling never did much good anyhow.

The village was too small to be considered a suburb of Ormoc, little more than a collection of huts that appeared peaceful enough.

Yet something wasn't quite right. There was an air of desertion about the place. No smoke rose from any cooking fires. No people were visible. The animal pens made from tree branches and scraps of wire stood empty. Not so much as a chicken scratched the dirt. Deke couldn't quite put his finger on it, but some instinct made him tense up and ready his weapon.

Danilo must have sensed it too. Up ahead, the Filipino slowed his pace, taking it all in. It was hard to say whether the settlement felt serene—or spooky.

Any thoughts that Ipil was a half-forgotten village evaporated when the Japanese opened fire as the company came in view of the dwellings.

"Take cover!" Merrick shouted as soldiers scrambled off the road.

The village provided good cover for the enemy, who had built dugouts under the huts or were taking advantage of the root cellars beneath. They were practically invisible as they opened fire. The tallest building seemed to be a kind of barn, almost like a hayloft, and there was a Japanese up there with a submachine gun, doing a good job of spraying the road with metal.

Caught in the open, several soldiers went down in the initial burst of fire. Deke saw a soldier throw out his arms in what might have been a gesture of welcome if it hadn't been for the gaping bullet holes coming out his back. The man dropped his rifle, rocked back on his heels, and fell into the road, blood running from his body. Poor bastard never knew what hit him, Deke thought.

Deke scrambled behind a log that had been knocked down during the shelling. He lay on his belly in the dirt, staying as flat as possible, head down as bullets chipped chunks off the log. Philly and Yoshio slid in beside him. The rest of Patrol Easy had scattered, finding cover wherever they could. Stray bullets kicked up dirt and sand all around them.

"Son of a bitch!" Philly shouted.

Behind them they could hear Captain Merrick shouting for his men to pour fire into the huts. Nearby, Lieutenant Steele was doing his best to direct the platoon that he'd been given command of when he had joined the company.

"Aim low," Honcho ordered. "The Nips are hiding under those huts."

The thin walls of the huts offered the Japanese little or nothing in the way of protection as the company began to get organized and return fire. Too many of the bullets passed right through the empty huts, though. Honcho had hit the nail on the head. The Japanese were under the huts, which made them difficult targets. As men figured it out, they took up the cry, "Aim low! The bastards are under the huts!" The satisfying sound of rapid fire from M1 rifles began to fill the air.

The thing about combat was that the sheer terror of it made

returning fire with any real accuracy difficult. Sure, these men were veterans of several fights, but in those first moments of the skirmish their aim was shaky, and their shots went wild. Officers like Merrick and Steele filled the all-important role of reminding the men to return fire. Eventually the soldiers' training kicked in. The sheer volume of fire from the superior M1 rifles began to have a telling effect on the enemy, especially as the soldiers calmed down and took more accurate aim.

Lieutenant Steele had been lying flat behind another fallen log. He rolled to one knee and fired a couple of quick shots from his combat shotgun into the base of the nearest hut.

"Goddamn Nips!" he shouted, then threw himself flat once again just before a fresh flurry of shots chipped splinters from the log he was hiding behind.

As it turned out, Lieutenant Steele also had another trick up his sleeve. He grabbed Rodeo by the shoulder and dragged him close. Rodeo had traded his heavy radio for a handset radio—or "walkie-talkie," as some called them. Steele took it from him, and everyone nearby could hear him shouting into the radio for the artillery to shorten its aim and bring some hellfire down upon the village.

Deke gulped. Everyone knew how risky that was. The smallest miscalculation would bring the shells down on their own heads instead of the Japanese.

He braced himself as the first shell came screaming in, literally burying his face in the dirt. The impact of the shell seemed to lift him up and shake him out like a rug. Then another shell hit, and another.

By some miracle, the gunners were right on target. Three artillery rounds arrived in quick succession. A couple of the huts simply disappeared. They were there one minute and gone the next, vanishing in a geyser of swirling dirt, palm fronds, and shattered lumber. A fourth shell exploded in the midst of the village, scattering debris in every direction.

Honcho called in a cease-fire over the handset. He then shouted, "Move! Move!"

Honcho led the way, shotgun held at hip level, blasting away. The artillery shells seemed to have stunned the Japanese, at least momentarily.

But the Americans weren't the only ones able to conjure firepower out of thin air. No sooner had the company begun its advance than a roar was heard overhead. The roar was caused not by more artillery shells, but by the powerful Mitsubishi engine of a Japanese fighter plane. Skimming the treetops, the plane dipped its nose toward the ground and unleashed a long burst from its machine guns. Men scattered as the bullets churned up the ground. The roar of the plane and then the fury of its guns was deafening.

Just as suddenly as it had appeared, the plane was gone, chased by antiaircraft fire from a battery at the beachhead. The proximity of the beach was a reminder of just how little the US forces had advanced. It was also a reminder that the Japanese were far from beaten as long as they still had a few aircraft to strike at ground troops.

Deke dove for the ground with the others, scanning the sky with his rifle in case the plane decided to come back. Incredibly, he heard cheering from the Japanese position as the sound of the plane receded.

The artillery barrage had left the Japanese battered but far from defeated. The appearance of the Japanese plane hadn't done much damage, but it had definitely been a morale booster. It had also put an end to the company's efforts to advance.

Loud and clear, cutting through all the noise, he heard a Japanese voice taunting them, "Hey, Charlie, how you like them apples?"

It might have been funny if the enemy's intent hadn't been so sinister.

"I got your apples right here!" Private Frazier shouted, then unleashed his BAR into the hut where the Japanese taunt had come from. The flurry of bullets ripped chunks out of the structure, filling the air with what resembled confetti.

As it turned out, the Japanese soldier might have been gloating too soon.

CHAPTER FIFTEEN

THE BRIEF BARRAGE had created another problem for the Japanese, igniting fires that began to spread among the village huts, sparks carrying from one burning hut to its tinder-dry neighbor. The huts that had provided such good camouflage were now turning into death traps for the Japanese soldiers in the cellars below.

They began to escape, crawling out from under the huts and making a run for it. Some continued firing as they ran, while others simply dashed away without so much as a look back over their shoulder.

Eager for revenge, the soldiers targeted the Japanese as soon as they appeared from under a burning hut. Some of the enemy waited as long as possible to attempt their escape, finally running out with their clothes literally on fire. They didn't get far before they were cut down.

Judging by a few of the screams that reached their ears, it was possible that some of the Japanese waited too long before trying to escape and had been trapped by the flames. The sickly-sweet smell of burning flesh reached Deke's nose. No matter how many times he smelled it in this war, he still found the cloying smell repulsive.

"Let them burn!" a soldier shouted. "Don't waste a bullet on the ones that are on fire. We're only putting them out of their misery."

"To hell with that," Philly said, and kept on shooting.

Deke lined up his sights on an enemy soldier whose shirt was on fire. The soldier was running away, and Deke shot him between the shoulder blades, sending him sprawling into the dirt. The dead enemy soldier continued to burn, looking like a pile of smoldering rags.

"What did you go and do that for?" demanded the soldier, who didn't want to waste bullets.

"Go to hell," Deke said.

The soldier looked as if he might say something in response, but then thought better of it when Deke turned his full attention on him. The look in Deke's eyes signaled that he wouldn't mind wasting another bullet right then and there.

Deke worked the bolt and searched for another target. But by the time another enemy soldier appeared, two or three other bullets found him instantly.

This was like the barge all over again, just shooting fish in a barrel. It was clear that the Japanese who still could were pulling out of Ipil.

Deke lowered his rifle, his head swimming from the noise and heat. *Damn this fever.* Just when he thought that he was feeling better, another dizzy spell washed over him all over again.

Just as quickly as it had started, the skirmish in the village of Ipil had come to an end in the Americans' favor. Not all the Japanese had made a run for it, and what followed was a mopping-up operation in which the soldiers moved from hut to hut, searching for Japanese.

Nobody bothered to ask if they wanted to surrender. Yoshio

could have translated, but his services were not requested. Instead, the soldiers went from hut to hut, tossing grenades into cellars. Sometimes a soldier bent down and sprayed a burst from a submachine gun into the space below the floor. Simply put, this was eradication of the enemy.

If the little village had seemed peaceful when they first approached, it was now being left a smoking ruin as the flames kept spreading from one burning hut to another. Thick, dark smoke roiled into the sky, the clouds of smoke bejeweled with flecks of red sparks and orange embers. The hamlet was now a scene of perfect destruction. Even some of the crops in the vegetable patches had caught fire, flames crackling through the dry vines and leaves. There were a few racks of fish drying in the sun, and these too caught fire. The whole damn place was going up in smoke.

Deke watched it all, wondering how the Filipinos were going to feel when they returned home. It was evident that the people who lived here must be subsistence farmers, scratching a living out of their fields, the nearby jungle, and even the sea. Like poor people everywhere, he reckoned that they would pick up the pieces and go on. At least they would finally be free of the Japanese.

The resistance in Ipil seemed to be at an end. Or most of it, anyway. It appeared that most of the Japanese had been killed or had slipped away into the surrounding forest.

So far he had managed to avoid the mopping-up action.

But he felt like he ought to be doing something rather than standing around gawking. He went to take a step and staggered, catching the attention of Lieutenant Steele.

"Are you all right?" the lieutenant asked. "Are you hit?"

"No, I'm just fine," Deke replied.

He paused to gather his strength before taking another step. The smoke, the flames, the heat—and through it all the nauseating pork-like smell of roasting flesh—it was all too much, and he felt his senses being overwhelmed. Another wave of dizziness left him swaying on his feet.

He had been doing his best to hide just how weak he was from the lieutenant. He had no desire to be sent back to the hospital area on the beach, perhaps to be deemed unfit for duty and sent to one of the hospital ships offshore. The last thing that he wanted to do was let down the lieutenant and the rest of the patrol.

"Goddammit, you're still sick, aren't you? I should have made sure those doctors kept you back on the beach." The lieutenant shook his head. "Make sure you drink plenty of water and eat something. You're getting so damn skinny that somebody is going to mistake you for a stick before too long."

Deke nodded in acknowledgment, the effort of speaking suddenly too much. He knew that the lieutenant was right about eating. The last real food that he'd eaten was the meal that Danilo had cooked on the trail. Fresh chicken and rice—couldn't ask for better. He doubted there would be more of that anytime soon.

The trouble was, the thought of a cold tin of stew made his stomach knot up. The only food items that sounded good were the hot buttered biscuits that his ma used to make. That and some hot coffee would have gone down good right about now. However, he had about as much chance of getting a buttered biscuit as he did of being promoted to general.

Deke's thoughts of food evaporated when he heard the crack of a rifle from the scrubby trees nearby. Deke and the lieutenant ducked just as someone yelled, "Sniper!"

Ducking was a reflex that wouldn't have done them any good if they'd been in the sniper's sights. A soldier about fifty feet away crumpled and fell.

Apparently not all the Japanese had retreated. There was at

least one sniper lurking out there. A trio of soldiers ran toward the trees, intending to take care of the problem. They soon returned, the sniper evidently having slipped away.

"All right, everybody keep your eyes open. We know the Japanese aren't done with us yet," Steele said to the men within earshot.

Captain Merrick was at the other end of the village, shouting orders that they couldn't quite hear above the pop and crackle of the flames from the burning huts.

The lieutenant moved off in Captain Merrick's direction, but not before giving Deke a long, doubtful look. Steele had a lot more men to worry about now than his handful of snipers, Deke included. Ostensibly, he had been put in charge of a platoon, but he had quickly become Captain Merrick's de facto second-in-command. He was now doing his best to get the men organized and moving, especially those who wanted to search the bodies of the dead Japanese for souvenirs.

It seemed as if even these combat veterans couldn't get enough Japanese gear and remained hopeful that they would pick up a coveted pistol or sword.

"Knock it off," Steele ordered the souvenir hunters. "For all you know, those bodies might be booby-trapped."

A kind of greed made one of the soldiers overly bold. He was not a big man, but he had a cockiness about him, like a bantam rooster. Wearing an insolent grin, he said, "You think they booby-trapped themselves in between running from those huts and us shooting them, Lieutenant?"

"Don't be a smart aleck," Steele said. "And if you call me by my rank again when there might be Jap snipers around, you won't have to worry about the Japanese, because I'll shoot you myself. Now get your asses ready to move out."

There was some grumbling about officers spoiling their fun. It was likely that some of them saw Steele as the new guy and he hadn't yet earned their respect. He might be a combat veteran, but he hadn't been in combat with them. Or not much combat, anyway. Also, some of the soldiers had reached that point where they were tired of being told by an officer what to do, or didn't much care about the consequences if they didn't.

But Lieutenant Steele could be an intimidating presence with his eye patch and shotgun. He was no butter bar fresh from Officer Training School. The soldiers did as they were told, even if they took their time about it.

Maybe this was why Steele had dodged any kind of promotion or command—Deke could see that being in charge was all one big headache.

However, the soldiers couldn't resist searching one more body. The man appeared to be an officer, which might prove to be rich pickings. The dead Japanese officer lay on his belly in the dirt. The soldiers could see a sword hilt half concealed under him. Whooping with excitement, they descended upon him like buzzards.

The soldier who had confronted Lieutenant Steele bent down to roll the dead Japanese over.

But they soon discovered that the officer was not dead. He was clutching a hand grenade to his chest. In a flash, he raised the grenade in his right hand. In his final act on earth, he planned to take out a few of the hated Charlies with him.

Taken by surprise, the soldiers did not have time to react before the grenade exploded. Two did manage to turn away quickly enough that the shrapnel caught them in the legs and buttocks. They rolled away, screaming in pain.

The bantam-size soldier hadn't been so lucky. Blood streamed from his chest and wounds in his face. He didn't make a sound but stumbled away in shock.

As for the Japanese officer, he was now well and truly dead.

After that, most of the soldiers gave up on collecting

souvenirs and took the precaution of putting a bullet into any Japanese bodies that they did have to approach.

Philly had the bug for souvenirs as bad as anyone.

"I'm going to have a look around," he announced as he started toward one of the huts. "Why let those guys get all the good stuff, right?"

"Hold on now, Philly," Deke said. "Didn't you hear what Honcho said about souvenirs? Didn't you see those fellas get blown up?"

"Aw, stuff a sock in it, Granny Deke. He meant those other guys. He didn't mean me. Besides, I'm not stupid like them."

"Don't go too far," Deke suggested. "Maybe take Yoshio with you. There might still be Japanese around."

"What about you?"

"Don't worry about me. I just need to catch my breath."

"All right. Come on, Yoshio."

The two moved off, but they hadn't been gone long before Philly gave a shout. "Hey, over here!"

Philly had stumbled upon a wounded Japanese soldier who was trying to lift his rifle, but it was clear that his hands were too badly burned to grasp the weapon. It was a pitiful scene. Standing with his back to the wall of the hut, the soldier refused to give up the fight and was clearly in pain, but literally not able to defend himself.

Considering the tense situation, he wouldn't be allowed to live for long.

Yoshio was saying something urgently to the Japanese soldier, who didn't seem to be listening.

The standoff ended when Deke walked up and snatched the rifle away. The Japanese soldier sank to his knees and glared at Deke. Deke raised his rifle to finish him off, and the Japanese soldier closed his eyes as if expecting the bullet.

"Hold on," Lieutenant Steele said, approaching them. "HQ is

always wanting prisoners, and there are precious few of them. Let's send him back to the beach."

"This guy is pretty banged up, Honcho. Hell, I don't even know if he can make it back to the beach."

"These Japanese are tougher than you think, Philly. Anyhow, let's see if he knows anything first. Yoshio, ask our friend here what we can expect up ahead."

Yoshio stepped forward and spoke a few words in Japanese. The captured soldier seemed surprised to hear his own language being spoken by someone in a US uniform. At first, all he could do was stare at Yoshio.

The prisoner closed his eyes and winced in pain. He stammered a few words in response to Yoshio's questions.

"What's he saying?" the lieutenant demanded.

"I asked him where the rest of his unit is hiding. He says there are concrete bunkers about a quarter mile from here on the way to Ormoc, hidden in the forest."

"All right, that's something. We'll ship him back to HQ and see what else he knows."

"Should we bandage him up first?"

"Hell no. We're not wasting bandages on the enemy. We've barely got enough medical supplies with us as it is. They can patch him up at HQ."

Steele looked around and ordered two of the men who had been wounded by the Japanese officer's grenade to escort the prisoner back to the beach area. One man who wouldn't be making the trip was the bantam rooster of a soldier. He lay on his back, blood-soaked bandages covering his face. His dead body looked even smaller, all the fight having gone out of it.

"Hey, you two, I'm going to check and make sure that this prisoner made it there. Larson and Walsh, right? Don't go shooting him and then say he was trying to escape. Guy like that, where would he go, anyway?"

"Yeah, I hear you, Honcho," Larson said sullenly. "I suppose you want me to give him a drink of water, maybe polish his boots for him?"

"Watch your mouth, soldier," Steele snarled. "Just be sure he makes it back to the beach. If he doesn't, I'll add some buckshot to that shrapnel in your ass. You disobeyed orders and got yourselves rendered unfit for duty. Last time I checked, that was worthy of a court-martial."

That got the soldier's attention. He pulled himself up straight, and it looked as if he might salute, but then he seemed to remember where he was. There wasn't any saluting on the battlefield.

He actually sounded convincing when he responded, "You got it, Honcho. We'll deliver this prisoner safe and sound."

Deke was relieved that Steele hadn't sent him back with the prisoner. He seemed to be reading Deke's thoughts as he turned to him and said, "Even half-sick, you're twice as good to us as those jokers. They must think this is all some kind of big souvenir hunt. That's why I'm sending them back to the beach to get stitches in their ass and keeping you here."

"You won't get no argument from me, Honcho."

Although the enemy had delayed their advance, the victory had come with some rewards. For one thing, the Japanese had left behind several trucks. The original plan must have been for the Japanese to withdraw from the village using the trucks, but the intensity of the fight had spiraled out of their control. Any survivors had simply fled on foot.

Immediately, these trucks were pressed into service. Later, when there was time, sloppy white stars would be painted on them. For now, it would have to suffice that someone had tied a small, ragged American flag to the lead vehicle. Hopefully they wouldn't be machine-gunned from the air by their own planes.

The vehicles were smaller than comparable US trucks—they

had found that everything from rifles to the interiors of tanks to the cockpits of Zero fighters was scaled to the smaller dimensions of Japanese men. Built by Isuzu, these were Type 94 six-wheeled trucks with canvas tops rigged across the beds to keep the sun off. The tall front grille, along with swooping running boards over the front tires, gave the trucks a vague resemblance to a working man's Packard.

The trucks might be cramped, but they sure beat walking. Even better, the trucks were fueled up and ready to go.

As they climbed into the back of a truck, Philly said, "Gee, it sure is strange riding in a Japanese truck. Might as well have been built by Martians. You could never sell a Japanese vehicle in the States, that's for sure. Nobody would buy them. I just hope these things don't fall apart—or blow up before we get where we're going."

"I hate to say it, but these are better built than our own trucks," Honcho said. "Maybe not as big, but sturdy as hell. The Japanese were planning for jungle conditions."

Deke, at least, was grateful for the ride. He closed his eyes and almost instantly fell asleep.

Captain Merrick wanted to know how many Japanese they had killed so that he could report it back to headquarters. The final tally was eighty-three dead Japanese and one prisoner.

"I suppose we were lucky to get a prisoner, even just the one," Honcho said. "Over in Europe, the push across France toward Belgium and Germany is in full swing. I heard they've taken hundreds of thousands of German POWs, maybe even close to a million German prisoners. We've captured around half a million Italians."

"Maybe they're all a bunch of cowards," Philly said. "Especially the Italians."

Honcho shook his head. "The Wehrmacht doesn't allow any cowards into the ranks, let alone the SS. Just ask our boys who have gone up against them. As for the Italians, didn't you ever hear of the Roman Empire? Italians make good soldiers. We've got any number of Italian Americans in *our* army. The ones over there are just poorly led. Anyhow, my point is that the soldiers we're fighting in Europe know better than to keep fighting when the odds are against them."

"I suppose you're right," Philly conceded.

"Altogether, that's far more than a million prisoners of war who have been captured in Europe," Honcho continued. "You know how many Japanese we've captured so far in the Pacific? Last I heard, it was about thirty thousand. You don't have to be a math wizard to know that's a whole lot less than a million. Say what you want about the Japanese, but they sure as hell don't like to surrender."

"That's not news to me," Philly said.

The company had lost just five men, and another handful had been wounded. While the soldiers keenly felt the loss of each fellow soldier, it was also clear that this fight in the village had been a lopsided victory.

"That is a ratio of sixteen to one," Yoshio noted. "That is quite impressive."

"Yeah? Ask our guys who got killed how impressed they are," Philly pointed out. "They're dead all the same."

Nobody had a response, because it was true. In the minds of the soldiers, dead Japanese didn't count no matter how many there were—only dead Americans mattered. Maybe it was wrong to think that way, but that was the way it was.

More shells began to arc overhead. The US battery was back in business, intending to clear a path for the company's advance. To their surprise, a few Japanese guns responded. The enemy still had operative artillery and was sufficiently organized to return fire, albeit sporadically. Overhead, the dueling shells crossed back and forth as the men looked up nervously.

It had become clear that the Japanese hadn't simply run away. Nor had they all been killed. That was just wishful thinking on the part of the American troops. Instead, the Japanese had fallen back to new defensive positions. The Japanese prisoner appeared to have been telling the truth during his brief interrogation by Yoshio before being sent back to the rear area.

They had won the skirmish, but there promised to be plenty of fighting ahead.

CHAPTER SIXTEEN

THE COMPANY ROLLED out on the trucks, although some men were still on foot, which slowed the pace of the advance down the dirt road. Swaths of forest bordered the road, intermixed with various crops growing in the Filipinos' fields. These trees and crops would provide good cover to any Japanese looking to ambush them on the road. All eyes scanned the roadside nervously.

The men riding in the captured trucks couldn't help but feel that the vehicles were something of a double-edged sword.

"We're sitting ducks in this truck," Philly complained.

"You want to get out and walk?" Deke wondered. "I don't. Hell, I'm not sure I could. I hope this truck can carry me all the way to Tokyo."

"Not unless it can float, you dope," Philly said. "We're on an island."

"I know we're on a goddamn island," Deke said irritably. "It's a figure of speech. Anyhow, keep it up and you ain't gonna have to worry about gettin' to Tokyo."

"Yeah, yeah," Philly said, but refrained from adding insult to injury where Deke was involved, even if he was sick.

"We are in Japanese trucks," Yoshio pointed out. "The Japanese might hold their fire, thinking that they would be firing on their own men."

"Let's hope that's the case."

As it turned out, they were headed toward Camp Downes, designated as the rallying point for US forces before the big push for Ormoc. The camp was, in fact, what remained of a former US military outpost left over from the years leading up to the Japanese occupation. The camp was named for a young officer from Texas who had died heroically while fighting insurgents not long after the Spanish-American War. Camp Downes had been in existence long enough to be shown on local maps, and the name was reassuringly American on maps dotted with mostly foreign names.

The collection of barracks and outbuildings had been taken over by the Japanese during the occupation. They had since cleared out to fortify their own defensive ring around Ormoc.

It wasn't long before they encountered those defenses. The convoy of captured trucks was moving up the road when they began to draw fire.

"Everybody out!" Lieutenant Steele shouted.

The trucks rolled to a stop. Men didn't need to be told twice to get out of the vehicles. As Philly had predicted, the trucks were sitting ducks. It sounded as if the Japanese had brought some of their twenty-millimeter antiaircraft guns into play, using them as ground defense weapons.

Chewed to bits by these heavy machine guns and tracer fire, the lead truck began to burn. This was a blessing in disguise, considering that the thick, black smoke created a smoke screen for the soldiers running for cover at the edges of the road. The remaining trucks backed up until they were out of sight around a bend in the road, leaving the soldiers on foot.

They could see a concrete bunker around the bend ahead, and soldiers began to return fire. However, rifles were no threat to the enemy soldiers behind thick concrete walls. Each bunker vaguely resembled a concrete jack-o'-lantern, with a low horizontal firing dugout, much like the pumpkin's smile, that accommodated the larger weapons, including the nasty Nambu machine guns and vertical firing slits for riflemen.

It was clear that the Japanese had been planning this defense for a long time, and the company had finally stumbled into it. The enemy had been waiting patiently for the appearance, but judging by the fire that poured from the bunkers, their fingers had been itchy on their triggers.

Seeing the situation, Steele had already waved Rodeo over and was on the handset. It was too close to their own men for an artillery strike, but Steele had another plan.

"We need some tanks up here!" he shouted into the handset. "They can bust right through those bunkers if they need to!"

Steele could shout all that he wanted, but that wouldn't make the tanks move any faster. It also didn't mean that whoever he was talking to at division headquarters would agree or that tanks were even available. Only a handful had arrived so far on the beach, but the sight of all that armored plating and firepower was always welcome.

For now, it was just infantry facing the heavily fortified Japanese position. They were good and truly pinned down.

Captain Merrick had reached the same conclusion. He ran over to Steele's position, dodging fire all the way. The man must have lived a charmed life.

"We need to get some grenades into those bunkers and clean them out," he said.

"Agreed," Steele responded. He turned to the members of

Patrol Easy, who crouched nearby. "Come on, fellas. Let's show 'em how it's done."

The patrol moved forward, slithering on their bellies, hugging the ground and using whatever cover they could find—piles of rocks, blasted logs, shell holes that they slid down into and crawled back out of.

They took fire the whole way. Most of it came from the Japanese machine guns, which seemed to cut the air above their heads or churn up the ground nearby. Lucky for them, the machine-gun fire was not aimed with any real precision.

However, in the first bunker was at least one sniper who kept up a withering fire. Each shot came too close for comfort. At one point Alphabet stuck up his head to get his bearings and paid the price for his curiosity.

"I'm hit!" he cried, clutching his neck. Blood seeped between his fingers.

Steele fired a couple of quick shots from his twelve gauge at the slit in the bunker that seemed to be where the sniper was shooting from, then rushed forward and slid down beside Alphabet. "Let me see that," he said, examining the wound.

"How bad is it, Honcho?" Alphabet asked, wild eyed with fear and pain. "Dammit, I always hoped it would be quick when my number was up."

"Not so bad," the lieutenant announced. He dragged out a sweat-stained handkerchief from a pocket. "Put that on it and apply some pressure. You're lucky. The bullet just grazed you."

Although the handkerchief quickly became soaked with blood, it was clear that the Japanese hadn't managed to kill Alphabet—at least not this time. Steele knotted the handkerchief as best as he could to create a makeshift bandage.

Once Steele had finished, Alphabet reached for the rifle he had dropped. "Better luck next time, you damn Nips!" he shouted, and fired a shot at the bunker. The bullet whined angrily off the concrete, sounding as frustrated as Alphabet.

In response, there was another shot from the Japanese sniper, causing Alphabet to duck as the bullet ripped the air just inches from his head.

"What the hell!" he shouted. "I'm getting tired of that son of a bitch."

"We're getting chewed to pieces here," Steele agreed. "Where the hell are those tanks?"

Watching from cover, Deke couldn't help but think about the sniper that he had battled earlier on Leyte. His name had been Ikeda. The two men had crossed paths more than once. Ikeda had seemed to outwit him at every opportunity, but Deke had finally turned the tables on the Japanese sniper and tricked him by rigging a scarecrow in the jungle as a decoy. Ikeda had been so sure of himself that he had fallen right into that trap.

As always, the Japanese seemed to have no shortage of snipers. Sniper warfare was just another tactic that the Japanese trained for. This sniper was likely not Ikeda's equal but simply had the good luck to be ensconced inside a concrete bunker.

Deke smiled to himself. That sniper's luck was about to change.

"Hey, Philly," Deke said. "Try and hold that Jap sniper's attention."

"How do I do that?"

"Shoot at him, that's how."

Without waiting for a response, Deke began to creep closer to the bunker, using whatever he could for cover—even, as it turned out, some poor bastard's body.

It was one of their own soldiers, killed by the Japanese. He avoided looking closely at the face to see which of the company's soldiers it was. For all he knew, he might have shared a laugh or a canteen with this man. He figured that it didn't matter now—the soldier was just so much dead meat, a backstop for bullets.

He stopped behind the body just long enough for the corpse to absorb a burst of machine-gun fire and for Deke to slide his rifle over the dead soldier's rump and squeeze off a couple of shots.

He tried not to think too much about the fact that he was using a dead man for cover. They were in the middle of a battle, and whatever he could put between himself and the endless hail of the enemy's bullets was just fine by him.

It was almost too much to hope that he wouldn't end up just as dead in the next minute. The well-defended Japanese in the complex of bunkers were tearing them to pieces.

Deke knew he couldn't take on the whole damn Japanese army. But he could fight at least one of them man to man, or sniper to sniper.

He could see the slit in the concrete, no more than six inches wide and a foot high, dark against the lighter face of the concrete, reminding Deke of the vertical pupil of a mountain rattlesnake.

That must be where the Japanese sniper was shooting from. Yet the man was well hidden behind who knew how many inches or even feet of concrete.

These Japanese had been preparing for the arrival of American forces for some time, and the entire island seemed to be so incredibly well defended that for every step forward that the Americans were able to take, they also seemed to be bleeding a gallon of blood for each one of those inches.

Time to make the Japs bleed a little of their own precious blood, he thought.

"Can you hit it?" Philly asked. He had scooted up near Deke and was on his belly behind a chunk of concrete that had been blown free by the artillery barrage. He had already emptied his own rifle at the trench slit without any success.

"Don't go talking nonsense," Deke replied. "Do you want me to shoot that Jap in the left eye or the right eye?"

"And here I always thought you didn't brag much."

"My pa always said it ain't braggin' if it's true."

Philly reloaded his own rifle. "All right, then. I'll keep him distracted."

Making the situation difficult was the fact that the Japanese were shooting at them the whole time, forcing Deke and Philly to keep their heads down, not to mention the rest of Patrol Easy.

"What we need is a tank," Philly said. "Honcho called for tanks, but I don't know how long they'll take to get up here."

"I don't see any tanks around, do you?" Deke snapped.

But he had to agree with Philly. What they really needed was more firepower. They couldn't do much good against concrete bunkers. The rifle felt like a puny instrument in his hands compared to what appeared to be an impregnable fortress in front of him.

He put the scope to his eye and kept focused on the firing slit, hoping for a sign of movement within. However, the Japanese sniper didn't appear eager to show himself.

He realized that, just maybe, he had been bragging to Philly, after all. Could he really put a bullet through that slit in the bunker?

The day's heat had continued to build so that the tropical sun beating down through the foliage felt like heated pinpricks. Sweat streamed into Deke's eyes, making aiming the rifle that much harder. Insects buzzed in his eyes and ears, as if the buzz of bullets wasn't bad enough.

Damn it all. He inched higher above the corpse, where he had rested the rifle, trying to get a better look at the Japanese position before him. Sure enough, there was machine-gun fire coming from the bunker, but it was the more accurate fire from the sniper that was proving to be even more deadly and taking a toll on the troops.

Maybe it was Deke's imagination, but he thought he saw a glimpse of movement through the slit in the concrete, even the black gaze of the Japanese sniper's eye.

But of course he was too far away to actually see that. He knew it was all in his imagination. Maybe he was still feverish.

Deke lined up his sights on the slit and fired. However, he had flinched at the last instant because a bullet had passed too close for comfort. He saw a puff of concrete dust through the scope but wasn't sure exactly where his bullet had struck.

"You missed," said Philly, who was watching through his own rifle scope.

"That ain't exactly helpful."

"Aim a little to the left," Philly said.

Deke wiped the sweat from his eyes and put his finger back on the trigger, lining up the sight on the target. Slowly, slowly, his finger took up tension on the trigger until he felt the satisfying jolt of the rifle stock against his shoulder.

This time there was no puff of concrete dust. The bullet sang right through the slit. When the sniper did not reappear, it seemed to indicate that Deke's bullet had done its job.

"Did you get him?"

"I reckon."

"What are you waiting for?" Philly demanded. "Shoot some more of those bastards."

Philly was right. Every sniper duel was so intense that it was easy to forget the bigger battle taking place.

Deke put his eye back to the scope and began to search for another target. Before he found anything to shoot at, he heard a sound behind him on the road and swiveled around to take a look.

Tanks. Two of them. Coming up the road toward Ipil. He turned to watch the behemoths approaching. The breeze carried the smell of exhaust as their powerful engines churned. Both tanks rushed forward, their treads clanking. To a man on the ground, the churning tracks appeared strong enough to pulverize anything in their way. The tanks were not buttoned up, but their commanders stood in the hatches atop the turrets, trying to size up the situation before them.

They held their fire for now. The fact that the tanks hadn't even brought their machine guns into play seemed odd.

At the sight of the tanks, a few of the men even cheered.

"Here comes the cavalry," Steele shouted. "I'm glad to see them, that's for sure."

"I don't know what the hell they're waiting for," Philly complained. "Why the hell don't they shoot?"

After coming up the road in a rush, the tanks took their time getting into position, like two bulls preparing to charge. When they began to draw fire, the tank commanders pulled the hatches shut, disappearing inside. They were soon seemingly oblivious to the rain of fire headed their way. Even the fire from the Japanese antiaircraft weapons that had been adapted to defend the bunker bounced off. The frustrated Japanese doubled their rate of fire, which made things only worse for the men on the ground.

Formidable as the tanks appeared, their guns were no match for the thick concrete of the bunkers, cleverly angled to deflect shells.

The tanks tried anyway, firing their main guns into the nearest bunker at almost point-blank range. *Whang!* With that awful sound, one of the shells bounced off without detonating and flew into the trees, where it exploded with an earsplitting release.

What the Japanese hadn't planned on were the flamethrowers. One of the tanks pulled back slightly, pivoted on its tracks, and then advanced again until its main gun was practically touching the bunker. A stream of orange-and-red flame suddenly shot from where the machine gun was normally located.

"I'll be damned. They're Satans!" Philly shouted, using the nickname for tanks that had been rigged with flamethrowers to release hellfire against the enemy. These tanks had first made their appearance on Guam and Saipan. They were both hated and feared by the Japanese.

The Satans had been aptly named. The tank had been aiming for the bunker's horizontal slit, from which the Japanese defenders were firing. Instantly the front of the bunker was covered in a fireball.

Deke shuddered at the sight of the flames. He could only imagine what it must be like to face a flamethrower. In fact, he didn't want to imagine too hard. Deke had given himself over to violence—there wasn't any other choice as a soldier if you wanted to survive—but some part of him remained amazed at the sheer cruelty of this weapon of war.

The scorching flame seemed so much more inhumane than a simple bullet. The fire would reach deep into the bunker, licking into every corner. The flames were sticky, in a sense, because they were fueled by a jellied gasoline that clung to whatever it touched. Those enemy troops who weren't burned to death often suffocated as the hungry fire sucked the oxygen from the confined space inside the bunker.

All in all, the flamethrower was a horrible weapon but was highly effective when there was no other hope of rooting out the enemy.

The tank gave one last burst with its flamethrower. No

sooner had the flames subsided than a couple of soldiers ran forward and lobbed grenades through the smoking, blackened gap. If anyone had managed to survive the inferno, the grenades would surely finish them off.

Nearby, Philly made a gagging noise. "Ugh, that smell! Makes me sick to my stomach."

Philly was more than right. The stink of the burning fuel from the flamethrowers mingled with the smell of burned flesh. "I won't mind getting out of this place and finding some fresh air," Deke agreed.

But they weren't done yet with Ipil. One by one, the tanks knocked out the bunkers and the enemy soldiers inside them, with teams of GIs following up with grenades. By the time that nightfall approached, the bunkers as well as the area surrounding the old US military base known as Camp Downes had been secured.

The next prize would be Ormoc itself, and they all knew that the Japanese would not give up the town easily.

CHAPTER SEVENTEEN

BY NIGHTFALL, Camp Downes and the surrounding area were back in American control, at least for the time being. They all knew from experience that darkness would likely bring Japanese infiltrators, if not a full counterattack.

Consequently, the outcome of the fight might depend on the next few hours. The US line was spread thin, extending tenuously from the beachhead. Military doctrine stated that a beachhead should extend at least a quarter of a mile from the landing zone itself, creating a defensive bubble that would reduce harassing fire or mortar attacks by the enemy.

It wasn't always possible to follow military doctrine. Sometimes the reality was that you had to hang on by your fingernails. The division barely had enough men to hold the beachhead. Fortunately for US troops, the Japanese had not tried to force the soldiers back into the sea but had fallen back to defend Ormoc and its airfield.

The situation meant that there would be no relief for Merrick's company or for Patrol Easy. Whatever came their way at Camp Downes, they would have no choice but to face it and try to hang on.

Being little more than a collection of old wooden barracks and outbuildings, Camp Downes did not provide much in the way of a defensive position. It hadn't been intended as a fortress. If it hadn't been for the war, the waterfront location of the camp would have been quite pleasant, situated to capture both the view and the cooling breeze off the water. The outpost had been intended as a presence during the days of the Filipino insurrection more than thirty years before, a jumping-off point for patrols into the nearby countryside.

The Japanese had done little to expand the former American outpost, but had focused their attention on building the concrete bunkers and other defenses. Those bunkers were now blackened and blasted ruins, still smoldering from flamethrower attacks by the Satan tanks. Within the smoking bunkers were the remains of the Japanese defenders.

No one was eager to occupy the bunkers under the circumstances, so the soldiers dug foxholes in the open ground around Camp Downes.

"If I'd known that I'd be digging so much, I would have stayed on the farm," Deke said, bent over his entrenching tool.

"Yeah, I'll bet you miss the sheep too," Philly said. He and Yoshio were digging nearby, their shovels loudly scraping into the dirt.

Deke snorted and threw a shovelful of dirt at him.

"Hey, you dumb cracker! Don't go filling this hole back up, goddammit."

It was enough to set a man's mind whirling, to think that he had faced down death earlier in the day and lived to enjoy some minor high jinks. The sound of Philly muttering indignantly under his breath brought a grin to Deke's face, and he realized that he must finally be feeling better.

This morning he wouldn't have had the energy to dig a hole. Still, it had been one hell of a day, and every bone and muscle seemed to ache as the sweat oozed out of his pores. The physical labor reminded him of being a boy on the farm, where there had been no shortage of hard work.

Strictly speaking, Deke knew that there hadn't been a family farm anymore when he had joined the army. He had been living in a rooming house in town with his sister, Sadie.

She was now in Washington, DC, working as a police officer. And here Deke was, digging holes on the far side of the world. It sounded to him as if his sister had come out ahead on that deal. Again, he grinned.

Just as quickly, the grin faded. Their family farm had been stolen away by a rich banker when the mortgage had come due. Bankers just like him had stolen a lot of farms—and people's houses, too—all around the Appalachians. The mountains had been slow to come out of the Depression, if they ever would.

Thinking about that banker, Deke supposed it was a shame that the man wasn't here, because the hole Deke was digging was just the right size to bury that banker in.

The sandy, volcanic soil was easy to shovel. That much was different from the farm, at least—the mountain soil was thin to the point of being stingy, except when it came to rocks. There were always rocks in abundance. It was little wonder that the mountain farmers struggled so much. He could see that the farms and fields here on Leyte were far more abundant.

For a change there were no tangled tree roots, because they were digging in what appeared to be the old parade grounds for Camp Downes. They were working by the last of the tropical daylight.

When the night arrived, it came quickly. Once again, the tropical sunset did not disappoint. The sun disappeared in a cloud of purple and orange that hugged the horizon. The last light of day vanished in a heartbeat, swallowed by the clouds. The coming night did little to alleviate the humidity, which groped at them like fingers dipped in sticky lard.

The forest canopy beyond Camp Downes fell into shadow, a tangle of vines and branches, lit by pinpricks of light from fire-flies and punctuated by occasional birdcalls. For all they knew, those birdcalls might be Japanese units signaling to one another. The soldiers doubled their pace, working to finish up their foxholes.

Beyond the land, the ocean reflected light like a giant mirror, empty of any ships, friendly or otherwise. A squadron of planes flew in the distance, too far away to tell if they were American or Japanese.

The threat of a Japanese night attack was just one of the problems they were dealing with. There was also the issue of the wounded, not just from their company, but from other units who had been working to push the Japanese back from the beach and pen them in closer to Ormoc.

There were also several dead soldiers, their bodies set out in neat rows and covered in their own blankets. Almost all of them knew someone who was dead under one of those blankets, and they were haunted by the thought, *Tomorrow that might be me*.

Normally, the wounded would be taken to the beach, and from there to hospital ships or naval sick bays that were better equipped to treat them. However, word had come down that there was going to be a delay in evacuating the wounded.

"The Navy pulled its ships back," Lieutenant Steele explained. "They're afraid of Japanese aircraft in the vicinity and also of the Japanese Navy."

"I thought they licked the Japanese Navy."

"Not completely," Steele said. "There are plenty of Japanese submarines around too. Anyhow, the bottom line is that the navy isn't sending any vessels to take our wounded off Leyte."

Nobody spoke up to accuse the US Navy of being captained by a bunch of grannies. The soldiers had been passengers aboard the ships, and so they knew better. They had seen what the squids were up against. It was different from being in a dark jungle, but constantly scanning the skies and horizons for an enemy that might appear at any moment to sink you with torpedoes or bombs was no picnic.

The Japanese Navy was no joke, and neither were their remaining aircraft—especially the new kamikaze attacks.

When they had first heard about those, nobody could believe it. It still took some getting used to, the idea of Japanese pilots committing suicide by flying into ships and taking as many US sailors with them as possible. For the average soldier, it was just further evidence of the death wish that seemed to possess the Japanese forces.

"What are we supposed to do with the wounded, then?" Philly asked, sounding disgusted. "Those poor bastards need help."

"Division is sending a surgeon up from the beach to do what he can for the wounded," Steele said. "I guess it's easier to send him here than to try and move the wounded."

As promised, the surgeon soon appeared, bouncing along in a Jeep with two orderlies. The Jeep was being driven in blackout conditions, its headlights reduced to slits to avoid drawing enemy fire. The flip side was that the dim headlights made navigating the jungle road more than a little challenging. It was a lucky break that there was still some lingering daylight as the Jeep pulled up.

An officer got out and dusted himself off as Lieutenant Steele approached.

"Welcome to Camp Downes, Doc," the lieutenant said.

"This is it, huh?" the surgeon asked, looking around. He was well into his forties, of average height, and was wearing wire-rimmed glasses. He took off his helmet to rub a sweaty bald head. He had a bit of a paunch that his baggy uniform didn't quite hide. Considering that nobody was going to get fat eating army food, the paunch must have been a vestige of civilian life.

"It's my understanding that it used to be one of our bases before the Nips took it over in forty-one, along with the rest of the Philippines," Steele explained.

"Glad we got here when we did. I don't think we could have found it once it got any darker."

"Yeah, it won't be long before it's as dark out here as the inside of a meatball," Philly added.

The combat surgeon gave Philly a quizzical look, as if he was wondering whether he had just found a genuine Looney Tune, but he didn't respond. He turned his attention back to the lieutenant. "I've got to say, this place isn't much to look at. But I'm sure glad we found you. I was half expecting to run into enemy lines by mistake. The way I understand it, this place is still crawling with Japanese."

"You wouldn't be wrong there," Steele said.

"You're in charge here?" the surgeon asked.

"Captain Merrick is the company commander, Doc. I'm just in charge of this little corner of paradise," Steele replied. "I'm Lieutenant Steele."

"That's good enough for me, Lieutenant. I'm Captain Harmon, by the way. Doc Harmon," the surgeon said. He studied the lieutenant's face—or rather, his leather eye patch. "Why, Lieutenant, I believe you only have one eye. That's not a fresh wound either. What the hell are you still doing in the field?"

"Just lucky, I guess."

The surgeon shook his head. "Most men I know would be more than happy to be sent home if they were in your shoes."

"I guess I'm just not ready to give up the fight yet."

"I know the feeling," the doc said. "All right, take me to the wounded, and let me see what I can do for them."

"This way, Doc."

The orderlies unloaded medical equipment, and the surgeon also carried a bag. It seemed like precious little equipment, considering the injuries of some of the wounded, but the surgeon didn't appear daunted in any way. He quickly fell into step beside the lieutenant.

The Japanese seemed intent on reminding the soldiers that this fight wasn't over. From time to time, sniper fire punctuated the darkness. There would be a muzzle flash somewhere in the forest and then the crack of a bullet. Sometimes a man went down, but mostly the sniper fire seemed intended to rattle the soldiers' nerves. It was harassing fire, pure and simple.

Nobody really knew what the Japanese were shooting at, but every soldier's natural inclination was to think that the bullet was aimed at *him*. Nobody blamed a guy for flinching. They were all a little jumpy.

To his credit, and showing that he was no stranger to a combat zone, the doc didn't even bother to duck at the sound of sniper fire.

The surgeon was guided to where the wounded had been placed on the ground, with a few shelter halves strung over them to keep off the nighttime damp. Under the circumstances, it was the best that could be done for them. The musty smell of the canvas mingled with the odor of blood and sweat, sweetened by the occasional breeze that had carried all the way from the sea, salty and fresh.

A few of the wounded lay moaning, one or two were cursing, and the worst off didn't make any noise at all. The exception was a soldier with a bad chest wound and ragged breathing. A couple of stretcher bearers had volunteered to tend to the wounded, and they went from man to man, offering water.

The men had a variety of wounds. Some had been shot, others hit by shrapnel. The ones who had been shot had mostly been hit by rifle fire rather than machine guns. That was because the Nambu machine guns tended to rip a man apart. One way or another, the Japanese were intent on killing them, all in the name of their emperor.

An American soldier could only view that motivation with a mixture of mystification and disgust. Also, no one had ever forgotten the sneak attack on Pearl Harbor. There was a measure of revenge in everything about this war.

They all knew that the cost in American lives had been horrific. Almost countless sailors had drowned, and thousands of airmen had been lost in the skies. That said, the fighting on land somehow felt more personal.

For the average soldier, there were plenty of ways to die in the Pacific that had nothing to do with the battlefield. These included sunstroke, fever, snakebite, and drowning. By and large, combat deaths across the Pacific islands were caused by blood loss, the exception being those who were killed outright. Basically, the wounded bled to death. Depending on the severity of the wounds, death could take several minutes.

A man's buddies might make some effort to stop the bleeding, but most of the time there was only so much that could be done. It was a hell of a way to go.

The lucky ones died instantly, which was what most soldiers hoped for.

Lieutenant Steele and the surgeon had reached the wounded spread on the ground. At a signal from the lieutenant, Deke and Philly had fallen into step behind them.

The wounded had lived this long, but could they survive the night? The arrival of the surgeon on the front lines had given them some hope.

The surgeon set to work. From the deft way that he handled

the wounded, it was clear that Doc Harmon knew his business. The surgeon moved from one injured man to the next, assessing their wounds, while his assistants readied the necessary instruments and supplies.

What he was doing was triage, seeing who was the worst off, who could be saved, and who should just be dosed up with more morphine and made as comfortable as possible. It was basically the way that wounded had been dealt with since the time of the Romans.

"Have we got any light?" the surgeon asked.

"Just flashlights, Doc."

"All right, I suppose that will have to do. Let's raise these shelter halves up. I want to be able to stand under here and have some room to move around. See if we can rig some kind of operating table."

Steele sent the men out to find materials before it was completely dark. A couple of boards that weren't charred too badly were retrieved from one of the bunkers, then set up on crates. The surgeon had to stoop down, but it would be better than working on the ground.

"What about the Japanese?" Deke asked.

"What about them?" Steele asked.

"They'll see the light and start shooting at us, that's for damn sure. Their snipers won't let us alone."

"All right, let's try to rig some sides and maybe block the light." More shelter halves were found, along with some blankets. Once they were finished, Steele asked, "How's that, Doc?"

The surgeon looked it over and nodded. "Better than nothing, I suppose. Get that man over there on the table."

Once the wounded soldier was positioned on the makeshift operating table, the surgeon set to work. One of his assistants held the flashlight as he began probing the man's wounds and extracting pieces of shrapnel. He did his best to clean the wounds and stitch up the gashes and cuts.

The so-called operating room that had been pieced together out of shelter halves and scrap wood was cramped, but Deke couldn't help but linger, watching the surgeon work. Philly had practically run out at the first flash of the scalpel, but Deke never had been squeamish about the sight of blood. He had to admire the surgeon's deft skill.

That was where his enthusiasm ended. He was glad that he wasn't the one under the surgeon's knife. He'd rather face a samurai sword than a scalpel.

CHAPTER EIGHTEEN

DEKE WENT OUTSIDE and joined Philly and Lieutenant Steele, who were smoking cigarettes that they cupped in their hands to contain the dim glow, gazing uneasily at the darkness. Not all the wounded could fit inside the tent, so several were spread on the ground, waiting for their turn with the surgeon. Their torn bodies lay in a rough circle around the tent, some on stretchers and others just on blankets on the ground. They didn't complain. Again, a couple of volunteers continued to circulate, bringing them water and doing what they could for the wounded.

"Thank God for that doc, or these guys wouldn't have a prayer," Honcho said quietly. "I hope to hell we can get them off this island tomorrow."

Philly spoke up. "I just wish—"

He never got to complete the thought. Two figures material-ized out of the darkness, rushing right at the wounded and the operating tent. At first it seemed as if two more volunteers had come to help the wounded. But then the shapes materialized into soldiers with rifles and bayonets, wearing Japanese uniforms. What light there was revealed faces twisted into savage expressions.

If they had wanted to, they could have had the drop on Deke, Philly, and Steele. But they did not attack. Instead, to Deke's horror, the Japanese began using their bayonets to stab down at the wounded.

To make it even more confusing, the Japanese did not utter a sound, other than a grunt of exertion as one of them jammed his bayonet down. This was followed by the awful sound of the blade cutting into meat. The other Japanese soldier stabbed one of the unarmed volunteers who had rushed to intercept him, then turned his bayonet on the wounded.

What the hell? Those damn Japs sure as hell want to finish what they started.

Honcho was the first to react. His shotgun boomed, the powerful blast of the twelve gauge catching the nearest Japanese infiltrator in the chest and lifting him clear off his feet. Honcho racked in another shell and shot the man again before his body had even hit the ground. At close range, the deep boom sounded like a cannon going off. Flame stabbed out from the muzzle, searing into Deke's vision.

Deke still managed to fire his rifle from the hip, hitting the second Japanese in the belly. The wounded attacker spun like a top, giving Deke time to work the bolt and raise the rifle to his shoulder so that he could deliver a second shot. Hit twice, the infiltrator went down and didn't move.

A third Japanese soldier appeared like a wraith, stealthy and silent, his arm cocked back as he prepared to pitch a hand grenade into the canvas tent.

Steele dropped him with a shotgun blast. The enemy soldier must have fallen on top of the grenade, which exploded an instant later with a muffled *whump*.

The attack was over as quickly as it had begun. The whole

medical team, along with the wounded, had come within seconds of being wiped out.

"Son of a bitch!" Philly shouted. "Where the hell did they come from?"

The three men kept their weapons leveled, but no more infiltrators appeared—at least not for the moment. The savage sneak attack had claimed two American lives—the wounded man and the volunteer who had been tending the wounded—both killed by bayonet.

All over Camp Downes, similar scenes were taking place. Japanese soldiers charged out of the darkness, wreaking havoc. The humid night air served as a cloak, muffling sound and hiding the attackers within its dark folds.

Mostly the enemy relied on their bayonets, a silent weapon that was both primitive and terrifying. Nobody wanted to get eighteen inches of steel rammed through their guts. Because the Japanese had opted not to use their machine guns or rifles, there was no warning and nothing to shoot at—not until the enemy was right on top of them.

A few infiltrators threw grenades into the foxholes, taking out whatever defenders sheltered there. Adding to the havoc was the fact that the infiltrators knew the ins and outs of Camp Downes all too well, having vacated the outpost only recently. The Japanese knew the paths that ran between the buildings, providing cover until they were right upon the Americans.

They also used the smallest shrubs for cover, creeping to within a few feet of the US sentries. Their war dog now played his part. Thor barked savagely, alerting the soldiers that they were not alone in the darkness. Egan strained to hold Thor's leash. Meanwhile, M1 rifles cracked, putting an end to the infiltrators who had been trying to creep up on them unseen.

Other Japanese managed to slip around to the waterfront and surprise the defenders by coming at them from behind the lines, rather than from the direction of the forest, as expected. Seemingly piecemeal at first, it became clear that the infiltrators were coordinated and organized, doing far more damage than a full-on attack, which would have been mowed down by the defenders' machine guns.

One thing for sure was that there wouldn't be any sleep that night.

"I got to say, this is like battling bedbugs in a cheap hotel," Philly said. "Soon as you squish one, you feel another one crawling on you."

"Remind me not to travel anywhere with you," Deke said. "Either that or stay in a better class of hotel."

Doc Harmon had emerged from the operating tent to see what all the commotion was about. The night was punctuated by shouts and gunshots. "What the hell is going on out here?"

"Jap infiltrators, Doc," Honcho explained. "I'm afraid that the sons of bitches got one of the wounded and one of our stretcher bearers."

The surgeon knelt to examine one of the men who had been bayoneted by the Japanese. Although it was dark, the man's blood appeared darker still as it pooled beneath him. Harmon finally straightened up, shaking his head.

"Gone," he said, a hint of anger in his voice. "I can't say that I'm encouraged by the fact that the Japanese keep killing them faster than I can patch them up. It's not exactly easy operating by flashlight, you know."

"Don't worry about the Japs, Doc," Honcho said, stepping forward and racking a fresh shell into his combat shotgun. "You concentrate on helping those wounded. I'll admit that the sneaky bastards caught us by surprise. It won't be happening again. We'll make sure not so much as a mosquito gets through. Deke? Philly?"

Deke nodded. He tightened his grip on his rifle. Something

about the thought of helpless wounded men being murdered in their blankets made him angrier than usual at the Japanese. What the hell was wrong with these people? "On it."

"All right," the surgeon said. "I appreciate it. Just try not to get yourselves shot or stabbed in the process. I seem to have all the work that I can handle."

Deke, Philly, and Steele kept vigil around the operating tent, fingers on their triggers. The rest of Patrol Easy, including Thor, were kept busy elsewhere. Yoshio was off with Alphabet and Rodeo, guarding what served as headquarters at Camp Downes. Captain Merrick seemed to like having an interpreter on hand, just in case Yoshio overheard any shouted orders. In any case, there appeared to be plenty of infiltrators to go around.

As for Danilo, the Filipino had not been content to play sentry. Wordlessly, he had left his rifle behind and crept into the darkness, armed only with his bolo knife. To merely call it a "knife" was something of an understatement, like calling an eagle a bird. The traditional blade was more like a machete or short sword. By comparison, even Deke's custom-forged bowie knife looked like the bolo's little brother—or maybe a toothpick.

For generations the bolo had served the Filipinos as both a tool and as a weapon when necessary. They were handed down from father to son and treated as heirlooms as valuable as Excalibur, even when they had the humblest workaday appearance.

In Danilo's hands, the bolo blade would be more than enough. Deke shuddered to think about the fate that awaited any Japanese that Danilo encountered. While the Americans fought the Japanese because it was their job as soldiers, Danilo and other guerrillas had suffered cruelly at the hands of the occupiers. The Japanese had taken away their freedom, their homes. For them, this was more than combat—this was revenge.

"Damn fool is gonna get himself killed out there," Philly muttered.

"Maybe, but he'll take a few Nips with him, that's for sure."

* * *

THEY SETTLED DOWN TO WAIT, which was always the hardest part at night when you were expecting an attack. It was only a matter of time before there were more infiltrators. The Japanese seemed to have plenty of tricks up their sleeves. One thing, at least—nobody was in any danger of falling asleep.

Once or twice Deke heard a distant shriek cut short. It was hard to say if the cries had come from a human or an animal. Either way, any hunter would recognize that sound as the dying cry of prey. Was it Danilo at work, or some other predator?

Deke stared out into the darkness until he saw spots. He blinked them away, looking for any movement. Given the depth of the tropical night, it wasn't easy. The darkness appeared to ebb and flow like the eddies and currents of some great, black river.

"How dark did you say it was out here, Philly?" Deke asked. Deke was poking at him because Philly had become somewhat infamous for his similes.

"I'd say it's as dark as my boot up your ass."

Deke snorted. "Yep, that sounds about right."

"All right, you two, knock it off," Honcho said irritably. Ever since he'd had to take command of an entire platoon within Merrick's company, Honcho's patience had worn thin. "Pay attention. I need to leave you and go check on the rest of these ladies."

Once the lieutenant had gone off to check on the rest of his platoon, Deke and Philly traded one-liners and insults to stay awake, and in part to be reassured that there was another man just a few feet away in the darkness.

Twice more that night, Japanese attacked the medical tent.

The first time, it was another trio of infiltrators who made the mistake of shouting some kind of battle cry. If the attack had been silent, the outcome might have been different, but the shouts of the Japanese jolted Deke's trigger finger awake. By then Honcho had returned from his rounds and taken up his guard duties again. Honcho's shotgun boomed beside Deke, and then Philly's rifle. All three infiltrators went down.

The next attempt was even more of a stealth attack, undertaken in total silence. They didn't even spot the two Japanese at first, not until they were already at the tent, using their bayonets to cut their way in through the canvas to get at the medical team and wounded inside.

Before the infiltrators could do any real damage, they were shot down by Honcho, Deke, and Philly.

At first Deke thought that Doc Harmon hadn't been aware of how close the Japanese had come to getting inside the tent. But then a hand appeared from within and tugged the slits in the canvas closed. It was as if the infiltrators were nothing more than a nuisance.

"I'll be damned," Honcho remarked. "That doc has got some sand, all right."

By first light, the Japanese attacks had subsided. Somewhere within the morning mist that enveloped the edges of the forest, they could actually hear the Japanese talking to one another, and even laughing at one point. The smell of cooking food drifted their way. Apparently the enemy troops were having a hot breakfast.

The Japanese did not depend on canned rations like the Americans did, although the Americans had occasionally come across caches of tinned Japanese crabmeat and even fish. Instead, Japanese troops were typically issued dried rice.

The rice was highly portable and easy to prepare, plus had the benefit of providing hot food. Theoretically US soldiers

could heat up their ration cans, but few ever bothered to do so
in the field. The distant talk and laughter, along with the smell
of the small cooking fires and the hot food, served as a reminder
that the Japanese defenders were not only well supplied but in
good spirits.

"I'd say those Japanese have a passel of fight left in them,"
Deke remarked.

"Yeah, they just don't know they're beat yet," Philly said. He
held out a chunk of cold, hard, bitter tropical chocolate,
designed not to melt in the tropical heat. First thing in the
morning, it was not very appetizing, but it provided instant
energy to weary men. "Want some breakfast?"

Deke took it, stuck the square of chocolate in his mouth, and
snapped off a bite. The chocolate crumbled like chalk and tasted
about the same. He washed it down with some canteen water.
"Mmm, mmm. I'll just pretend it's scrapple."

Philly shuddered. "Scrapple? I can't believe you eat that hillbilly crap."

"In case you ain't noticed, I *am* a hillbilly. Proud of it too."

The surgeon emerged from the operating tent, which was
covered in a heavy dew from the previous night's damp
jungle air.

Honcho offered the surgeon a cigarette, which he accepted
with a nod.

"How did it go, Doc?"

"I fixed them up as best as I could. Hopefully the wounded
will be transported out to a hospital ship as soon as possible. A
couple of them need more surgery, but I patched up the worst of
it. Some of them need plasma, too, and we're damn low on that.
It would be helpful if nobody else gets shot today."

"We'll see what we can do about that, Doc, but that's really
up to the Japanese." Honcho grinned. "You can see that the
Japanese weren't too keen on you fixing up the wounded. It

doesn't make sense, being so intent on attacking them. Those men are out of the fight."

"It's their way of getting at us mentally," the doc said. "When they kill our wounded, it makes us feel vulnerable."

"Then I've got to say, it works pretty well."

Despite his air of nonchalance, it was clear that the doctor was exhausted. He had worked through the night, operating by flashlight, under constant threat of enemy attack. He yawned wide and rubbed his face.

"I don't suppose there's any chance of getting some hot coffee around here? Maybe with two sugars?"

"If you find any, Doc, let me know."

"I guess a cigarette will have to do."

"Say, aren't those bad for your health?"

"So is being on a battlefield, but that hasn't stopped me yet either."

The surgeon sucked the cigarette smoke deep into his lungs, exhaled, and then walked around the tent, inspecting the dead Japanese with what appeared to be professional curiosity. Like most dead men, they looked smaller than they had while animated by life.

However, the enemy soldiers looked relatively well fed, and their uniforms were in better shape than those of some of those worn by the Americans. Cleaner and not as ragged. These were indications that at least some supplies must still be getting through to the Japanese. The army brass always pitched the idea of the enemy being on the ropes, starving and low on ammo. The GIs in the field knew otherwise.

Even in death, the enemy casualties did not have the look of troops who had been fighting out of desperation.

A few feet away, they could see Yoshio sitting on a crate, skimming the documents that soldiers had collected from dead Japanese scattered across other sections of Camp Downes. The hope was that he would find maps or orders, documents that gave a hint of the Japanese positions and strength. So far, all that he had come across were letters from home. It was a reminder that the Japanese might not be as monstrous as they had seemed during the night.

When their bodies had been searched, it revealed that many of the Japanese were wearing colorful "thousand-stitch belts" around their waists. Even die-hard souvenir hunters among the US soldiers left them alone. The embroidered belts had been made for the enemy dead by loved ones at home—mothers and wives, sisters and sweethearts. The belts were intended to keep their men safe from harm, much in the way that many US soldiers wore a cross or religious scapular under their uniforms. It was evident that neither crosses nor thousand-stitch belts did much to stop bullets, but a soldier took hope where he could.

In truth, there were a surprisingly small number of dead enemy troops. During the night, it had felt as if hordes were infiltrating the camp. It went to show just how effective the infiltrators' tactics had been.

"I have to say, these enemy soldiers appear to be in good physical condition," the surgeon observed, unwittingly echoing what Deke had said earlier to Philly. "It's not going to be an easy fight."

"Yeah, well," Honcho said. "At least these fellas won't be helping."

CHAPTER NINETEEN

THE SOLDIERS EMERGED from their nighttime ordeal dazed and exhausted. Some moved stiffly from being cramped into their foxholes all night. Early-morning jungle dew beaded their helmets and dampened their uniforms.

They had survived the series of piecemeal nighttime incursions by the enemy, but those had taken their toll in a way that was almost as devastating as a coordinated daytime attack, whittling away at their spirit and energy. The night had left their nerves feeling as raw as their bloodshot eyes, tired from straining to see into the darkness.

Now that it was daylight, there was a new threat that the Japanese might be trying a different tactic and launching just such an all-out attack.

"If the Japanese do attack, I hope it's sooner rather than later," Deke told Philly. The two men sat side by side in a foxhole, eating what passed for breakfast and washing it down with metallic canteen water.

"How about if they don't attack us at all?" Philly suggested.

Deke shook his head. "One way or another, we're gonna have

to fight some Japanese today. At least we're dug in here at Camp Downes. If they hit us once we push on toward Ormoc, we'll be caught out in the open."

"Caught with our pants down, you mean," Philly said. "Wouldn't be the first time. It's not a pretty sight."

"No, it ain't," Deke agreed.

Overhead, a single reconnaissance plane made slow sweeps over the frontline area. Nobody paid the plane much attention because it was one of their own.

The plane was designated as an L-4 Grasshopper, basically known in civilian life as a Piper Cub. With a fixed upper wing, a top speed of 85 miles per hour, and a maximum operational altitude of twelve thousand feet, the unarmed army plane wasn't about to tangle with any enemy fighters. However, the plane's ability to chug overhead at just under 40 miles per hour made it ideal for observation missions. Typically the pilot got in close while the aerial photographer clicked away.

Honcho paused near Deke and Philly's foxhole as he made his rounds, then lit up a cigarette and watched the plane overhead.

"He'll let headquarters know if he sees any sign of the Japanese," Honcho said. "I just hope to hell the Japanese don't pull a Saipan on us."

"If they come, I'll be ready," said Private Frazier, who was listening nearby, holding on to his BAR.

"That's the spirit," Honcho said. His expression didn't match his words, however. His sad frown spoke volumes. It was as if the lieutenant had seen and heard it all before—which he had.

By now they had all heard about the fight for Saipan, where the cornered enemy had launched massive waves of banzai charges involving thousands of Japanese troops. At first the US Marines had been overwhelmed. Hundreds of Americans had died in the savage close-quarters fighting as waves of the enemy washed over them like surf dashing upon rocks.

Sheer firepower had eventually carried the day, securing the American lines and wiping out thousands of Japanese troops. In all of the war, including in Europe, there had been no other example of close-quarters fighting on that scale. You would almost have to go back to medieval times for something like that. No one was eager for that scenario to play out here.

So far the enemy seemed content to dig in and let the Americans come at them.

"Everybody get something to eat," Honcho said to Patrol Easy and the platoon under his command. Although he had made no secret of the fact that he didn't want to be in charge of anything bigger than the sniper squad, it was clear that he took his duties seriously. He looked around to make sure that the hollow-eyed, exhausted men were listening. "Make sure your canteens are full. It might be a long day."

Honcho might have said more, but at that moment a warning shout was heard. Somebody was pointing at the sky. The US reconnaissance plane was still overhead, flying low and slow, but that wasn't what they were pointing at. As the men on the ground looked up, they saw two aircraft drop out of the sky and begin vectoring toward Camp Downes. The roar of approaching aircraft engines was getting louder by the second.

"Holy hell!" Philly cried. "Those are Japanese planes!"

In disbelief, Deke looked up and heard the roar of approaching aircraft engines just seconds after he spotted the planes themselves, shooting like arrows above the treetops, almost impossibly fast. No wonder—top speed for a Japanese Zero was 350 miles per hour, thanks to its powerful Mitsubishi engine.

Deke's sharp eyes managed to get a glimpse of the meatball insignia on the wings.

Zeros, all right. Two of them. Headed right for Camp Downes. Even with their foxholes, the entire unit was vulnerable to attack from above.

There was barely time to react. Soldiers caught in the open ran for cover or threw themselves flat.

Deke hit the dirt like everybody else, but he kept his eyes on the planes. Part of him couldn't help it—he had never seen enemy planes this close before. It was both terrifying and fascinating. He gripped his rifle tight, cursing the fact that the weapon was useless against the fast-moving planes. By the time he got it to his shoulder, they would be gone.

The planes must have been launched from an interior airfield, possibly even the one at Ormoc—a perfect reminder of the urgency of capturing the airfield. Two airplanes weren't going to win the war, but they sure could rain destruction upon the soldiers clinging to the beachhead and defending Camp Downes.

A new sound could be heard over the whine of the racing engines. This one sent chills down Deke's spine. It was the chatter of machine guns blazing down at soldiers who scrambled to get out of the way of the line of fire. Each Zero was equipped with twin 7.7-millimeter machine guns, which were unleashing their fury at the targets below.

Some men were too slow getting out of the way of the bullets digging stitches into the ground. Hit multiple times, they went sprawling in the sand, never to get up again. One man wasn't killed outright, but the heavy slug had broken his arm, leaving it dangling. As the second plane began hammering the ground, the man just stood there in shock.

Seeing the dazed and wounded man, Doc Harmon and one of the orderlies broke cover and ran to help him. Deke couldn't decide if the medical men were brave or foolish. They got on either side of the wounded man and guided him toward the hospital tent. Its thin canvas walls could provide no protection from air-to-ground gunfire, but it served as cover, if nothing else.

"Take cover!" Honcho yelled, but it was too little, too late. The planes were already on them like hawks on a rabbit, chewing up the men on the beach with their heavy-caliber machine guns.

As if the machine guns weren't enough, the planes each carried two bombs that they dropped with unnerving precision. These were small bombs, weighing just over one hundred pounds, which was just about all the extra weight that the Zero could manage. But what they lacked in size, they made up for in accuracy. Flying at such a low altitude, there was almost no way that the planes could miss their targets below.

Seconds later, the ground shook as the bombs detonated, filling the air with fire and smoke, shrapnel and concussion. Deke found himself diving for cover with everybody else. He got a mouthful of sand for his trouble, but it was better than tangling with the debris that spread overhead. When he raised his head, he saw a chunk of red-hot metal the size of a silver dollar embedded in the sand nearby, still smoking. *If that shrapnel had come just a foot closer—*

One of the bombs managed to hit a tank. It was hard to say if the tank had been targeted or if it was just bad luck, but the so-called Satan tank exploded in a fireball of its own, probably helped along by the fuel it carried for its flamethrower. The combustible jelly fed flames that spewed from every crevice in the tank. It was clear that the tank crew never had a chance. Maybe they never even knew what hit them, which would have been a blessing.

The result of that bomb strike was one less behemoth with which to dislodge the Japanese defenders around Ormoc. Here in the middle of the Pacific, a wrecked tank wasn't something that could be easily replaced.

The twin Zeros rushed out to sea and turned as if on a dime, heading back in for a second pass. Those Japanese Zeros were nothing if not nimble.

The men on the ground were also quick. They had been through this before on other landings. The beach was not undefended. Antiaircraft batteries sprang into action, filling the sky with tracers and flak, trying to knock down the Zeros.

One of the planes was hit and began trailing smoke, but rushed away and disappeared toward the interior of Leyte. It would remain to be seen whether the plane reached its hidden base. The second plane strafed the beach one last time for good measure, its machine guns churning up the sand. Then it, too, vanished.

"That was exciting," said Philly, picking himself up off the ground and brushing sand and gravel from his uniform and helmet. "I guess those Japanese still aren't ready to give up. Nobody told them that the battle was over."

"Nope, not until we've killed off the last one," Deke agreed.

Looking around at the devastation, he felt a bit stunned by the attack. In addition to the burning tank, bombs had also hit one of the buildings at the camp, so that the building was on fire, its flames spreading to the thatched roof of a neighboring building. A handful of soldiers rushed to carry supplies out of the burning buildings before it was too late. Several wounded men lay on the ground, some struggling to get up, some not moving at all.

Deke hadn't been wounded, and he was relieved to see that none of the other snipers had been either. But at the same time, the air attack made him feel defenseless. After all, how could anyone defend against such fast-moving planes? A lone man with a rifle couldn't do much. Deke shook his head, reminded once again that modern warfare was a whole lot bigger than a man with a rifle and a bowie knife.

"I'll be damned," he muttered.

As it turned out, the Japanese fighters hadn't been the only planes in the sky.

Philly pointed. "Look, it's one of ours. He's been up there this whole time!"

The lone American reconnaissance plane was still airborne over the beach. The pilot had evidently decided that the plane was too slow to make a run for it. Instead, he had dropped even lower, apparently hoping that the two Japanese Zeros would be too busy to notice him.

That strategy had worked—to a point. However, the reconnaissance aircraft was far from being out of danger. The storm of flak was intended for the enemy planes, but the airbursts were indiscriminate.

From the uneven flight path, it was clear that the pilot was struggling for control of his plane and trying to dodge whatever ground fire he could. Lucky for him, the ground troops seemed to be doing their best not to shoot down one of their own.

But the sturdy plane wasn't out of danger yet. At any moment, one of the fast-moving Zeros could wipe out the recon plane like a bird snapping its beak on an insect, without so much as a second thought.

The pilot's flight path carried him directly over the spot where one of the Japanese bombs was detonating. At that instant an explosive geyser clawed its way upward in a tornado of high explosives, ripping off the entire tail of the small reconnaissance plane. One moment the tail had been there, and the next moment it was gone. The front section of the plane and the wings were untouched.

Fighter pilots got all the glory, but it spoke to the pilot's skill that he was able to wrestle with the controls as the plane plunged toward the beach. It wasn't going to be a controlled landing, but it looked like the pilot was going to avoid crashing altogether—just barely.

Soldiers ran out of the way as the plane came down, swinging wildly from side to side and dipping up and down like a paper airplane caught in a whirlwind. The wheels touched down, and the plane skidded across the sand before coming to a halt. Soldiers ran to help the pilot and copilot get out. By some miracle, the plane had not caught on fire.

Allowing himself to be led away, the pilot looked back at what was left of his plane and stared at the missing tail section.

Technically, he had not been shot down, but it was hard to find a term that explained that the tail of a reconnaissance plane in flight had been blown off by a Japanese bomb on the ground. Some clerk down the line would likely put it down as mechanical failure and leave it at that.

"How about that," he said. "I *thought* something was wrong."

"I'll say, buddy," a soldier replied. "It looks like the whole back half of your plane is gone!"

Then the pilot shook off the helping hands and walked nonchalantly away.

CHAPTER TWENTY

ONCE THE EXCITEMENT of the attack by the Japanese Zeros had died down, the men prepared to move out.

"That was just two lousy Japanese," Honcho pointed out. "There's a lot more where those came from, and we're gonna go find them."

"I think they already found us," Philly pointed out.

Whether or not the lieutenant heard, he chose to ignore Philly. "Patrol Easy, you're on point. I want my snipers out front. Keep an eye out for the Japanese. I'm sure they have more than a few surprises waiting for us up ahead."

Leaving Camp Downes behind, they moved out through the ruins of the Japanese defenses that they had cleared out during the previous day's fight. The bunkers still smoldered, stinking of burned gasoline from the flamethrowers. There were other smells, too, and not even the most desperate souvenir hunters wanted to find out what was in those bunkers.

No soldiers were left to hold Camp Downes—the hard-fought position was simply abandoned as the troops rolled on. While it might have been better to hold the ground, there simply weren't enough troops. The invasion force was spread that thin.

The division commander, General Bruce, had made it clear that he "wanted to pull our tail in behind us." In other words, his strategy was to keep his men moving forward and not concern himself with holding the territory that they moved through. The exception was the beachhead itself, where a rear-echelon support area included mechanics, clerks, supply staff, and even cooks to feed them all. Although essential in their own way, these men were not considered frontline combat troops.

The overall strategy meant that between the beachhead and the units converging on Ormoc, there were only splintered trees, empty foxholes, and enemy corpses.

The advance was far from easy. Snipers hid in spider holes, harassing the soldiers, then disappearing from view before popping up again once the infantry had passed to shoot them in the back.

One effective method to deal with the spider holes was to run a tank ahead of the advancing infantry, with a few soldiers clinging to the exterior of the tank. Although the attack by the Zeros had wiped out one of the Sherman tanks, leaving it a burning hulk on the perimeter of Camp Downes, two more of the so-called Satan tanks had been brought up from the beachhead.

Their flamethrowers were not much use against the Japanese hiding in the spider holes, many of which had makeshift covers made of woven mats covered with earth or moss. The covers not only disguised the hiding places, but were rather effective at blocking the flames.

What proved more effective was having a tank run right over any spider holes they spotted, forcing the enemy soldiers within to duck down. At the back end of the tank, soldiers fired down into the spider holes as soon as the tank cleared them. At that moment the Japanese often threw back the covers over their holes, ready to hurl hand grenades at the tank.

The soldiers had to be quick, firing at the first opportunity. Submachine guns proved especially useful. A Japanese soldier with a bolt-action Arisaka rifle was no match for an M3 "grease gun" spitting .45 slugs literally into his face.

It was gruesome work at such close range, when you were just a few feet away from the man you were shooting and could clearly see his face. But without it being done, the Japanese would pop up again to shoot the advancing soldiers in the back.

"I don't like this, not one bit," one soldier said.

The soldier beside him slapped home another thirty-round magazine into his M3. "Aw, quit your griping," he said. "As far as I'm concerned, it's just another day at the office."

"Doesn't mean I have to like it."

"Hey, it's them or us, buddy. Them or us. Don't you go forgetting that."

The tank rolled on, and the soldiers opened fire in its wake.

* * *

IN ADDITION to the network of cleverly hidden spider holes, individual units of Japanese troops had dug defensive positions into the forest and fields, waiting to throw themselves at the first American troops that appeared. These units varied in size from a handful of men who had survived the previous day's onslaught and chosen to make their last stand, to entire companies.

There wasn't really any strategic objective here other than to delay the American advance. None of the Japanese planned to survive, and they would take as many American soldiers with them as possible.

Deke and the others led the rest of Captain Merrick's men forward, wary of walking into one of these ambush attacks.

"We ought to get Egan's dog up here," Philly said quietly as he pressed forward with Deke and Danilo. "That mutt can sniff out the Japanese for us."

"Hush now," Deke muttered, aggravated by Philly's voice in his ear. His full concentration was on the landscape ahead.

Danilo moved forward a dozen feet to Deke's right, just as tense and wary. They could hear the whir and grind of the tanks, along with the occasional rattle of gunfire as the spider holes were cleared out—it was the sound of annihilation.

But the ground was climbing quickly, rougher and rocky, so that the tanks were becoming less effective. Rocky outcroppings and large trees halted their forward motion. The tanks moved to the flanks, where the ground was flatter, searching for a way around the ridge ahead. Deke and Danilo would have to be the unit's ears and eyes now.

Deke didn't mind. He was feeling much better today after the bout with fever had left him weakened. *I'm almost feeling like my old self,* he thought. In the distance, a Japanese sniper rifle cracked. *Yessiree, feeling better just in time to get myself killed.*

Despite the fact that a rough, unpaved road ascended the slope, the ridge ahead posed a serious obstacle. Adding to the difficulty was the fact that the ridge was almost without trees toward the peak as it emerged from the forest, like a full head of hair with a bald spot on top. Shouldn't they follow the lead of the tanks and go around it? After a brief confab of the officers and scouts, Captain Merrick made it clear that he wanted to climb the ridge.

"If anyone is going to take the high ground around here, it's going to be us, not the Japanese," he said. He turned to Lieutenant Steele. "I know I can count on you and your snipers to make that happen."

"Will do," Honcho said.

Deke was studying the ridge. "We best go ahead and take a look-see before everybody else," he said. "Ain't no telling what's on the other side."

"All right," Steele agreed. "Take Philly and Danilo with you."

"You got it, Honcho," Deke said.

Together, the three scouts scrambled up the steep slope, trying to be quiet and feeling exposed as the trees fell away into an open landscape of brush, shrubs, boulders, and clumps of kunai grass that offered perfect concealment for any enemy sniper. The road that they had been following seemed to run out of energy and ended at a terraced field that some farmer had carved out of the slope, whatever crop had grown there long since given over to weeds.

They bushwhacked their way forward. The ridgeline itself had been hit by naval artillery shells, leaving it looking like a badly plowed field. At the same time, all those shell holes created perfect defensive positions.

"I tell you what, I sure hope that the Japanese didn't get up here ahead of us," Deke whispered. "If they did, they can just throw rocks down on us."

Danilo grunted as if he understood and agreed, although Deke still hadn't puzzled out just how much English the Filipino understood. The Filipino guide's eyes never wavered from the landscape ahead, where any number of enemy troops might be hiding.

The navy had done a spectacular job of lobbing shells ahead of the Ormoc landing. As usual, it had been quite a show, but it didn't appear that the naval bombardment had done much more than blow hell out of this hilltop and surrounding patches of jungle. It would have been nice to have the support of those big guns now, but the fleet had pulled back out of sight of land for fear of Japanese planes and ships. The fleet didn't want to be penned in by the confines of the bay, where its ships couldn't maneuver effectively if they came under attack.

"What do you think, Deke?" Philly asked quietly as they made their way up the slope, ever so cautiously. Slowing their progress was the fact that all three of them were trying to keep their rifles at the ready, but they kept having to sling their weapons in order to scramble across the larger spills of boulders or up and down shell holes.

"I don't like it," Deke replied. "Something doesn't feel right, like I can almost feel a Japanese soldier holding his breath up ahead. But come on, we've got to check it out."

Their pace slowing, all three of them were breathing heavily by the time they reached the top of the ridge. It was almost knifelike up there, no more than just a few feet wide. The company would have to scramble across that ridge before coming down the slope on the opposite side, which by all appearances was equally as steep.

Considering that their orders were to keep moving rather than hold any ground, Deke wondered at the wisdom of crossing the ridge at all, other than the obvious necessity of making sure that there weren't any Japanese troops up there. So far they hadn't seen signs of any.

All three men lay on their bellies and edged forward. Philly seemed content to let Danilo take the lead, but Deke slithered faster until he came even with the Filipino.

The two of them peered down the opposite slope, and what they saw made them both freeze.

Philly was slightly behind Deke, who held up a hand, indicating for him to stop. Philly started to ask a question, but Deke signaled for him to be quiet.

Deke said a silent prayer that for once Philly would be able to keep his mouth shut. If he so much as asked anything in his usual loudmouth voice, which was better suited to hailing a taxi than to scouting within a stone's throw of the enemy, then all three of them were as good as dead.

Blinking through the sweat in his eyes, trying to ignore the hammering of his heart, Deke looked down at a trench dug into the slope a few feet beyond the ridgeline. He could see the helmets of what appeared to be an entire Japanese company dug into the slope. The soldiers all had fixed bayonets and looked ready to use them.

Deke held his breath. The soldiers were so close that Deke could almost have reached down and tapped the nearest soldier on the head.

They were so close that he could *smell* them, that slightly fishy, oily scent that seemed to hang around the Japanese. He knew from his boyhood spent hunting in the mountains that all game animals had a smell that clung to their lairs and bedding places—the muskiness of a fox den was different from the pungent smell where deer in rut bedded down, for example.

He wrinkled his nose, hoping the Japanese couldn't smell *him*. Whatever an American smelled like, he was sure it was oozing out of his sweaty pores.

It was only by some miracle that he and Danilo hadn't been spotted.

Deke and Danilo eased back from the ridgeline, still crawling on their bellies. Both men could move with the silence of a caterpillar, or maybe a snake in the grass, as they reverse-wriggled away from the Japanese. Finally they settled in beside Philly.

"What?" Philly had the good sense to whisper the question. "From the look on your face, it can't be good."

"Japs," said Deke. "Lots of Japs. There must be an entire company dug in just on the other side of that ridge, waiting for us, well, waiting for *somebody* to show themselves."

"I'll be damned," Philly said. "It's a good thing we took a look-see first."

"Yeah," Deke agreed. "The Japanese won't be happy that we've gone and spoiled all their fun. We'd better scoot back down this hill and warn the others. Whatever the hell you do, don't make any noise, or we'll have the whole damn bunch down on our heads."

"You got it," Philly said. "You know me. I'm quiet as a Caddy rolling on new tires."

They started to move down the slope toward the rest of the company waiting at the base. Philly hadn't gotten more than ten feet when his foot kicked a loose rock that tumbled down the slope. Ordinarily it would not have been very loud, but in the tense silence, the rolling stone sounded like thunder itself.

"Dammit!" From the look on his face, it was clear that Philly realized what he had done.

The Japanese would have their own scouts, and they'd be listening for just such telltale sounds. He and Danilo had managed to climb up and back without making any noise, but Philly had just blown it.

Deke knew what was coming and got his rifle ready. Sure enough, seconds later, a Japanese head popped above the ridge. The soldier spotted them, pointed, and started to shout something.

Deke got off a quick shot and worked the bolt, then sprang to his feet. The time had passed for stealth. Now it was all about speed.

"Let's get the hell outa here!"

Philly didn't need to be told twice. He started running down the slope, Deke racing after him. Danilo took the slope in a series of running leaps, agile as an old billy goat.

The steep slope made running downhill difficult, so the men were half falling as they made their way back toward the company. Philly was shouting and waving a warning as they ran, getting the attention of the others below.

Deke paused long enough to spin and fire again, just as several Japanese soldiers appeared over the ridge, coming after them. The Japanese could run only so fast, but their bullets could move a whole lot faster. Fortunately for the three American scouts, shooting downhill and hitting anything was notoriously difficult, as the Japanese soldiers were discovering.

Still, dust and dirt exploded all around them as bullets struck at their feet, ricocheting off rocks and careening through the stands of kunai grass. The wave of Japanese soldiers had launched themselves over the ridge and were sweeping down toward the American line, which had spread out to meet them.

The US troops were firing at will. Bullets filled the air along with the crackle of rifle fire. Very few men went down on either side for the simple reason that the GIs and the Japanese were in motion, trying to get into position, and the fire was not very accurate as a result. It was a firefight on the fly.

Deke reached the American lines and threw himself down, breathing hard. He brought his rifle to his shoulder but found it hard to keep it steady. The Japanese were spread out on the slope and made difficult targets. He could have fired, but he hated to waste ammunition, even if it was courtesy of the US government. Meanwhile, it was hard not to feel as if the whole damn Japanese company was headed down the slope right at him.

Private Frazier stepped up beside Deke and unleashed the full fury of his BAR at the oncoming Japanese. Several toppled, their bodies sliding down the slope out of sheer inertia.

With the company forming a defensive line at the base of the hill, the Japanese attack soon lost momentum. However, Deke's fears came true about the terrain being ideal for defense. Enemy soldiers used the shell holes, boulders, and even clumps of grass as cover; plus they had the advantage of occupying the hill. As if the situation wasn't bad enough, more Japanese came pouring over the ridge to add their numbers to the attack. Captain Merrick's company was already spread thin. There was real danger that they would be forced back toward Camp Downes, maybe even all the way to the beach.

"Dammit, what we need are reinforcements," Honcho observed.

But as far as they knew, there weren't any to be had.

Deke had finally caught his breath, so he lined up his sights on an enemy soldier, squeezed the trigger, watched the man go down through the scope, and then worked the bolt.

At the rate things were going, he was going to run out of ammo before he ran out of targets.

* * *

As soon as he'd seen what they were up against, Captain Merrick had been on the radio, requesting support before his company was overrun. He knew what the answer would be—that there wasn't anyone to send. But he had to try. It was a shame that the navy boys and their big guns weren't available—they would have made mincemeat out of the Japanese on the slope.

Much to Merrick's surprise, division headquarters informed him that reinforcements were being sent.

He got off the radio, feeling a little incredulous. The question was, What reinforcements could headquarters possibly be sending?

They would find out soon enough. Until then they had to stand firm against the Japanese. He'd be damned if his company would give up an inch of ground.

For a change, the Japanese were not launching any pointless banzai attacks. Instead, they were steadily advancing down the slope, using the natural cover to fire from. The Japanese had sometimes gotten the reputation of being like bowling pins for being easy to mow down. This was not the case today. Whoever the commander was, he knew his business. Merrick had his hands full.

His own men were not dug in and thus were more exposed. They kept up a steady fire, but the situation was getting desperate.

Doc Harmon had moved out with the company that morning, leaving the wounded with his assistants. The surgeon had wanted to be available to help the wounded at the upcoming fight for Ormoc. Merrick was glad to have him come along, considering that they were short on medics and medical supplies. The situation was so desperate that Doc Harmon had put his medical equipment aside and picked up a rifle, which he was firing steadily at the Japanese.

They would hold on as long as they could. They had to.

In the distance, he heard the rumble of trucks coming in a hurry up the jungle road. He looked behind him, and his heart sank. There were trucks coming up the road, all right, but the trucks were clearly Japanese—not the familiar Studebakers.

The radioman had seen them too. "Sir?" he said, a nervous catch in his voice.

But then Merrick caught sight of the stars that had been hastily painted on the vehicles and realized that these must be more of the Japanese trucks that had been captured already in the push toward Ormoc.

"Those belong to us, son," the captain told the radioman. "If those really are reinforcements, Christmas just came early."

CHAPTER TWENTY-ONE

IF CAPTAIN MERRICK had known just who these reinforcements were, he might have been slightly less enthusiastic.

But beggars can't be choosers. The entire division was short handed. Low on men and with no hope of getting additional troops across a sea that was fraught with enemy ships and planes, Division Commander General Bruce had been forced to make do with whatever men remained in the beach area.

To call it the rear echelon wasn't exactly accurate, because this implied an area that was safely behind the front lines. Technically, the front lines were still just a few hundred feet from the beach landing area.

Consequently, all the support staff had been rounded up. This included mechanics and supply staff, clerks and cooks. These men had important jobs—no army was going to run with broken-down tanks and Jeeps, empty bellies, or even without paperwork, for that matter.

While their military role might be different, it was also true that you weren't going to meet any tougher soldiers than mechanics and supply sergeants. They were already unsung heroes.

However, they were not frontline combat troops. The actual fighting was usually left to soldiers like the men in Captain Merrick's company. Much to their surprise, these rear-echelon men had been told that they were headed for the front lines.

Loaded onto the captured Japanese trucks, they had been given whatever weapons were available. Technically, every man in the division was a potential combat soldier, but it had been a long time since some of these men had handled a weapon, much less fired one. From the sounds of the firing in the not-so-far distance, it sounded as if they were going to have plenty of opportunity to get reacquainted with the use of their rifles.

Looking dazed, these men jumped down from the trucks to reinforce the beleaguered company.

Merrick was also taken aback when he saw that one or two of the relief troops still wore the aprons they'd had on back in the mess area, as if they had been rounded up in the middle of slinging hash. But what he really cared about was that these were men with rifles. A cook could still shoot.

He shouted orders, getting them into position.

* * *

ONE OF THE newly arrived soldiers was Private Dean Rafferty, a clerk whose chief skill was that he could accurately type sixty words a minute on his military-issue manual typewriter. Anyone who had ever tried to type on one of those clanking beasts would realize that this was no small feat. Clearly Private Rafferty had fingers like steel claws.

Still, Rafferty was on the scrawny side, being five foot six and weighing 125 pounds soaking wet. He was so skinny that it looked like he might fall between the typewriter keys if he wasn't careful. He'd barely made it through boot camp. His drill sergeant had never once used his actual name, but had dubbed him "Pencil Neck." It was probably no wonder that he had quickly been designated as a clerk. Nobody seemed to think he would get very far marching with a rifle and a fully loaded haversack.

Watching the battle-worn soldiers trudging through camp, young Rafferty had often wondered what it must be like to experience combat. He had even daydreamed now and then of leading a charge, or single-handedly wiping out a nest of Japanese. However, the headquarters tent back on the beach was as close as he'd come to the sights and sounds of battle —until now.

Nearly tumbling out of the truck that had rushed reinforcements to the front line, he had stumbled around in confusion until he found himself shoved into position, literally landing on the ground next to a tough-looking soldier with bad scars on one side of his face.

Holy cow, what happened to him?

The soldier gave him a glance out of the corner of his eye, a look so cold that Rafferty felt his blood chill a bit despite the tropical heat. The soldier went back to firing a rifle with a telescopic sight. *A sniper, then.*

The noise of battle was deafening and confusing, but Rafferty figured out what he was supposed to do fairly quickly, helped by the fact that an officer with an eye patch was shouting, "Shoot the bastards!"

Another clerk who'd been brought up from the beach suddenly slumped over, shot through the head. Too late for that poor soldier, the officer added further instructions, "Dammit, keep your heads down while you're at it!"

Rafferty focused on the stretch of land in front of him. He was amazed to see actual Japanese soldiers on the hillside. The officer had reminded him that his job was to shoot at them. The enemy soldiers were scurrying from rocks to clumps of bushes, running low, making difficult targets.

He fired off a shot that went wide. He tried again, but in his nervousness he ended up yanking on the trigger before he had even picked out a target. He'd forgotten to put the rifle butt tight against his shoulder, so that each time he fired, the stock leaped back and kicked him. His shoulder soon ached, and he felt like he'd been punched in the jaw.

His own rifle was beating him up worse than the Japanese.

* * *

During a pause while reloading, Deke glanced at the scrawny soldier beside him. It looked like he was trying to wrestle with the rifle as much as shoot it. Deke shook his head. Where did they find these dumb bastards?

He wasn't sure why, but he took pity on him. Judging by the soldier's clean uniform, he was not used to frontline duties, probably a clerk. Something safe back at HQ. The kind of fella who typed up long lists of soldiers killed in action, confident in the fact that his own name wouldn't be on that list anytime soon. All that had changed with the Japanese advance threatening to overrun the beachhead.

Deke had to give him credit. This clerk was fighting as best as he could against the oncoming Japanese. He just couldn't shoot that rifle worth a damn.

"That ain't a typewriter," Deke growled. "Put that rifle butt snug against your shoulder. Squeeze the trigger. Just like you were taught in basic training."

The clerk looked at him, fear mixed with determination in his eyes as he nodded and did as he was told. The next three shots were better—at any rate, he didn't appear to be wrestling with his rifle anymore. Whether or not he had hit anything remained to be seen, but at least he was sending bullets in the direction of the enemy with enough accuracy to make them keep their heads down, instead of all his shots going wide.

"Keep at it," Deke instructed him. "Aim and fire. If you miss one, shoot at him again. If you don't, he'll just shoot at you."

The clerk didn't respond, but fired two more shots. The stripper clip ejected, and the soldier fumbled with the fresh clip of rounds for the M1.

"Give it here a minute," Deke said. Deftly, he showed the clerk how to reload the weapon, then handed it back. "Don't slam your thumb in there. Think you can do that yourself next time?"

"Yeah, I think so."

"All right, then. Do some good with that."

Up and down the line, similar scenes were playing out as men who didn't normally handle weapons were getting reacquainted with the M1. More than a few got their thumbs slammed by the action as they tried to reload, a common hazard that often resulted in a swollen and bruised thumb, known as "M1 thumb." However, with so much enemy lead flying at them, a mashed thumb was the least of their worries.

Mashed thumbs or not, the influx of fresh men began making a difference, bolstering the number of defenders on the line.

The firing continued hot and heavy, neither side willing to pull back and admit defeat. It had become a grudge match.

"Hey, Charlie!" shouted one of the Japanese, hidden in a pile of rocks no more than fifty feet from the American line. "We kill you now!"

"To hell with that!" shouted an outraged Private Frazier, who poured fire from his BAR at the rocks. Dirt and bits of rock flew in every direction. It was hard to say whether he'd gotten the enemy soldier, but the flurry of lead had certainly shut him up.

Setting aside the clerks and other support staff, the backbone of the defense was made up of veteran soldiers. For the past few months, they had lived and breathed combat. They knew their M1 rifles and other weapons better than they knew the contours of their wives and girlfriends. The combat veterans were tough and stubborn, even when the Japanese were equally so.

The Japanese made one last, mad push down the hill. The US line had been holding steady and hadn't appeared in danger of being overrun—but this renewed attack made it waver and buckle, similar to a sail billowing in a strong wind.

Handfuls of attackers reached the US line, screaming their battle cries, resulting in hand-to-hand combat. Most of the Japanese had already fixed bayonets, which was a popular tactic. The idea was to rush in close with the Americans, overwhelming their defenses. On the US side, knives were drawn. Rifles on both sides were fired from the hip, no aiming necessary.

The supply staff and mechanics proved to be an ace up the Americans' sleeve, because they were excellent brawlers. Maybe operation of the M1 gave them some trouble, but they understood well enough how to smash the butt into the skull of an enemy infantryman. The tactic being used by one big sergeant was simply to grab the enemy soldier's rifle and twist it away, then punch the man in the face.

But as fast as they dealt with the Japanese, more appeared. Once again, the outcome of the battle balanced on a knife's edge.

Captain Merrick came running at a crouch and slid into position beside Deke, like he was sliding into home plate. A burst of tracer fire stitched the air that his body had occupied just an instant before.

"Deke, everybody says how you're a great shot, so don't let

me down now. You see that Japanese officer near the top of the ridge? I've been watching him through my binoculars. The son of a bitch must lead a charmed life. He's up there directing the whole damn attack. I need you to take him out."

"All right," Deke said.

"He's pretty far away," Merrick said doubtfully.

"He ain't that far. Not as far as Japan, anyhow. As long as I can see him, I can hit him," Deke said, then looked around for Philly, who was twenty feet away, busy dealing with a Japanese soldier who had run close to their position. He looked around some more and his gaze settled on the skinny clerk. "Soldier, I need you to cover our asses. Don't let any Japanese run up and stick us with a bayonet. The captain here is gonna watch through those binoculars of his and tell me how to correct my aim if I miss."

"You got it."

Deke had managed to tell Captain Merrick what to do without giving him orders. The captain was now watching the ridge intently through his binoculars.

Deke's telescopic sight was not as powerful, but he could still see the officer up there. The man held a stick and was pointing it here and there, directing the additional soldiers who crossed the ridge. He appeared to be shouting orders. From his vantage point on high ground, the Japanese officer could evidently see where the US line was weakest and send his fresh troops to attack.

Go on and yap, little dog, Deke thought. *You won't be yappin' long.*

Deke lined up the crosshairs on the Japanese officer. The tendency when firing uphill was to aim too high, which Deke compensated for. There was a little wind off the ocean, so he adjusted his aim accordingly.

Deke couldn't have explained how he knew where to aim. He just did it out of natural instinct. It was no different from shooting at a big buck up on a ridgeline back home. A buck that thought he was safe up there, beyond the reach of any two-legged hunter.

The target had ceased being a person in Deke's mind. He was simply the prey, and Deke was the hunter.

His concentration was interrupted as a bullet whipped past. He'd even heard the crack of a rifle, much too close for comfort. Startled, he pulled his eye away from the scope, losing track of the target. He refocused on a patch of ground about fifty feet away, where a Japanese soldier was running at him, bayonet leveled and screaming his fool head off.

"You still with me?" he asked the scrawny clerk. "Now would be a good time to start shooting."

"On it," came the reply. There were three quick shots off to his right, and the attacker went down.

"Don't let him get so close next time," Deke said.

He turned his attention back to the rifle, putting his eye back to the scope. The ridgeline sprang closer. There was the Japanese officer, pointing his stick downhill, right at the American line and shouting something that needed no translation. Another few minutes and there wouldn't be any American line.

The officer had cleverly spaced out his men rather than commit them in a single attack that could have been wiped out with a well-placed machine gun. Pure and simple, his plan was to grind them down.

Deke lined up the sights on the Japanese officer, once again doing the mental calculations that placed the crosshairs slightly above the man and to the right.

Off to one side, he heard the skinny clerk's rifle fire two rapid shots. He must have stopped another attacker in his tracks.

This time, there was no interruption as Deke squeezed the trigger.

He missed.

He hadn't seen where his bullet had gone, but the man was still standing. It didn't help that the officer kept moving around.

Quickly, Deke worked the bolt and ejected the spent shell, which flickered away in the sunlight. A little whiff of smoke came out, followed by the refreshing acrid smell of burned gunpowder; then the smooth brass casing of a fresh round slipped into the chamber.

He had almost forgotten that Captain Merrick was watching through the binoculars.

"Come on, take out that son of a bitch," Merrick said, a sense of urgency in his voice, which didn't help Deke feel any calmer. The captain added, "You hit a little to the left."

The second part was more helpful, considering that Deke hadn't seen where his bullet had gone. Deke didn't respond, already concentrating on his next shot, his eye glued to the round disk of glass on the telescopic sight. For Deke, the battlefield had shrunk to just the few feet of the slope visible through the scope, and he shut out everything else.

He let the crosshairs hover even more to the right, aiming at thin air, then squeezed the trigger.

Through the scope, he saw the Japanese officer crumple to the ground, his lifeless body sliding a few feet down the slope.

"You got him!" Captain Merrick cried, still watching through the binoculars. What appeared to be a junior officer had run to the fallen officer and crouched over him.

Deke was still hunched over the rifle, so he shot the junior officer for good measure.

Merrick finally lowered the binoculars and stared over at Deke, clearly impressed. "I could have taken potshots at that officer all day and not even have come close. I've got to say, you are pretty good with that rifle, son."

Deke worked the bolt. "Who do you want me to shoot next?"

"Any son of a bitch in a Japanese uniform, that's who."

Having lost the officer managing the attack, the Japanese assault began to fall apart. Some Japanese even began to retreat back up the slope, which they wouldn't have dared to do if the officer had still been up there with his swagger stick.

The icing on the cake came when the soldiers heard the familiar rumble of clanking tracks and roaring engines. The tanks had returned, having given up on their mission of trying to go around the ridge. Long stretches of rice paddies had blocked their advance, with the heavy tanks unable to cross the water-filled fields.

The two Satan tanks opened fire on the slope covered with Japanese forces. Their main guns punched new holes in the rocky slope.

A few soldiers even cheered.

A brave Japanese soldier ran right at the tanks, brandishing hand grenades in both hands as if he single-handedly intended to take them out with nothing more than his frenzy and the grenades. He was mowed down by a machine gun before he'd gotten nearly close enough to hurl the grenades.

Once the tanks were within range, they unleashed the fury of their flamethrowers. The flames licked at clumps of grass and brush that had provided concealment for the Japanese. Enemy soldiers were forced to run, some of them on fire as the jellied gasoline clung to them. The ones who had escaped the flames were cut down by machine guns and rifle fire.

It was all too clear that the back of the Japanese assault had been broken. The remaining troops began to withdraw back up the slope, at first in groups of two or three, and then by entire patrols.

Captain Merrick gave the order to advance, and men began

racing up the slope, herding the Japanese before them like a pack of frightened sheep chased by demented shepherds. The loudest and wildest of the pursuers turned out to be some of the rear-echelon troops, shouting like banshees and waving their rifles like clubs as they went after the enemy.

The retreating Japanese forces ran past the body of their fallen officer without a second glance, then crossed over the ridge and disappeared.

The battle had finally been won. The beachhead was safe for now. In a sense, the fight had been an important turning point in that it was now unlikely that the Japanese would mount another meaningful offensive. Their tactics now would be purely defensive.

Exhausted and bloodied though they were, the soldiers would push on past the ridge to bring the fight to the Japanese dug in at Ormoc. The airfield there still needed to be captured.

Patrol Easy, Deke included, had not joined in the chase. They were content to hang back and save their energy for the next fight, which wouldn't be long in coming. Deke looked around and saw Honcho and Yoshio in the distance, along with Rodeo, Alphabet, and Philly.

Only Private Egan and Thor weren't there—they had joined the hunt for Japanese who had opted not to run, but who were trying to hide on the hillside. Thor's sharp nose rooted them out, and the crack of a rifle announced the quarry's end. No prisoners were being taken.

As was increasingly becoming the case in the Pacific, the fighting felt personal. Killing any Japanese they found was more about revenge than it was about military necessity. Such were the vicissitudes of war.

After all, there were a handful of bodies scattered around the American line. Good American boys who wouldn't be going home. Their buddies were taking out their anger on the Japanese survivors. Neither Captain Merrick nor Honcho made any effort to put an end to the killing.

Deke took note of the skinny clerk still hovering nearby. He nodded at him and said, "That was some good shooting, kid."

Private Rafferty grinned a bit sheepishly, but with evident pride. He hadn't come through the fight completely unscathed, however. Sure enough, he had managed to mash his thumb in the action of the M1, the painful M1 thumb, but had kept fighting. From the looks of it, he had managed to get his thumb caught in the slamming action more than once. The thumb was swollen and bloody.

Deke noticed and said, "Let me see that hand a minute." He used a scrap of cloth to bind it up. "Good as new."

"Aw, why are you even bothering with him, Deke?" Philly wanted to know. "He's just a clerk. How's he gonna type with his thumb wrapped up like that?"

"Oh, I don't know about that. We might just make a soldier out of him yet."

His face was now grimy with dirt and blackened by gun smoke. The uniform that had been relatively clean that morning as he'd performed his clerical duties beneath a tarp erected on the beach was now muddy, torn at the knee, and soaked through with sweat.

Deke's words had summed it up perfectly. You could almost see the man swelling up with the kind of pride that was hard earned. It didn't matter how big he was or what his job in the army had been or what he would go back to once the Japanese were contained, for above all things, army clerk Rafferty was now a combat veteran.

CHAPTER TWENTY-TWO

THE AFTERMATH of that combat was evident on the hillside. It wasn't pretty. In places the earth was stained red, so savage had the fighting been. Already a few soldiers were calling it the Battle of Bloody Ridge. The name quickly caught on.

Teams of GIs had retrieved their own dead and wounded, but no one was going to clear away the enemy dead.

And there were a lot of them.

"I'll be damned," Deke said, looking across the slope. In the heat of battle, his fight had been limited to what he could see through his scope. Now he took in the overall panorama of the battlefield. A few fires still burned where the flamethrowers had touched. But what really caught his attention were the large numbers of corpses. "That's a lot of dead Japanese."

"What I want to know is, When the hell are they going to run out of soldiers?" Philly wondered.

"They didn't run out today, and I reckon they won't run out tomorrow," Deke said.

"The bastards would've kept coming if it hadn't been for the tanks."

"Saved our bacon," Deke agreed.

Philly grunted. "And fried theirs," he said, nodding at a black-ened enemy corpse.

Nobody liked to talk about it out loud, but there was some-thing horrible about a flamethrower. Bullets, knives, and bayo-nets were bad enough. A flamethrower was the stuff of nightmares, the war of the future.

Deke leaned over and tried to spit but came up empty, his mouth too dry. The tangy smell of gunpowder still filled his nostrils.

After being laid low by that fever, he had rallied enough to do some good in the fight. He had managed to shoot that Japanese officer, after all.

But he didn't feel quite right. He could feel sickness trying to get back in, like some critter gnawing at the edges of a door. A feverish tremor went through him now and again. Deke did his best to ignore it. He had been warned that malaria was like that, coming and going in fits and starts.

Victory at Bloody Ridge felt bittersweet. They had won the fight against the Japanese, but a glance at the wounded lined up on their stretchers showed that the price had been steep. Some of the men had their faces covered, having lost their lives on this nameless ridge. Covering the faces of the dead, even with nothing more than a muddy and bloodstained blanket, was the least that they could do.

After the firefight, many of the survivors slumped down on the ground, exhausted. Adrenaline had coursed through their veins, fueling the fight-or-flight response that stretched back to the dawn of humanity, when the first humans had tangled with lions or maybe a saber-toothed tiger. In this case their only choice had been to fight.

Their bodies had burned through that evolutionary jet fuel, leaving them feeling hollowed out and spent, as if they had just run a marathon. Mixed with the exhaustion was a euphoria at still being alive.

A few men managed to get food into themselves. They craved anything sweet, even wolfing down the tropical chocolate bars that had the consistency of chalk. Others sat quietly, too dazed for words, smoking cigarettes, their hands shaking.

The rear-echelon troops who had plugged the gap and experienced their first real combat felt the most dazed of all, but also proud.

However, there would be no resting on their laurels. The newly blooded soldiers weren't being given a chance to process what they had just been through, not with more fighting ahead.

"We're moving out!" shouted Lieutenant Steele, once again reluctantly thrust into a command position. The fight at Bloody Ridge had left another lieutenant under one of those blankets. That left the company with just two officers. Honcho had found himself second in command as Captain Merrick's company prepared for the final push toward Ormoc.

"But I was just getting comfortable, Honcho," Philly complained, pushing himself up from where he had sprawled on a patch of soft ground. "How about letting us rest for a while?"

"Get your ass up and moving," Honcho snapped, sounding uncharacteristically short tempered. "That's an order, goddammit."

Surprised, Philly hurried to stand up. "Yes, sir."

Nearby, the others got to their feet as well and prepared to move out. They could see that this wasn't the laid-back Honcho who had commanded their sniper squad. He certainly commanded respect, but he had never appeared angry before —until now.

The lieutenant stalked away and shouted at other men who were slow to get to their feet.

"Gee, I wonder what got into his craw?" Philly wondered aloud—once the lieutenant was safely out of earshot.

"Yep, he's crankier than a moonshiner with a hole in his still," Deke agreed. It was clear that Honcho was stretched thin, and his customary patience with Philly's banter had finally snapped. "I wouldn't go poking at him, if I were you."

Philly snorted. "No worries there. Where the hell are we going, anyhow? I hope it's not far. Maybe we can hitch a ride on one of those captured Japanese trucks, or even better, a tank."

"I don't think we're goin' anywhere good. We cleared those Japanese off the ridge, so our next dance is gonna be in Ormoc, sure as an egg-suckin' dog finds the henhouse."

They glanced hopefully in the direction of the trucks, the captured Japanese vehicles painted with the lopsided US stars. There was a wide road ahead that would have meant a smooth ride to Ormoc. However, the trucks were being loaded with the wounded, pointed in the opposite direction, apparently for transport back to the beach. Maybe word had gone out that the navy was ferrying the wounded to the hospital ships once again.

They could see Doc Harmon directing the effort, checking each man as he did so. Some were being left behind on the ground, too badly wounded to transport. It would be only a matter of time before there was a grimy blanket covering their faces, to keep off the flies and the heat of the sun.

Philly sighed. "Looks like we're walking."

The men were ordered to assemble at the base of the ridge, in the road that had formed their line during the battle. The sun beat down, and men jostled to get under what little shade was offered by the roadside trees.

Once again they donned their battered helmets and loaded up on ammunition. More C rations were handed around and stuffed into haversacks. Some men slung their rifles, which were starting to feel heavy, but others preferred the reassurance of having a fully loaded M1 in their hands.

They were a motley crew, these fighting soldiers, their fatigues alternately filthy with mud or streaked with white from the soaking in the salt water when they had landed on Leyte. But this was no dress parade. This was setting out to finish the job of liberating Ormoc. These men meant business, and there was no doubt that they looked the part.

* * *

WITH THE JAPANESE finally pushed off the ridge, the road toward Ormoc had been opened. Patrol Easy followed the road through the fields and forest, taking point ahead of the rest of the company.

"I'm waiting for the other shoe to drop," Philly whispered, nervously scanning the surrounding landscape for any sign of the enemy.

"I hate to tell you this, Philly, but it ain't gonna be a shoe that drops. It's gonna be a boot," Deke said. "And that boot ain't gonna drop. No, sir. It's gonna kick us in the ass. Keep your eyes open."

"What the hell do you think I'm doing? I wasn't planning on taking a nap."

Like his buddy, Deke moved cautiously, alert for any sign of an ambush. Despite the scene of destruction that they had left behind, they had not completely wiped out the Japanese back on the ridge, so the question was, Where had the enemy gone?

Ideally, Deke thought, the enemy would have jumped in the ocean and swum all the way back to Japan, but that was wishful thinking.

If the enemy wasn't out here somewhere waiting for them,

then they had fallen back to Ormoc and would be waiting for them there. Neither prospect was particularly appealing.

Their battered company wasn't the only one moving into position. Most of the entire division was converging on Ormoc. In the distance, when there were breaks in the trees, revealing a vista of open rice paddies, Deke could see another unit following a path parallel to their own. Deke had waved at them, making sure that they had seen *him*, in order to avoid any surprises down the road.

There had been more than one situation where soldiers had been killed by friendly fire, which was easy enough in the confusion of the jungle landscape.

The day's heat bore down, the air feeling heavier by the moment. Sweat slicked the men's faces, rolled down the backs of their necks, soaked their uniforms. It was almost enough to make them wish for another beach to storm, just for the chance to cool off in the surf.

Like a pot of old stew simmering on the back of a hot stove, Deke had felt troublesome waves of the fever that had afflicted him earlier returning. At first he had tried to ignore it. Then he had stumbled now and again, starting to feel dizzy.

Danilo had given him a knowing, concerned look. The Filipino guide was more than aware of the ebb and flow of the various jungle fevers. They receded like the tide and then came racing back in.

"Are you all right?" Philly asked, after Deke stumbled for a second time.

"Just tired, is all."

"If you say so. I can tell Doc Harmon about it. Maybe he's got some pills to fix you right up."

Deke might have argued that this was a bad idea, that the surgeon might put him in a truck with the other wounded and send him back to the beach, but he was feeling too tired to argue.

It was true that their numbers had been bolstered by the cooks, truck drivers, and mechanics who had not returned to their field kitchens and maintenance yards but had been set on the road to Ormoc. For the fight at Ormoc, where the Japanese planned to make a stand in the streets, the division was going to need every man it had to be carrying a rifle.

They followed the road toward the city, occasionally passing detritus left behind by the retreating Japanese, everything from broken crates to discarded gas masks and an occasional dented canteen. Once or twice they passed a wounded soldier who had succumbed and whose body had been left behind. The GIs studied the bodies with curiosity, hoping for some clue to the enemy. But dead men told no tales. The GIs trudged on down the road.

In places the road ran through wide rice paddies, the sun sparkling off the water that lay in the flooded fields. They passed a few small houses that looked abandoned and forlorn. There was no sign of the Japanese.

* * *

ORMOC WAS a place that few Americans had heard of before late 1944, and it was a name that few would remember in the intervening years, with the exception of those who had been there and perhaps lost a buddy in the street fighting or during combat with Japanese holdouts in the surrounding jungle.

The name itself had come from "Ogmok" in the old Visayan language—a precursor to the modern Tagalog spoken by Filipinos—from a word that meant "low-lying place." The name hinted at the abundant rice fields on the city's outskirts.

Perhaps it was not an auspicious name, but the sprawling,

small city always had been a busy port, going back centuries, so it had a worldliness to it that belied its remote location.

Stretching back centuries, Ormoc had been a seaside trading village. The Spanish had arrived in 1595 but had never seemed to put their stamp on the place, as they had in larger towns. Ormoc looked and felt very much Filipino.

Given this history of watching the world come and go, there wasn't much that the people of Ormoc hadn't seen, and not much surprised them.

Yet it remained a welcoming place. The seaside port had the easy, languid feel of many tropical towns. There was an innocence about the city when the Japanese were out of sight and the city wasn't under threat of imminent attack. It was rare to see a man in a suit. Younger teenage boys rarely wore anything more than shorts, and the girls went about barefoot in colorful skirts.

You might say that Ormoc was busy but not ambitious. Few buildings were more than two stories high, and judging from the humble nature of even these taller buildings, there was very little wealth in the town. It didn't help that the war had squeezed dry what little commerce there was, wringing out the local businesses like a sweaty bandanna.

Although the town was pleasant and friendly, it had a ramshackle appearance and made no effort at order or neatness. Even the houses along the waterfront, with its beautiful view of the bay, looked as if they had survived one typhoon too many. These buildings near the waterfront tended to be the largest structures in town.

The streets were winding, unpaved, passing between tightly packed small houses covered in stucco and with tin roofs. Many of the houses occupied miniature compounds with fences or even walls around the cramped yards. Muddy brown chickens scratched in the dirt, and friendly, tan-colored dogs wandered everywhere.

Despite the poverty and oppression by the occupiers, the residents had not lost their love of plants. Entire fronts of houses were taken up with rows of potted plants, sometimes stacked on rickety wooden shelves several rows high. Lush greenery grew in every yard and untended corner, giving the town the appearance of being one sprawling garden. All in all, Ormoc was a town that a Western visitor found easy to love—as long as there weren't any bullets flying.

Considering that the Japanese preferred everything to be neat and tidy, which was the opposite inclination of the average Ormoc resident, it was easy to see how from their perspective the occupants of the city might be inferior. The residents had been treated accordingly.

To that end, an entire element of the port city's population was absent. The older boys and men had long since been rounded up to work as slave labor on the Japanese defensive projects, such as the bunkers at Ipil. Without any heavy equipment, most of the work had been done with buckets and shovels, requiring backbreaking effort in the tropical heat. There was little food or rest.

The Japanese were harsh taskmasters. Treated cruelly, given little to eat and forced to work long hours, many of these Filipinos would never return home.

With a battle imminent, it was fortunate that most of the residents had fled. Where they had gone was anybody's guess, but they had likely hidden in the surrounding forests and rice paddies.

It was only the Japanese who now occupied Ormoc, and they had turned the entire city into a fortress. Sandbags had been placed around the sturdier stucco houses, which now bristled with machine guns. Soldiers had dug trenches at key crossroads and corners, enabling them to command long fields of fire along the city streets.

A few of the bunkers even contained field artillery or antiaircraft guns that had been turned from the skies to the streets to deal with any tanks that appeared.

The tropical buildings typically did not have cellars or basements, but soldiers had created dugouts in the crawl spaces, enabling them to shoot from beneath.

Snipers hid themselves in the upper floors of shops and houses. With some water and a few rations, they waited patiently for the arrival of the Americans.

All in all, capturing Ormoc wasn't going to be easy.

Ultimately, it was a fight that the Japanese must have known that they could not win, but they were prepared to sacrifice themselves and the city itself if it meant slowing down the US advance.

* * *

IN A SENSE, the fight taking place at Ormoc was a microcosm of the Japanese situation. All around the Pacific, the noose was tightening around the Japanese. The strands of the web that held their sprawling empire together were snapping, one by one.

Had the Japanese really believed that they could command an empire that stretched across such a vast expanse? True, Japan was a powerful and determined nation, but it lacked the necessary natural resources to maintain its war machine—chiefly rubber and oil. Its army and navy operated independent of one another, and joint operations were undertaken more in a spirit of grudging cooperation than under a combined command structure. It was no way to fight a world war—but no one seemed to have told that to the Japanese.

Finally, their attack on the United States at Pearl Harbor seemed to have been an act of supreme hubris. They had provoked a powerful nation in the worst way possible. Admiral

Yamamoto had said it best, saying that Japan had awoken a sleeping giant.

The people of the United States had willingly joined forces with the beleaguered nations of Europe to fight Nazi Germany. In the view of the US government, the war in Europe came first. For all Germany's aggression in Europe, Nazi forces had never attacked the US outright—although they had certainly schemed to do so. Sure, Americans fought Nazi Germany because it was a job that needed to be done.

But the Japanese had attacked in the most despicable way possible. In the minds of many, the attack on sleepy Pearl Harbor seemed more like an act of murder than an act of war. Consequently, many Americans felt a special enmity toward the Japanese that had carried over to the island battlefields across the Pacific.

They may have found themselves increasingly surrounded, but the Japanese only fought harder. Their backs were to the wall. Despite tremendous losses, they provided a seemingly endless supply of soldiers and planes and ships. Fewer each day, perhaps, but still a threat.

Although it was far beyond the pay grade of the average soldier, plans were already being made at the highest levels for the eventual assault on the Japanese home islands. Iwo Jima, the smaller Ryukyu islands, and then Okinawa would be in the crosshairs. Losses promised to be heavy.

No one liked to talk about it, but after those large stepping stones would come the attack on Japan itself. Knowing the way the Japanese fought so desperately, the combat losses promised to be almost incalculable. Would the American public be able to stomach such losses? These were the sort of thoughts that kept men like Douglas MacArthur and the president, FDR, awake at night.

But if the military planners remained two steps ahead, the

troops on the ground still needed to deal with the business before them. Ormoc and Leyte itself could not be left in Japanese hands.

In Ormoc, there had been fewer blatant atrocities than in other population centers in the Philippines. Instead, the Japanese had primarily controlled the population by threatening to starve them and by abducting their men and boys as slave labor. If they behaved, there were vague promises that their men might be returned.

The vast rice fields in the region were quite productive. Most food production had been channeled to feed the Japanese military, with whatever the farmers produced being taken from them.

If local officials did not cooperate, the supply of rice to the civilian population would be cut off. The threat of famine made a very effective whip.

Although local officials gave the appearance of collaborating with the Japanese, they also walked a dangerous tightrope by also staying in communication with guerrilla forces. It was a dangerous game that they played with the *Kempeitai*—the Japanese military police, who surely suspected what the local officials were up to and used all the informants at their disposal to catch them in the act.

It didn't help matters that the *Kempeitai* was itself corrupt, with everyone from the commander on down working to fill his own pockets with bribes. In addition to black market foodstuffs, there were the profits from brothels and bars to consider. All in all, occupied Ormoc was a tangled web, indeed.

* * *

GIVEN THIS TABLEAU OF MISERY, the people of Ormoc had cheered when news arrived of the US landing on the other side of the island. But now the war had arrived within the city itself, with all its destructive force. There would be a price to pay for liberation.

The sun was still high in the sky when the first US troops crept cautiously down the empty streets. The Japanese held their fire, letting the enemy get well within firing range.

Their fingers on their triggers, they waited.

Deke, Philly, Yoshio, and Danilo were among the first of those soldiers entering the city. Right behind them came Honcho and a handful of the rear-echelon troops who had been pressed into service, mixed with veterans from Captain Merrick's company.

The more inexperienced men were doing their best to follow Honcho's orders and imitate the combat men who scurried from one building to another, covering one another in the process.

"It's awfully damn quiet," Philly whispered to no one in particular. "I don't like it."

"Don't you worry your pretty head," Deke said. "I reckon it's about to get real noisy around here."

CHAPTER TWENTY-THREE

THE AMERICANS ADVANCED into the city, moving house by house, street by street. Still, the Japanese did not open fire. The deserted streets seemed to be holding their breath.

Deke had to admit that Philly was right about one thing. The advance into Ormoc took place in an almost eerie quiet, punctuated only by the crackle and pop of flames. Several fires burned in town as the result of the heavy artillery bombardment that had preceded the advance.

Following the usual strategy, the bombardment had been intended to soften up the Japanese defenses. The hope was that any civilians who remained in the port city had found shelter.

While it was true that most civilians had fled, it was always the poorest, the youngest, and the oldest who got left behind. The shacks built of concrete block, scrap wood, and corrugated metal looked even more flimsy in the face of advancing troops and armor. Where artillery shells had rained down, the houses had been reduced to piles of rubble.

Poor bastards, Deke thought. The people here clearly didn't have much.

The destruction might have been even worse except for the fact that the bombardment effort had relied on the division's own artillery and whatever aircraft could be sent to aid the fight.

The navy guns that usually handled the job—and surely would have absolutely leveled the town—remained far out to sea to avoid the Japanese planes that still managed to launch attacks from small airfields on Leyte.

Perhaps the Japanese planes no longer appeared in the numbers that they had, but the navy had a healthy fear of the new kamikaze strategy. Turning planes into bombs was a weapon that was hard to understand and difficult to defend against, so it was best to remain farther out to sea for now.

Despite the bombardment, the division's big guns wouldn't be enough on their own. Sacking Ormoc was a job that would have to be done on foot, street by street, house by house. It would be similar to the fight they had experienced in Palo on the other side of Leyte, but that had been more of a running battle through the streets.

At Palo, the Japanese had even pushed a wall of refugees ahead of them, using the Filipinos as human shields. Here the enemy had dug in and prepared for them. Thankfully, no civilians remained in sight, so it was unlikely that the events of Palo would be repeated.

Having entered the town, Deke put one foot in front of the other, his eyes locked on the rooftops and windows of the taller buildings, basically scanning any position that enemy snipers might be using as a vantage point.

The trap had been set. Japanese forces had been expecting them for some time. The fighting promised to be fierce.

Deke was moving along the edge of the street, keeping to the shadows cast by trees and front porches. He found himself thinking wistfully of the jungle, which offered much better cover. Besides, Deke always felt more at home in the forest or fields, rather than making his way up a street, feeling too exposed.

He moved like a prowling cat, keeping to a pace that was unlikely to draw much attention to himself. His fever seemed to have abated for now, for which he was grateful. He needed to be sharp.

Behind him came the bulk of the soldiers, who ran between buildings in small squads, crossing the street at a scramble while the men awaiting their turn to cross were prepared with covering fire that wasn't needed yet.

Deke figured that the rest of the advancing forces could worry about the machine-gun emplacements inside the street-corner bunkers. He could see some of those up ahead, or what he guessed were machine-gun emplacements. It was hard to know for certain because they remained quiet, the Japanese waiting for the GIs to get closer.

Deke would worry about enemy snipers.

Along with Danilo, the rest of Patrol Easy was doing the same thing, watching any likely sniper positions. There were so many possible ones, and yet no one was shooting at them yet.

The peace and quiet didn't last for long.

A shot rang out. The men behind Deke scrambled for cover, but not before a soldier had fallen. The sniper's aim had proved deadly. The GI lay sprawled in the dirt street, a pool of crimson spreading around him.

Nobody ran to drag the dead man out of the street, because that would have been suicide, making them an easy target for the Japanese sniper.

"See him?" Philly whispered, his eyes on the rooftops.

"Not yet," Deke whispered in reply.

The way that the rifle crack had echoed along the street made it hard to tell where the shot had been fired from.

Deke crouched in the shadows, waiting.

Captain Merrick called a halt, and the wait lengthened.

Now and then shots were exchanged, the two sides pecking at one another.

Truth be told, Deke was glad for a chance to rest. They had been in almost constant motion since leaving Bloody Ridge.

The only bad part of taking a rest was that it gave his malaria or whatever bug he had to rear its ugly head. Advancing into Ormoc, maybe he'd just been too busy to be sick.

But he could feel his fever gradually returning—if not at a full boil, then definitely a simmer. Between the fever and sheer exhaustion, all of a sudden he could barely think straight.

Deke knew that he wasn't the only one who was half-asleep on his feet. Nobody had managed to get much sleep in the days leading up to the beach landing or during the long initial night after that landing, which they had spent fighting off Japanese infiltrators. Half the men were walking around like zombies, even if they weren't sick like Deke.

He caught himself swaying as a shiver ran through him, despite the high air temperature. It was an awful thing to have fever chills at the same time that you were sweating in the tropical heat.

Speaking of which, from time to time he got a good whiff of himself, the stink of his dirty uniform mixing with feverish sweat. Whenever he moved, his stiff and grimy shirt stuck to his skin, as if it had taken on a mind of its own. The smell was somewhere between a dead woodchuck on the side of the road and the sickly-sweet odor of hay that had been rained on and left to rot. He wrinkled his nose. It was a good thing that everybody else smelled just as bad.

Meanwhile, the tropical heat was nearly overwhelming, and the humidity clung to him like the grasping hands of a thousand greasy beggars. He wiped the sweat out of his eyes but felt it run down his chest and pool in his navel.

He was finding it hard to concentrate, because what he really wanted to do was lie down and take a nap, preferably a nap that would last for a week. The lack of sleep from the last several nights was taking its toll. Unfortunately, the war was not being fought on his schedule, and nobody was going to call a time-out.

Behind him, Captain Merrick's company had been held up, but not for long. The advance could not be halted because of a single sniper.

"Let's go!" Honcho shouted.

More soldiers ran across the street, presenting themselves as targets.

Sure enough, the sniper fired again.

Another man went down.

Feverish as he was becoming once again, Dekes seemed to be having a harder time focusing on the windows and rooftops. But like a sudden glimpse of an enemy ship through the fog at sea, he spotted movement in the window of a house across the street. He could just see the sun outlining the shape of a Japanese helmet, neatly framed by the window.

There. He put the rifle sights on the other sniper's head and ever so slowly squeezed the trigger.

The rifle bucked against his shoulder, jolting his already aching bones.

Had he hit the target?

When he looked through the scope again, the window frame was empty.

"You got him," Philly whispered. It was hard to say if his tone indicated grudging admiration or disbelief at the skill involved. "Hey, you all right? You don't look so good. Did your fever come back?"

"Like a freight train."

"You know what? You picked one hell of a time to get sick again. We're in the middle of another battle."

"I'll keep that in mind."

It soon became clear that the elimination of one enemy sniper was just a drop in the bucket. The Japanese snipers were scattered throughout the city, taking shots at any US soldiers who appeared in their sights. It was a highly effective strategy for pinning down the advance through the city streets.

And those were only the snipers. Far more daunting were the well-placed bunkers, covering the streets with machine-gun fire. Men scrambled for cover, pinned down one moment, running for their lives the next. They had known this wasn't going to be an easy job, but it looked as if breaking the enemy stranglehold on Ormoc was going to be even more bloody and costly than expected.

Fortunately, the Americans had at least some aces up their sleeves.

What the Japanese hadn't counted on were the tanks. Once again, the tanks were the heroes of the hour, able to advance into a hail of machine-gun fire. Even fire from the antiaircraft guns that the Japanese had turned into ground defense weapons bounced off the tanks' thick steel hides.

The tanks rolled right up to the defensive emplacements and opened fire at nearly point-blank range, obliterating the enemy defenses. For the most part, the tanks refrained from using flamethrowers for fear of incinerating the largely stick-built city —the resulting inferno might trap any civilians or US soldiers within.

Frustrated Japanese defenders attempted to take out the tanks by rushing them with so-called sticky bombs, or they tried to hurl satchel charges under the tanks. However, the infantry moving forward in support of the tanks made quick work of the attackers, turning their efforts into nothing more than another suicide mission. Flesh never won against steel.

The Japanese fought back strongly as ever, employing interlocking fields of fire and rushing reinforcements into the gaps to slow the American advance. However, the army advance moved forward like a grindstone, wearing down the Japanese despite their determination.

Powerful as they were, the tanks could do only so much. Many of the Japanese were scattered around the town in smaller groups, often in the houses, fighting as independent units. A few tanks couldn't deal with them all. In places, the streets narrowed to the point where the tanks couldn't reach some of the houses being held by the Japanese.

That job fell to the soldiers. They were forced to go house to house, fighting their way up the streets, each dwelling having been turned into its own version of a fortress. It was a slow and bloody process, considering that the Americans didn't want to leave behind any defenders who could literally shoot them in the back.

"What a mess," said Philly, grabbing some shade alongside Deke during a lull in the fighting. "I feel like we're fighting in all directions."

"That's because we are," Deke said. His head was swimming from the fever, and he took a drink of water from his canteen, hoping that it would help quench his thirst. It didn't. "I reckon we're just in the eye of the hurricane."

More shots spattered around them, and they ran for cover.

* * *

THE REMAINING soldiers of Patrol Easy had plunked themselves down nearby, spread out along a low stone wall. Yoshio was nearest to Deke, then Rodeo and Alphabet.

Danilo sat a little apart as always, if "sitting" was the right term. He tended to squat on his haunches. It didn't look very comfortable to Deke, but it was how most of the other Filipino guerrillas sat when they were out in the open or in the jungle. Danilo kept his rifle across his knees and his mean-looking bolo knife slung across his back.

Deke felt functional despite the fever, but it didn't help that his movements seemed to be taking place in a fog. He also felt oddly removed from the situation, almost as if he were watching someone else from a distance, maybe an actor in a movie. Again, fever and exhaustion were to blame.

He shook his head, trying to get back to reality. He needed to get with the program, and fast.

If he wasn't careful, he was going to have an eternity to catch up on his sleep.

Somehow a handful of rear-echelon troops had gotten mixed up with them, including the skinny clerk, Private Rafferty, that Deke recognized from the fight back at the ridge. It was a reminder of how thin the division was spread, when every man was needed for the fight. There would be no reinforcements coming—every spare soldier in the division was in the field.

Things in Ormoc might quickly go south if the Japanese turned out to have more men than expected.

"Look at that. You're still alive," Deke said to the clerk.

"You sound surprised," Rafferty replied, offering him a lopsided grin.

"Keep your head down, and don't do anything stupid if you want to stay that way."

The clerk gave him a quick nod to show that he understood. "These Japanese don't know when to quit."

"Don't you worry, kid. They're saying the same thing about us right about now."

Missing from the group was Lieutenant Steele, who was trying to bring up the rest of the company. They were a couple of blocks back, held up by a hail of machine-gun fire. The dreaded Nambu machine guns hammered away, their deadly rhythm making them sound like bloodthirsty woodpeckers. *Tap, tap, tap.*

To make matters worse, the Japanese had planned their fields of fire for maximum efficiency. They also set traps, luring the advancing American units with a lull in the fire, then opening up when they had multiple targets in front of their guns.

Another absent member of Patrol Easy was Private Egan. He and his war dog, Thor, were toward the rear of the company, sniffing out any enemy soldiers who might be trying to hide, so that they wouldn't cause problems later. The enemy soldiers had a nasty habit of attacking the advancing units from the rear with rifle fire and grenades.

However, the battle clearly had been taking its toll on the enemy. Nearby was a dead Japanese soldier. Deke was surprised to see that the dead man bore a chrysanthemum and anchor symbol on his helmet. He recalled that he had seen this symbol before, when Honcho had pointed out that it designated these troops as part of the Japanese Special Landing Forces. These were elite troops who had seen combat around the Pacific, especially in China. Essentially, they were the Japanese equivalent of marines. Crack troops with a fearsome reputation that was well deserved.

No wonder this had been such a tough fight so far. It was clear that the Japanese were throwing everything they had at Leyte.

Studying the body of the elite soldier, Deke thought, *At least that's one less for us to deal with. Not so tough now, are you, fella?*

Yoshio scurried out and quickly went through the dead Japanese's pockets, returning to the safety of the wall with a few items clutched in his hand.

"Anything?" Philly asked as Yoshio scanned the papers. Yoshio was under orders to gather any intelligence that he could.

Yoshio shook his head, then held up a snapshot of a young woman and child. "Only letters from home."

It was yet another reminder that the enemy was all too human, even soldiers from an elite unit.

Not only were the snipers doing what they could to take out any Japanese marksmen, but they were also seeing what lay ahead for the advancing troops by serving as their eyes and ears. From time to time, Captain Merrick sent a runner to relay that information.

"Heads up," Philly said. "Here comes the runner. Poor bastard."

They could see the man coming, using whatever he could for cover, including the burned-out carcass of an automobile that was still smoldering, licks of flame fed by what was left of the seats, tires, and engine grease. The reeking smoke provided him with some cover.

It was a job nobody envied. Dodging enemy bullets and machine-gun fire was a dangerous game. Here in Ormoc's streets, it was also a game of cat and mouse.

"All right, looks like he's gonna make it. We need to send word back about that bunker up yonder," Deke said. "Can't have the boys walk right into that."

"Cover fire," Philly said.

Patrol Easy began firing at the bunker, but the Japanese defenders were so ensconced behind their sandbags that they made difficult targets.

They watched the runner make the final dash toward the wall that Patrol Easy sheltered behind.

He almost made it.

At the instant before he reached cover, he was caught by a burst of machine-gun fire. The soldier spun around and collapsed in the street.

What unfolded next was difficult to watch. Badly wounded,

the soldier managed to drag himself by his elbows toward the shelter of the wall.

Yoshio started to go over the wall to help the wounded man, but even in his fevered state, Deke grabbed the back of his belt and tugged him down. "No, you don't. You'll end up just like him."

Watching a wounded man without being able to help him was one of the most heart-wrenching situations that a soldier faced. In rushing to help him, a soldier tended to be operating on sheer emotion rather than thinking things through. More often than not, that would get him killed. The Japanese machine gunners and snipers liked nothing more than to use a wounded man as bait, luring others into their sights.

Rodeo shouted at the man, "C'mon, buddy. You can make it. Keep going!"

Slowly and desperately, the soldier crawled closer to the safety of the wall.

Evidently the Japanese decided that their trap wasn't going to work and lost patience. A single shot rang out, and the wounded man went limp.

"Son of a bitch!" Philly said through gritted teeth. "A sniper finished him off."

"We need to get word to Captain Merrick," Deke said. "Maybe he can get a tank up here to clear them out. Otherwise, the whole damn company is gonna walk right into this mess. They're gonna get the same as that poor bastard."

"What are we supposed to do about it?"

"I'll go," Deke said. "Hell, I'm half-dead anyhow."

Deke started to get up, staggering a little, but Philly pulled him back down. "Hold it right there, Corn Pone. You wouldn't let Yoshio go, so how would you do any better? You're sick. You shouldn't even be on the front lines at all."

"I said I'd do it, didn't I?"

"You want to play hero, do it another day when you're not running a fever," Philly said. He took a good look at Deke's face and shook his head. "Look at you. I swear to God that even your eyeballs are sweating. I'll bet you can't even see straight."

Philly hadn't let go of him, and Deke found that he didn't have the strength to shrug him off. In his current state, he was reduced to glaring and muttering a few choice words. Normally he wouldn't have let anyone put hands on him like that, not even Philly.

To their surprise, the clerk spoke up, offering to make a run for it, but he was ignored. The snipers still didn't consider rear-echelon men like this clerk to be real soldiers—not yet.

Alphabet spoke up. "I'll go."

"You sure?"

"I've always been quick on my feet. Just ask the girls at the USO dances."

"I think they'd say you were quick with your hands."

"Yeah, yeah. Listen, just make those Nip snipers keep their heads down, will ya? I don't want to end up like that guy."

Feverish though he was, Deke heard himself saying, "Don't you worry about that sniper. I'll take care of him."

He didn't know if Alphabet had heard him or not. He was busy stripping off his gear to the bare essentials, removing even his utility belt with its spare ammo and canteen. It was clear that he didn't want to carry anything that would slow him down.

He crouched behind the stone wall, getting in position like a runner at the start of a race.

"Go!" he shouted, as much to himself as to the men around him. Immediately, the men behind the wall poured fire at the bunker area.

Alphabet vaulted the stone wall. He didn't get more than a few paces before he went down, shot through the legs—not by the machine gunners, but by an unseen Japanese sniper. It literally looked as if the rug had been yanked out from under him—if that rug had been a dusty street.

"I'm hit, I'm hit!" he screamed.

To everyone's amazement, it was the skinny clerk who was the first over the wall. He moved so fast that he must have caught even the enemy sniper by surprise, because the next shot went wide, ricocheting off one of the stones in the wall.

"Where the hell is he?" Deke shouted, desperately scanning the rooftops and windows for the Japanese sniper. Each open window looked dark and menacing, but empty.

He had no idea where the enemy sniper was hiding.

Nonetheless, he fired at an open window. With any luck, the sniper wouldn't know that the bullet hadn't been headed in his direction. He might just keep his head down long enough to get Alphabet to the wall.

He fumbled with the bolt, struggling to get another round in the chamber. Damn, this fever had left him weak as a kitten.

The clerk was struggling to drag Alphabet to safety. Alphabet was trying to help him, but his legs were almost useless. He was just so much deadweight.

Another bullet struck the ground near them, closer this time.

They needed to get moving, because the sniper wouldn't miss again.

Deke heard the shot but still had no idea where the enemy sniper was lurking. Frantically, he used the scope to scan the windows up and down the street, but he came up empty.

Yoshio went over the wall to help retrieve Alphabet. Like the clerk, he was small and spry, and the two of them working together managed to get Alphabet to the wall.

A bullet bounced off a rock and careened away with a spine-shivering twang. It was clear that the enemy sniper was about to zero them in.

Philly helped drag Alphabet over. All four men sprawled in

the shelter of the wall, breathing heavily. By some miracle, they had just escaped with their lives. Maybe Deke had rattled the other sniper just enough to keep him from getting a clear shot.

But Alphabet was not out of the woods. He was bleeding heavily, blood running everywhere. This wasn't like the previous bullet that had only grazed his neck.

"Dammit, it's just my luck to get shot again," Alphabet said.

"He's hit bad," Philly said. Automatically, he shouted, "Medic!"

But out here at the knife's edge of the advance, there were no medics to be found.

"Forget it," Rodeo said. "We've got to stop the bleeding ourselves. Yoshio, you're the closest thing we've got to a doc. What should we do?"

It was clear that Alphabet had been shot through the legs, one bullet passing right through both thighs. The copious amount of blood now staining the ground could only mean that the bullet had struck an artery.

They had seen it all before. A wound that a soldier might have hobbled away was a different story when the bullet had opened up an artery.

A man had only so much precious blood inside him. They were in a race against time if they hoped to save Alphabet.

"We need a tourniquet," Yoshio said.

"Here, use this," said Deke, who had stripped the sling off his rifle. He tossed it to Yoshio, who quickly wrapped the sling around the upper part of the leg that was bleeding the most. He used a stick to twist the sling tight—then tighter still.

Alphabet yelped in pain.

"I am sorry," Yoshio said, grunting with the effort of tightening the tourniquet. "The bleeding must be stopped."

"You sure as hell don't have a gentle touch," Alphabet complained. "I've had prettier nurses too."

Yoshio gave one last twist of the tourniquet. The flow of blood from the bullet wound eased to a trickle, which was a good thing—Alphabet was starting to look an unhealthy pale color beneath the sheen of sweat on his face.

"We need to get you back to Doc Harmon," Deke said. "He'll fix you right up."

They knew that the surgeon had set up a makeshift field hospital at the edge of Ormoc to accept casualties from the fight. From there, the wounded could be taken back to the beach, then evacuated to a hospital ship when the time came. The trouble was that they were far in advance of the rest of the unit.

"I'll help take him," the clerk offered.

He had made the offer to Deke, and the others waited to see what he would say. Deke had long since become the de facto squad leader. It was a job he had taken on reluctantly, because he had no desire to be in charge of anyone but himself. However, the other men seemed to trust his decisions. Even Philly didn't argue.

Deke weighed what to do. There were several decisions that had to be dealt with. His fevered mind felt like it was lifting heavy rocks, but he tried to stay focused.

He knew that the clerk had made a selfless offer under the circumstances, considering that he didn't really know Alphabet —two stretcher bearers would make an irresistible target for any enemy snipers in the area.

Doubtfully, Deke looked Rafferty up and down.

Despite his considerable spirit, it was clear that the jockey-size headquarters clerk would have struggled to carry his end of a stretcher all the way back to the field hospital.

"You know what? I've got another job for you," Deke said.

The clerk would serve as Deke's new spotter and watch his

back while he was on the telescopic sight. This was a job that didn't require any heavy lifting.

In the end it was decided that Philly and Rodeo would carry their wounded comrade back to see what Doc Harmon could do for him.

That wasn't their only problem. Word had to be sent back to Captain Merrick sooner rather than later so that the company didn't walk into the Japanese trap. There was an awful lot of firepower hiding within that bunker.

"I will volunteer to take the message back to headquarters," Yoshio said.

Nobody argued with that. It was a dangerous job that had gotten them into all this hot water in the first place.

"Go," Deke said.

A moment later Yoshio was over the wall and gone. Fortunately, he was also one of the patrol's swiftest runners. A rifle cracked, but he kept going and was soon out of sight.

Danilo had been covering him, but like Deke, he had not seen where the sniper's shot had come from. The Filipino muttered in frustration. The echo from the rifle shot was distorted by the buildings lining the street, making it even more difficult to determine the source.

The stretcher bearers prepared to leave.

"Good luck, boys," Deke said. "Whatever you do, don't lollygag."

"No worries there. We're gonna haul ass."

Then they, too, were over the wall and gone, with both Deke and Danilo firing at any spot where they thought the sniper might be hiding. The Japanese sniper held his fire, Deke and Danilo having forced him to keep his head down.

Or had they? Deke wondered. The fact that the enemy sniper had held his fire was almost like a taunt.

He was still out there, along with who knew how many other

hidden Japanese defenders. They were just waiting for fresh targets.

For now, Deke, Danilo, and the clerk were the point of the spear that was the advance into Ormoc. Deke felt like that point had been blunted.

But they were not alone. A handful of other troops were there with them, an ad hoc mixture of veteran soldiers and rear-echelon troops. It would be up to them to clear the way as best as they could for the rest of the company.

If the enemy tried to advance with a counterattack, it would be up to them to hold the line.

Or die trying.

CHAPTER TWENTY-FOUR

ADDING to the frustration was the fact that the sniper was still out there.

"Where the hell is he?" Deke whispered. Bleary eyed, he peered through the rifle scope, searching once more for the Japanese sniper he knew was just biding his time.

"I don't see anything," the clerk whispered back, glassing the street with the binoculars.

"He's out there, all right," Deke replied.

He could sense the Japanese sniper, even if he couldn't see him. Deke didn't know whether to call it instinct, intuition, or just a gut feeling. It was as if he could *feel* the enemy marksman out there, eye to the rifle sights, waiting with a patience that matched Deke's own.

But Deke's patience was wearing thin, thanks to his fever and the heat. Sweat trickled into his eye, and he tried blinking away the stinging, salty tears. More sweat blurred his vision, which only added to his frustration.

He was tempted to swipe at it with the back of his hand, but that would require pulling his gaze away from the scope. He didn't want to do that, not even for a moment.

When he blinked again, his eyelids felt so heavy that he wanted to keep them shut. It wouldn't have taken much for him to fall asleep right there behind the rifle.

He forced his eyes back open.

Where are you at?

Somebody had shot that runner, and then in turn had shot Alphabet, and Deke hadn't been able to do a damn thing about it.

That sniper was still out there, awaiting his next victim.

He glanced over at Danilo, motionless as a lizard behind his own rifle. But he hadn't had any luck spotting the enemy sniper either.

That sniper was a slippery character, that was for damn sure.

But they couldn't wait forever for him to show himself. There was a town to capture.

They had to get a move on.

The urgency to seize Ormoc before the Japanese could regroup or mount a counterattack reminded Deke of being a boy on the farm, rushing to put up hay before a summer storm. Still feverish, he was suddenly carried away by the memory into a kind of waking dream, so intense that he could almost smell the clean, fresh scent of newly mown hay.

The hay had been cut, drying on a perfect summer day before it could be raked and stowed in the hayloft. But perfect weather in the mountain country seldom lasted long. The heat had spawned dark clouds on the horizon, heralding a thunderstorm. If the cut hay in the field was rained upon, it would turn moldy and be ruined.

They counted on that hay to feed the stock when the high-country grass turned dry and stingy.

They had all rushed to get the hay put up—Deke and Sadie, Ma and Pa. Even Old Man McGlothlin from the next farm over had come by to lend a hand, same as they would have done for him.

Pa occasionally feuded with McGlothlin over property lines —Pa claimed the corner boundary was an ancient oak tree, but McGlothlin favored a large boulder that his own pappy had told him was the corner. Sometimes the older farmer's hogs wandered onto their land and rooted up their fields.

In the mountains, shooting had started over less.

Grudges were often set aside when someone needed help. That was the way it had always been among the mountain people.

The wagon went around with Ma driving it, keeping the horse following the rows. Pa, Deke, and McGlothlin forked the dry hay onto the wagon. Sadie, being the most agile, climbed on top, stomping the hay down to fit more. When the wagon was loaded, they rushed to the barn and forked it up to the hayloft, Deke and Pa lifting it up with their forks, and Sadie and McGlothlin taking the load and pulling it into the loft.

It was backbreaking work, Deke forking hay until his arms trembled but not daring to take so much as a moment's rest, not working alongside his pa. Even Old Man McGlothlin wasn't a day under sixty, bald as a tom turkey, but he set a grueling pace.

There was no better feeling than those tired muscles after work that meant something.

Years later, Deke's arms were still like iron bars from all those farm chores. Boot camp had been like a church picnic compared to his daily efforts on the farm. All that running and all those push-ups seemed like wasted energy to a farm boy. You might as well do something useful if you were going to sweat.

The clerk interrupted his trip down memory lane.

"Do you think the Japanese are gonna come for us tonight?"

"I don't know, kid. Maybe just this once they'll be as tired as we are."

"You think?"

"Like I said, maybe. Just keep on your toes. If they do come, we'll send them packing in a minute."

As for the Japanese not coming at them tonight, he didn't believe they wouldn't, but he hoped it might reassure the clerk. It was like something Honcho would have said, just to give them some hope to hang on to.

Deke returned to his reverie. Revisiting those memories was a far more pleasant place to be than this war-torn town.

Once the wagon was empty, they rushed back to the field and did it all again. They got the last load into the barn just ahead of the storm, then watched from the shelter of the barn door as the rain and lightning swept in. Hail and sheets of windswept rain dissolved the woods and fields into a gray blur. After the heat of the hayloft, the sudden drop in temperature had chilled Deke to the bone, leaving him shivering.

No matter. They had gotten the hay in.

All that Pa had said to him and Sadie had been, "You two done good."

He could remember it all clear as yesterday.

He reckoned that he had put those words in his pocket and saved them, all these years later.

"Hey, you all right?" the clerk asked.

"Never been better."

* * *

THE DAY HAD TRUDGED toward nightfall following an exhausting pattern of street fighting. House by house, corner by corner, street by bloody street, the US forces advanced. The Japanese almost literally had to be dug out along the way, so firmly entrenched were they in their defensive positions.

Deke thought it was like rooting out gophers, or maybe turnips.

All the while, the heat and the sun bore down. Deke's fever settled into a steady burn.

The Japanese snipers haunted their every step. Deke wasn't sure if it was one sniper—possibly the same one who had shot Alphabet—or a series of enemy snipers. He supposed that it didn't really matter. The enemy was the enemy.

What did matter to Deke was that he seemed to have lost the ability to fight back. A shot would be fired at them, and he would frantically scan the surroundings for the most likely location for the sniper. Even when he could find the window where the bullet had probably come from, the enemy soldier would slip away before Deke could shoot back. Once again, it was a game of cat and mouse—in which he was mostly the mouse.

The sun was sinking lower, lengthening the shadows across Ormoc. The shadows only served to add to the camouflage for the enemy, their positions revealed by the occasional stab of flame from their muzzle flashes. Often those sudden flashes led to another soldier falling. The fight had turned into a slow and frustrating slog.

Even now the fighting had not ended for the night. For a change, it was the US forces who were still pushing forward . Tracers and muzzle flashes lit the night like the Fourth of July.

Deke was exhausted, feverish, and disheartened. All he could do was slump down against a wall with his rifle across his knees.

With night the temperature dropped, and a cool sea breeze carried across the city. Deke tugged his olive drab shirt tighter, feeling chilled.

He knew that he ought to eat something to keep his strength up, but he had no appetite. Yoshio, Rodeo, and Philly had not returned yet from their missions. Out here on the leading edge of the fight, it was just him, Danilo, and this typist-turned-soldier.

Defeated in body and soul, Deke had gone up against the Japanese snipers today—at least one, maybe more—and come up lacking. He hadn't brought his best game.

Worse than that, he had allowed Alphabet to get shot. Alphabet had been part of Patrol Easy from the start. They had fought together on Guam, survived a behind-the-lines mission to Leyte, then returned as part of the invasion force. He hoped to hell that Rodeo and Philly had gotten him to help in time.

It would have been ideal to take a chunk out of that Japanese sniper and make him pay for what he'd done. After all, Deke was a firm believer in an eye for an eye and a tooth for a tooth. And yet the Japanese sniper or snipers had eluded him. Sure, he had been brought low by this fever. But he had to wonder, *Was the fever entirely to blame?* Maybe he had finally lost his edge.

"Dammit," he muttered.

The clerk seemed to know what Deke was thinking. Mind reading? Maybe the kid had more skills than he'd given him credit for. "Don't worry," he said. "You'll get those Japanese tomorrow."

"I'm no damn good at this anymore, kid," Deke complained to the clerk. "The Japanese have got me whipped."

"I don't know about that," the clerk said. "We wouldn't have gotten this far without you. I've seen you in action. You're a real soldier. I'm just a clerk."

"You don't fight like any clerk that I've seen," Deke said. "You've got some stones, kid. I'll say that for you."

"But I'm not you," he said. "I saw you pick off that officer back at Bloody Ridge. The whole damn company was probably taking potshots at that guy, but you were the one who took him down."

Deke grinned in the dark. It had been a fine shot.

"I done lost my mojo."

"Then you had better get it back, for all our sakes."

"I wouldn't know where to look."

The clerk snorted. "It's not hiding under a rock somewhere, if that's what you mean. It's inside you. You just have to find it again."

Deep down, Deke knew that the clerk was right, which gnawed at him a bit. But he still felt feverish and weak. All that he wanted was to curl up and sleep for a few days.

A rifle cracked in the distance, a reminder that the Japanese weren't going to let him get that rest.

Deke began to disassemble his rifle. It could use a good cleaning. He got out the gun oil and a rag, almost lovingly wiping down the dully gleaming metal surfaces. He'd heard that in the Japanese religion, places and even sacred objects could be occupied by a kind of god or spirit. Feeling the rifle almost come alive in his hands, he thought that maybe they were on to something.

Other men had their prayers, cards, or fantasies about women, but when Deke needed to escape, he turned to his rifle. The need to concentrate on the task at hand gradually made him feel better.

But he remained in a sort of feverish fog, so much so that he was startled when he felt someone touch his shoulder. He was surprised to see Danilo squatting on his haunches nearby, offering Deke another steaming mug of his mysterious tea.

"Drink," he ordered. It was just like Danilo to play dumb about knowing English until it suited his purposes.

Deke put aside the rifle and accepted the cup in both hands. It was so hot that it scalded his lips and the roof of his mouth, even after he blew on it. Once again, the bitter taste and pungent odor made him wrinkle his nose. It tasted better hot, or maybe it was just that the scalding liquid helped render his taste buds useless.

His senses rebelled, but he drank it down, feeling the liquid burning as it flowed into his belly. The heat seemed to spread through him, chasing away the fever chills.

Deke gave the Filipino a nod of thanks. Once again, he was reminded of how generous these people could be. They were doing the right thing, fighting to liberate their country.

Danilo produced fresh-cooked rice, along with some kind of dried meat, not unlike deer jerky. Deke was certain it wasn't venison, but he didn't ask any questions. Smoky and salty, the jerky tasted a hell of a lot better than another cold tin of rations. Deke ate slowly at first, then more greedily. Danilo gave a grunt of satisfaction and brought him another mug of tea to wash it all down.

The stars had disappeared, and soon came flashes of lightning and the boom of thunder—nature's artillery. Rain came down in a torrent, although there didn't seem to be a breath of wind. Deke and the others relocated to a large porch that kept off the wet, though the drumbeat of falling rain on the corrugated metal of the roof was deafening. It was almost loud enough to drown out the permanent ringing that had begun to develop in Deke's ears.

Deke finished cleaning his rifle, then set it within easy reach. As the rain let up, a crescendo of tropical insects filled the void. A lonely dog barked somewhere, the mournful tone indicating that he was probably wondering where his owner had gone to.

I know how you feel, fella.

Looking around, Deke could see that the clerk was sound

asleep, looking baby faced and innocent in his slumbers. Nearby, Danilo still sat on his haunches, his own rifle between his knees, staring out into the darkness. He caught Deke's eye and gave him a nod.

With Danilo keeping guard, Deke slept.

CHAPTER TWENTY-FIVE

JUST AFTER FIRST LIGHT, Philly and Rodeo reappeared, Yoshio with them. Deke was already awake, wondering what the day would bring. He watched the trio scramble to safety before the Japanese had gotten warmed up for the day. He had to admit that they were a sight for sore eyes.

"Well now, ain't this a surprise," he said. "I thought you three would stay back at the beach if you could, tanning your hides."

"What, and miss all the fun?" Philly asked. "Not a chance. Besides, somebody needs to show you how to fight the Japanese. I'd say you've done a bum job of it so far."

"Bum job? Philly, I don't know what the hell you're talking about."

"What I mean is, the Japanese are still here, aren't they?"

Deke nodded toward the streetscape with its myriad hiding places. "I hate to say it, but you'd find more Japanese here than you'd find cats at a fish fry."

"That's just what I thought, but without the fish and the cats. Where the hell do you come up with this stuff?"

Yoshio had come straight from Captain Merrick, with the

message that the rest of the company would be coming up behind them. The captain had made it clear that he planned to make one more push today in hopes of having the Japanese cleared out of Ormoc.

It wasn't going to be easy, and it promised to be bloody. Deke just hoped that he could hold up his end of the bargain.

"How is Alphabet doing?" Deke asked.

"Doc says he'll make it. He got lucky. Chances are that he'll be on his way back to the States before long." Philly shook his head. "It was touch and go there for a while."

Deke nodded. "Alphabet always was a tough customer."

"You look like hell, by the way," Philly said. "You've got bags under your eyes as deep as foxholes. Anyhow, take these. Doc Harmon's orders. I saw him when we brought Alphabet in."

He dropped a couple of large pills into Deke's palm.

"What the hell are these?"

"Got me. But Doc said that it will cure what ails you."

The pills were so big that they looked like something you would give a horse. He shrugged and choked them down with the help of a few gulps from his canteen.

Even without the pills, Deke was feeling better. Thanks to Danilo having kept watch through the night, Deke had finally gotten some much-needed sleep. That deep and dreamless sleep was like a healing tonic for his tired body. The aftermath of the fever had left him feeling hollowed out, but functional.

He had slept so deeply that he'd woken up in a confused panic, looking for his scoped Springfield.

"Where's my rifle? Where's my rifle?"

"Hey, take it easy," said the clerk, who had been trying to snatch a few winks before the sun rose fully. He stared at Deke's hand, which was clenched around the hilt of his large bowie knife. A little madness danced in the sniper's eyes. "Nobody took your rifle."

Deke realized that the rifle was right where he'd left it, within reach. He took it in both hands, reassured by the familiar heft of wood and steel. The rifle felt alive in his hands, ready for action.

And so was Deke. To his relief, his fever had broken. Danilo's tea must have worked its magic. Maybe it had been the doc's pills. Did they act that fast? Either way, he felt better. He realized that he had spent the previous day feeling as if he were looking through a veil of gauze. Thankfully that veil had lifted.

He raised his head, sniffing the air like a wolf before the hunt.

The morning air carried the smell of burned wood, sweaty soldiers, mud, gunpowder, and a whiff of rotting flesh and jungle decay from the distant hills. The rising sun felt warm on his face as it chased away the night's shadows.

"Let's move out," he said.

What was left of Patrol Easy got to their feet—worn, tired, battered. Nobody griped or argued. The second day of the battle for Ormoc had begun.

* * *

THEY MOVED out through the streets, keeping to the shadows as much as possible. Every step was fraught with the possibility of carrying them into Japanese fields of fire that had been set up to ambush the Americans.

"Where the hell are these bastards?" Philly wanted to know.

"They're here, all right," Deke said. "I can smell 'em."

Seconds later, a rifle cracked, sending them all scrambling for cover. Philly dove behind the remains of a cart, while Yoshio tumbled behind a pile of rocks that had once been someone's garden wall. Danilo simply crouched in the street, his eyes scanning the city landscape.

At the sound of the shot, Deke had frantically searched the street ahead, looking for any sign of movement. They were looking at a street filled with small houses. The Japanese sniper might be hiding in any of them.

There was only one thing to do, and that was to go house to house, clearing out any Japanese.

"Pair up and let's sweep this street clean," Deke said. Nobody had put him in charge, and he didn't actually outrank anybody, but he had stepped into the role naturally. Anyhow, this wasn't their first rodeo, and they all knew what needed to be done. "Kid, you're with me. Who's still got some grenades?"

They all looked at one another, but nobody had any grenades left. There just weren't enough to go around in the first place, but a grenade was extremely useful for clearing a house.

"Everybody's out," Philly said. "I knew it. Dammit, why don't they get us some grenades?"

"Don't worry about it," Deke said. "Everybody knows what to do."

The men fanned out, Danilo with Yoshio, Philly with Rodeo. There were a few of the rear-echelon men with them, the poor bastards trying their best to look like they knew what they were doing. To their credit, they carried out Deke's orders without complaint. Everybody just wanted to stay alive.

A rifle cracked again. This time the sniper had found his mark. One of the other soldiers crumpled and went down. His grease-blackened hands, still clutching his rifle as he fell, indicated that he'd been a mechanic before being sent to the front lines. He had done his duty to the fullest, dying a hero, but dead all the same.

By firing, the enemy sniper had given himself away.

Deke was almost certain that the rifle shot had come from a nearby house. It was a poor-looking place, made mostly of thatched walls with a tin roof. There was a burned patch where debris from the artillery bombardment had caught fire but had not managed to burn down the whole place. The thatch walls wouldn't have been any good at stopping bullets, but there did seem to be a lot of windows, which offered the sniper an advantage.

"He's in there," Deke whispered to the clerk. "Cover me."

Without waiting for a response, he ran toward the house, bobbing and weaving as he went. When he ran, Deke had a naturally loping gait that made him a difficult target—which was a good thing, considering that whoever was in there took a potshot at him. The bullet kicked up mud in the street. In reply, Deke heard a couple of quick shots from the clerk behind him. He probably couldn't hit a damn thing, but the enemy sniper wouldn't know that.

Deke sprinted the last few feet, praying that he wasn't suddenly going to feel a bullet strike him in the chest.

The door to the thatch hut was closed. Deke gave it a kick and thundered inside, figuring that the enemy sniper would be right in front of him.

Nobody.

He worried that the Japanese soldier had given him the slip, but then saw the interior door leading to another room. The door was shut tight, and the sniper would certainly have heard him kicking the door open. He'd be on the other side of this one, waiting for it to open so he could put a round from the Arisaka right into Deke's guts.

But it couldn't be helped.

He kicked the door and stormed in.

There was the Japanese, right in front of him.

Even at this point in the war, Deke had rarely been up close and personal with many enemy soldiers.

The Japanese was a squat, sturdy man, with a long torso and short legs wrapped to the knees in puttees. He had a flat face big as a pie pan and an orange-yellow coloring that did, in fact, remind Deke of a pumpkin pie. This close, the enemy soldier smelled like sweat, and something vaguely fishy emanated from his pores.

The two men faced each other. They weren't more than twelve feet apart, and yet Deke held his fire. The Japanese hadn't shot at him. Did this Jap intend to surrender?

Not at all. It became apparent that the Japanese sniper's Arisaka rifle was hung up in some kind of harness that the Japanese had rigged to steady his aim. The harness had been tied off into the window frame, giving the soldier the ability to swivel instantly and fire accurately at whatever target presented itself— as long as that target was outside. The Jap was having a hard time getting his rifle free, and the narrow window frame prevented him from turning the rifle into the room and pointing it at Deke.

The soldier's frantic movements seemed to border on panic, but not for long.

With a frustrated bark that might have been a curse, the Japanese soldier let go of the rifle and reached for the knife at his belt. It sure as hell wasn't a gesture of surrender. The look on the other soldier's face said it all—it was an expression of sheer outrage. He barked again as he drew the knife.

There was no need to aim the Springfield at this proximity, only to point it at the enemy soldier.

Deke fired.

The sound of the gunshot in the small space made Deke's ears ring. The bullet hit the soldier in the chest. The smaller man made a sound like *oomph* as all those foot-pounds of muzzle energy knocked the breath clean out of him.

The Japanese soldier's look of anger instantly transformed into one of shock and surprise.

Knife forgotten, his hand shifted to the oozing hole in his

torso. He took his hand away and looked at the bloody fingers as if inspecting them, then almost absently touched his face, leaving streaks of red like war paint.

Then the soldier began to slide down the wall.

Deke had won the fight, but he wasn't sure that he would call it a victory.

There was a sound behind him, and Deke dropped and spun, coming within a split second of shooting the clerk, who had finally followed him into the thatched hut.

"You got him!" the clerk said, eyes widening at the sight of the enemy soldier. "I've never seen a live one up close."

"Go on and finish him off if you want to," Deke said. "You can tell your grandkids how you killed a Japanese face-to-face."

It was clear from the way that his eyes flicked back and forth between them that the Japanese soldier was still alive, listening to their conversation, even if it was unlikely that he understood a word.

"Maybe we can capture him," the clerk said, moving closer to the soldier. "Get Yoshio in here, talk to him—"

Deke stepped around the clerk and pulled the trigger again, the sharp rifle blast like a thunderclap. The Japanese slumped, sightless eyes staring.

"Why the hell did you do that?"

"He was done for. Might as well put him out of his misery," Deke said.

Already a fly had come out of nowhere and settled on the dead man's open eye.

"Do you think he's the one that shot your buddy?"

"Doubt it," Deke said. "He'd have to be up higher, not hiding in a hut. But look at the sniper rig he had. I'll bet this son of a bitch shot plenty of our boys. Don't go feeling sorry for him."

"I guess you're right."

Deke headed toward the door. "Come on. There's lots more

where he came from. Maybe one of them will even surrender for you, but I doubt it."

Up and down the street, soldiers were clearing the houses. Most of the houses were empty, but in others there was a short, sharp firefight. By some miracle it was a lopsided affair, with none of the soldiers even being wounded.

"Do you think we got 'em all?" the clerk asked.

The answer came soon enough, when they were met by more sniper fire.

Deke didn't know where the shot had come from.

But the clerk had seen movement. He pointed excitedly. "There he is, in that window!"

"I'll be damned, but you've got good eyes for a typist," Deke muttered, then ran for cover.

He slid behind a pile of rocks next to a burned-out vehicle, the clerk running up right behind him.

Deke reached up and pulled him down.

Another bullet whipped down the empty canyon of the street. So far their progress through the city had been slow, hampered by enemy snipers.

When Deke peered over the pile of stones, another bullet came zipping past.

"Stay down," Deke said. "He's got us in range, that's for damn sure."

Philly came sliding in next. "What's the plan?"

Deke thought it over. It would be hard to see where the sniper was, considering that he now had them pinned down. He picked up a sliver of mirror that was lying in the street, a relic from the destroyed car. By angling the mirror low and studying the reflection, he was able to study the street behind him.

It was a good thing they had found the mirror, because Deke did not feel confident about raising his head up—it would likely get blown off.

"He's in that farthest window on that second-floor house. Got to be."

This was a time when Deke thought it would be nice to have a couple of grenades, or even Private Frazier with his BAR. But they didn't have any of that.

"Far," Philly observed.

"You'd be right about that," Deke said.

But not too far.

Deke grinned.

What he needed was a target. Something to shoot at.

They had to get the sniper to show himself, at least for a moment.

"Hat on a stick?"

"Nah, he ain't gonna fall for that."

He knew they had only one chance at this.

"Get ready," the clerk said. "I'm going to stand up. When I do that, you shoot him."

"Wait—" Philly said.

"Get ready," said Deke, gripping his rifle. Nearby, Danilo gave Deke a nod.

An instant later, the clerk stood up, then bobbed back down like a jack-in-the-box. The Japanese sniper shot at him.

But at that exact moment, Deke leaped up and fired.

The Japanese sniper fell, his body draped over the windowsill.

Philly whistled in admiration. "That was some shot, Corn Pone."

"I reckon I had some help with that one," Deke said, catching the clerk's eye. "I wouldn't go making a habit of that, you crazy dang fool."

The clerk looked away, but not before a shy smile lit his face.

Everyone seemed to be holding their breath, waiting for the next crack of sniper fire.

The silence was interrupted by shouts behind them and the rumble of a tank. The rest of the company was moving up, possibly with the rest of the division, from the sounds of it, steamrolling up and over the enemy. At least there wouldn't be any enemy snipers lurking in the ruins to shoot them in the back.

The troops rolled forward, engaging with any Japanese who stood in their way.

Hour by hour, the firing died away.

Before dark, General Bruce, the division commander, had rolled into the city in his Jeep. He was able to walk freely down streets in a manner that a few hours earlier would have gotten him killed.

Pleased, he sent a simple message back to headquarters:

"Have rolled two sevens in Ormoc. Organized Japanese defenses wiped out. Bruce."

The general's message said it all.

Ormoc, the last large town on Leyte, was now in US hands.

CHAPTER TWENTY-SIX

ABOVE ORMOC, massive clouds of foul black smoke billowed into the Pacific sky. The retreating Japanese had set their gasoline supplies on fire rather than have it fall into American hands.

"Dammit, we could have used that gas," remarked a driver who had volunteered to take the wheel of a captured Japanese truck that was now doing double duty, hauling supplies from the beach and serving as an ambulance on the trip back. One arm, and the leg on the opposite side of his body, were heavily bandaged.

Disappointment over the loss of the gasoline was a sentiment shared by many, considering that each drop of fuel had to be laboriously brought ashore. If there was any consolation, it was that the Japanese had no hope of replacing any of the destroyed fuel.

All around Ormoc could be heard the popping sound of exploding ammunition—some of the booms were quite large. In addition to their fuel, the Japanese had also set their ammunition and other supplies ablaze. Their goal was to leave nothing behind that the Americans might be able to use, now that the Japanese had gotten out of Dodge.

The roiling smoke from the burning Japanese stockpiles was proof that the town and nearby airfield were now in American hands, at long last. There remained the threat of Japanese planes pestering the fleet in Leyte Gulf or strafing the GIs on shore, but the threat was much diminished by the capture of the airfield. Of course, there were still many much smaller airfields dotting the Leyte jungle. Light and agile, a Japanese Zero did not require much of a runway to take off and land. One by one, these small air bases would need to be rooted out.

In addition to the wreckage, the toll in human life had been high. Scores of Japanese were now dead. US losses had been surprisingly light—on paper at least. The official number of combat deaths in the fight for Ormoc was listed at thirteen. However, the small number belied the fact that each combat death had been felt severely by his fellow soldiers. There had been a much larger number of wounded, Patrol Easy's own Alphabet among them. Conditions were not ideal for treating the wounded, but the medical personnel were doing the best they could.

At the edge of town closest to the beachhead, Doc Harmon had set up a rudimentary field hospital—nothing more than a makeshift operating table, some piles of supplies, and tarps set up to keep the sun and weather off the wounded.

As for the tropical flies that settled everywhere, not much could be done about that. Worst among them were the biting flies, a shiny blue-green variety that packed a nasty wallop and raised red welts on unprotected faces, arms, and necks.

Taking a lesson from the night of attacks that the aid station had endured at Camp Downes, several of the walking wounded had been posted as guards. Able-bodied men could not be spared because they were needed for the mopping-up operation. Other troops had been sent—finally—to guard the areas around Ipil and Camp Downes, protecting the US rear as well as the supply road from the beach.

That road would soon be busy carrying supplies to Ormoc. The town would quickly be transformed into the jumping-off point for expeditions deeper into the interior of Leyte, where the remaining Japanese forces would be making their last stand.

It was typical of army operations that once an area was secure, the emphasis shifted to logistics. Bullets might win the battle, but an efficient supply chain was going to win the war.

The supply road was not long in terms of miles, but it was vulnerable to attack. The small bands of Japanese that had evaded capture soon targeted the road, ambushing trucks and even troops moving toward Ormoc. The supply road was now the soft underbelly of the US advance.

Mother Nature also weighed in. A brief but heavy tropical downpour during the night had turned it into a quagmire. Or, as some soldiers liked to say, "King Mud" had arrived. Even the toughest truck driver had to bow down before him.

More than a few of the Japanese trucks were soon stuck up to their axles, so that it took a considerable effort and a steady stream of cursing to get them moving again. Even a tank coming from the beach got so bogged down that it had to be abandoned —at least until the road dried out. So far it was the only tank that had been lost in the fight for Ormoc.

Under these conditions, it would take the better part of two days to carry the wounded to the beach, and another two days for the trucks to return with supplies. The enemy's destruction of the gasoline stockpiles was felt even more keenly.

Trucks were ready and waiting to take the wounded to the beach. As with the guards, many of the drivers were lightly wounded but had nonetheless volunteered to drive the trucks. Some of them managed to work the clutch using a foot swathed in bandages or steer a bucking bronco of a truck with bandaged hands.

Once they got the wounded to the beach, they would be ferried from there to the superior medical facilities provided by the US Navy. With Ormoc and its airfield knocked out, word had come that the navy would be sending transports once more to carry the wounded off the beach. There were still Japanese planes to worry about, but they were willing to take that chance.

There was enough of a respite from the fighting that Deke was able to walk back to the field hospital to check on Alphabet. Doc Harmon caught sight of Deke passing by and paused in his work long enough to shout, "You look like hell, soldier!"

"You ought to see the other guy, Doc. He doesn't look like hell. He *is* in hell." Moving closer, Deke asked, "How's my buddy Alphabet doing?"

"He's already been trucked back to the beach. With any luck, he'll make it." Doc Harmon looked Deke up and down with an appraising eye. "What about you? How's that fever?"

"I'm feeling pretty good. Say, what was in those pills you sent me, Doc?"

"You don't want to know. Let's just say you'll be feeling good for a while. Hell, a horse would be feeling good for a while."

"You got any more where those came from?"

"Son, if I gave you any more, it'd probably kill you."

"All right, then. I'll just stick with that nasty tea our Filipino guide brewed up for me."

The doc's eyes widened in mock alarm. "I've heard about some of the local folk remedies. Sounds like that might kill you too."

"I'll take my chances. You take care, Doc."

"You too, Deadeye."

* * *

THE BATTLE MIGHT BE OVER, but there was precious little in the way of peace and quiet in Ormoc. Much of the town of Ormoc lay in a smoking ruin. The townspeople who crept back in would find a terrible shambles, but at long last the occupying Japanese had been cut out like the infection from a festering wound.

The Japanese had not been completely defeated on Leyte. They had simply retreated into the hills and jungle to make their last stand. Knowing the Japanese, they would fight until the last man. The soldiers could expect a bitter conclusion.

All around the Pacific, the noose was tightening around the Japanese. But they only fought harder, churning through a seemingly endless supply of soldiers and planes and ships. Fewer each month, perhaps, but still a threat.

There remained the rest of the Philippines to conquer. The nation comprised a series of islands that would have to be removed from Japanese control, one by one. Leyte was just the first. The biggest prize, the pearl itself, was the city of Manila, located on the island of Luzon. There the Japanese had vowed to fight to the last man and had already vowed that there would be no surrender.

Rumors were already trickling in about terrible atrocities that the Japanese were committing in that city, now that they knew the end was near. It seemed that across the Philippines, the enemy occupiers were taking out their anger on the local population for being disloyal and ungrateful.

This was a far cry from what had happened on Guadalcanal and Saipan, where the population had been brainwashed into thinking that the Americans were intent on rape, murder, and torture. There were even mass suicides in those places. In the Philippines, US flags that had been hidden away on pain of death if they were found now flew from many houses and businesses.

The brutal actions being taken by the Japanese surpassed any sort of military strategic need. Instead, all across the Philippines, as defeat became an increasingly foregone conclusion, they seemed intent on leaving nothing but destruction and punishment in their wake.

* * *

DESPITE THE FACT that Ormoc was now firmly in US hands, the Japanese weren't quite ready to wave the white flag of surrender. From time to time, there was the crack of a rifle as a hidden Japanese soldier opened fire. It was hard to say whether the lone soldier had managed to remain hidden as US troops swept the city, or if he had slunk back in as an infiltrator. The sniper attacks were more of a thorn in the side of US troops than a serious threat, but they also took a psychological toll. Having survived the battle, the last thing a soldier wanted to do was fall victim to a sniper.

Just past noon on the day after General Bruce had sent his message announcing the capture of Ormoc, a Japanese sniper had gone to work near the harbor. Every few minutes he fired from the upper floors of a ruined building. Several soldiers had been hit.

The scout-snipers of Patrol Easy—and Deke in particular— had been called into action. It was what they did best, and as far as Deke was concerned, it beat the hell out of having to unload supplies.

"Deke, go get that son of a bitch," Honcho ordered. "Philly, see if you can help him."

"No rest for the weary," Philly complained, picking up his rifle with all the enthusiasm of a man reaching for a shovel, and following Deke.

"Quit your griping," Honcho said. "Keep it up and you'll find yourself driving a truck instead."

"Yes, sir."

Once they were out of earshot of the lieutenant, however, Philly did continue to gripe. "I've got to say, Honcho has been in an ugly mood since we landed on the beach. He's never in what you might describe as a good mood, but this really takes the cake."

"I reckon he's got a lot on his mind," Deke said. "Being an officer ain't no picnic."

"He was an officer before we got to Ormoc. He sure as hell didn't act this way back on Guam."

"Yeah, but back then he only had your sorry ass to boss around. Now he's got a lot more men to worry about. He's second in command of the company."

"What's left of it, anyway," Philly said. "We really got chewed up and spit out capturing this place."

Another shot rang out, causing a truck to veer sharply, a bullet hole leaving a spiderweb pattern of cracks on the windshield. Given the scarcity of trucks, they could scarcely afford to lose any.

"Come on," Deke said. "The war will be over by the time you get a move on."

"Yeah, yeah."

Deke felt good—better than he had in days, at any rate. He'd had another dose of Danilo's tea that morning. He was sure that the stuff could take the rust off nails and maybe even remove paint, but it seemed to keep the fever at bay. It reminded him of some of the folk remedies back home, like sumac tea to cure fever.

There were some who rolled their eyes at folksy medicine, but Deke had seen it work wonders. It sure seemed to be working for him better than any pills that modern medicine provided.

"How are you feeling, anyhow?" Philly asked. "You look all right."

"I've been worse," Deke said.

Philly nodded. "Nobody out here feels like a million bucks, that's for damn sure."

They set out toward the piles of rubble that lined the road on the waterside. Bricks, rubble, and concrete blocks were rowed up as if they had been put there by a giant plow. Boards poked out of the piles. They approached from the shaded side to remain out of the sniper's line of sight.

To Deke's mind, the rubble created a perfect sniper's nest, giving him a full view up and down the street. He crawled down into a hole and tugged a rusty section of corrugated tin over them. They had started out in the shade, but the shade did not last for long. They were now in the full sun, which beat down on the tin, heating it up like a stove lid.

Though they were sheltered from the direct sun, they started to sweat profusely in the tropical heat and humidity. What little sea breeze there was off the gulf didn't reach down between the piles of rubble.

Deke had no need of his hat because they were covered by the sheet of corrugated metal, so he took the hat off and tied a strip of cloth across his forehead to keep the sweat out of his eyes.

"You look like an Indian with that headband," Philly said.

"Well, I reckon I'm part Cherokee somewhere back down the line, so there's that."

Philly took off his own helmet, mopped his head with a rag, and put the helmet back on. "Couldn't we have picked a cooler spot? It's like an oven in here."

"Sure, and we should have brought some ice cream too. Hush now and pay attention."

"All right, don't get your shorts in a twist."

"The main thing is that he can't see us, but we have a good view of where he's hiding."

Philly glassed the buildings opposite them with the binoculars. Deke considered Philly to be a better-than-average shot, at best, maybe a distant third to Alphabet—now out of commission. However, Philly was a damn fine spotter. They made a good team.

Being a good shot wasn't everything. You also had to be sly and stealthy, a natural-born hunter. Danilo came to mind in that regard. Deke sure as hell wouldn't want to go up against him out in the jungle.

Hidden somewhere in the ruined buildings across the street, the sniper proved to be a slippery character. He would take just one shot, then move to a different location.

Deke found it disconcerting that this was the exact technique for sniper warfare that Honcho had recommended. The longer that you stayed in one place, the better your chances were of being detected. It was as if the Japanese sniper had been listening in. Usually they stayed put until someone rang their bell for good. Maybe the enemy's tactics were evolving.

Lying there waiting, Deke thought about the other snipers he had fought. Most recently there had been the nameless enemies in Ormoc who had given him so much trouble. During his feverish state, they'd almost had him licked.

There had been Ikeda, a very tough nut to crack, whom he had finally defeated with a clever ruse during a nighttime fight on a jungle trail.

The sniper that had eluded him was the one that he thought of as the Samurai Sniper, whom he had faced on Guam. That sniper had been more than Deke's match, but he felt that he had grown more skilled since then. If they ever met again, the outcome might be different.

Anyhow, that marksman had made it onto one of the few

boats evacuating Japanese troops as US forces closed in. With any luck, the boat had been sunk by a passing American plane. It was easy for snipers to get caught up in their own private game, one man against another, but even the most skilled sniper wasn't immune from the whims of the tremendous war going on around him.

Deke's thoughts were interrupted by the high-pitched crack of an Arisaka rifle.

Feeling pestered and angry, the GIs trying to unload supplies around Ormoc harbor immediately peppered the buildings across the street with a fusillade of angry shots. Their bullets hammered chunks of stone from the walls, kicking up spurts of dust, but it was doubtful that they'd gotten the sniper.

"Now that right there is a waste of government property," Deke remarked. "It doesn't take more than one bullet."

"Sure, if you know what you're shooting at—and if you can hit it."

"Shouldn't be a problem," Deke said.

The firing died away and they waited.

A lone shot from the ruins verified that the volley had completely missed the enemy sniper.

It seemed impossible, but it slowly got hotter. Sweat accumulated in Deke's headband. In the heat and quiet, it would have been easy to fall asleep. But there was no chance of that. Never taking his eye from the scope, he slowly swept the muzzle up one side of the street and down the other, then back again, like a restless shark.

"Hey, I see the son of a bitch," Philly whispered. "See that building that's kind of pinkish? He's on the second floor, third window from the left."

"Yep," Deke said.

He settled the crosshairs on the window Philly had indicated. Through the telescopic sight, he could just see a shadow, set back from the window itself. No wonder the boys on the ground hadn't been able to get at him. Wisely, the enemy sniper was firing from deep within the shadows of the room.

Deke felt reassured that the enemy sniper hadn't spotted him, hiding under the sheet of rusty tin. The wait in the heat had been worth it.

One shot would be all he got before giving away his position. Could he do it?

Easy now, easy. His finger took up tension on the trigger.

He prayed that the shadow wouldn't move. So far he still had the enemy sniper in his sights.

He held his breath. The crosshairs never wavered. The rifle fired, the concussion deafening in the cramped hole under the sheet of tin.

He worked the bolt, the still-smoking brass casing spinning away, and immediately resettled the sights on the window. The shadow that had been his target was gone. He had no doubts that he'd taken out the enemy sniper. It was hard to explain, but he had *felt* the bullet hit.

"That's that," he said.

"About time you nailed that son of a bitch," Philly replied. "Let's get the hell out of here before my brain melts."

* * *

THEY FOUND the rest of Patrol Easy gathered nearby, diminished by one from the loss of Alphabet. They had also lost one of the patrol members back on Guam, but that felt like years ago, before the bonds had really grown between them all. It was not to diminish the man's death but to be honest about the fact that they hadn't had the time to get to know him all that well. Maybe that had been for the best.

Egan was there, too, with his war dog, Thor. He was a beautiful German shepherd mix, mostly a golden tan, with just enough black markings on his coat to give him some natural camouflage. As the breeze ruffled his fur, the dog almost seemed to smile with enjoyment, pink tongue lolling between strong white teeth.

Deke had grown up with dogs on the farm and always had a soft spot for them. The way that Deke figured it, you could trust a good dog more than you could trust a human.

"He's the smartest dog I've ever known," Egan was fond of saying. "Sure, he's a mutt, not a purebred, but I like to say he's part German shepherd and part Albert Einstein."

He'd lost his first dog, Whoa Nelly, during the fighting on Guam, and had taken it as hard as if he'd lost a human buddy.

In Ormoc, Thor had been busy sniffing out any Japanese who had been hiding in the city's ruins. For the dog, it had all been a game, but one with a deadly outcome for the enemy troops who were discovered. The Japanese had come to despise the war dogs. Given the choice between shooting an American officer or one of the hated war dogs, they would target the dog every time.

The dogs were certainly useful, but more than that, they were also a psychological weapon. The message seemed to be that the Americans planned on using dogs to hunt the Japanese like beasts. Sure, Thor was friendly toward the GIs, but one look at those teeth and you could understand why the Japanese might both detest and fear the war dogs.

Glancing at the dog stretched out at Egan's feet, sound asleep, Deke felt a pang of envy. *Talk about a dog's life.* Given half a chance, he would have liked to do exactly the same thing and snatch a few minutes of sleep, but that was not to be.

Deke felt his spirits lift at the sight of Lieutenant Steele approaching, carrying his trusty combat shotgun, ugly and brutal as a stump. It appeared that Honcho had escaped his duties as an officer, at least for a short while. His familiar grin had even returned.

Among the GIs laboring at the docks, word had gotten around that one of their own marksmen was taking care of the Japanese sniper. They had heard the crack of a rifle on their side of the street, and the Japanese sniper had troubled them no more.

Some of them spotted Deke and Philly returning, Deke conspicuous with his Springfield rifle and its telescopic sight. They had cheered and whooped.

"Nice shooting!"

"You got him, Deke!"

Deke felt a sense of surprise that some of the soldiers knew him by name.

"You're getting famous," Honcho said, grinning.

"Watch out or the Japanese will put a price on your head," Philly said. "Hell, I might shoot you myself if the money is right."

"Yeah, I'd shoot Deke for a hundred bucks," Rodeo agreed.

"I was thinking that I'd do it for twenty," Philly said. "Hell, there are times I'd do it for free."

Deke snorted. "Keep it up and you won't be around to collect the reward."

"Listen up, you degenerates," Honcho said. "We've been summoned to HQ. Word is that General Bruce has another mission for us."

"Uh-oh, I don't like the sound of that," Philly said. "Last time we got sent on a mission, taking out that big gun on Hill 522, we almost got killed."

"How is that different from any other day?" the lieutenant asked.

"Good point, Honcho," Philly said. "I can see why somebody

put you in charge. What is it, do you think? Are there more snipers they want us to deal with?"

"There's always going to be more snipers, Philly. The Japanese are good at it, and that's not going to change. No, this is something different, but I'm as much in the dark as you guys. I guess we'll find out."

Deke nodded. Whatever it was, he and his rifle would be ready.

NOTE TO READERS

Thank you for once again choosing to follow the adventures of Deacon Cole and Patrol Easy in the Philippines. I didn't plan to spend so much time in the Philippines but have found it fascinating with many stories to tell. I have enjoyed exploring the era and bringing to life what the troops went through, at least in some small way.

The inspiration comes in large part from reading the unit histories and memoirs of those involved. Several actual events and actions have been used here, although they have been fictionalized for the sake of the story.

Speaking of story, the armchair admirals and generals out there may notice that the date of the sea battle of Leyte Gulf does not quite mesh with some of the events on land. In reality, the sea battle took place earlier in the Leyte campaign, but it worked better for the book to include it later in the timeline.

My relative Tom O'Connell makes another appearance in the sea battle pages. I know that many of you had fathers, grandfathers, uncles and great uncles who served in WWII. We should not overlook the many mothers, grandmothers, aunts and great aunts who also served or who filled vital wartime roles on the homefront. Thanks to all those who have proudly shared their stories with me in emails and on Facebook.

Once again, I want to express my deep appreciation to the advance readers and editors who gave advice and corrected my errors. As noted in other books, the language and slang used by the soldiers has been included here to reflect that era.

Deke and the gang will be returning soon in another adventure, so back to the writing!

—DH

ABOUT THE AUTHOR

David Healey lives in Maryland, where he worked as a journalist for more than twenty years. He is an author member of the International Thriller Writers. Join his newsletter list at:

www.davidhealeyauthor.com